JAYA AND RASA
A LOVE STORY BY SONIA PATEL

JAYA AND RASA

A LOVE STORY BY SONIA PATEL

Cinco Puntos Press

• EL PASO, TEJAS •

FIRST EDITION
10 9 8 7 6 5 4 3 2 1

Library of Congress Cataloging-in-Publication Data

Names: Patel, Sonia, author.
Title: Jaya and Rasa: a love story / by Sonia Patel.
Description: First edition. | El Paso, Texas : Cinco Puntos Press, 2017.
Summary: "In Hawaii, seventeen-year-old Jaya Mehta is a transgender outsider with depressive tendencies and the stunningly beautiful Rasa Santos thinks sex is her only power. Will their love transcend and pull them forward or will they remain stuck, separate, in the chaos of their pasts?" —Provided by publisher.
Identifiers: LCCN 2017018314| ISBN 978-1-941026-86-1 (hardback : alk. paper) | ISBN 978-1-941026-87-8 (paper : alk. paper) | ISBN 978-1-941026-88-5 (ebook)
Subjects: | CYAC: Love—Fiction. | Family problems—Fiction. | East Indian Americans—Fiction. | Racially mixed people—Fiction. | Transgender people—Fiction. | Hawaii—Fiction.
Classification: LCC PZ7.1.P377 Jay 2017 | DDC [Fic]—dc23
LC record available at https://lccn.loc.gov/2017018314

Cover Illustration by Zeke Peña

(keep yr. eye out for Zeke's first graphic novel, coming soon! This graphic novel was written by Isabel Quintero. Zeke first met Isabel when he Illustrated the cover for her debut, GABI, A GIRL IN PIECES. And Sonia Patel, being drawn to GABI, A GIRL IN PIECES by that very cover, sent her book RANI PATEL IN FULL EFFECT to us, wanting, maybe, to also have Zeke draw her cover. Which he did. Things going around and coming around.)

Design and layout by Rogelio Lozano / Loco Workshop

FOR T

CHOCOLATE AND VANILLA SOFT-SERVE

The late morning Hau'ula sun hurled fiery beams onto seven-year-old Rasa Santos' back. But she didn't feel a thing. She was frozen below the window of her mother's bedroom by the sound of strange groans bursting through the thin wall of their green shack. The grating, throaty noise reminded Rasa of a sick dog she once stumbled across in their sleepy Hawaiian town nestled in the northeast corner of Oahu.

She listened closer. Her mother moaned as if she were in pain.

Rasa raised her head a little so that she could peek inside. Her eyes widened. She watched as her mother's brownness entwined with white. Like chocolate and vanilla soft-serve swirling in slow motion. She recognized the white skin—it belonged to a man named Paul.

Rasa ducked her head. She turned around and sunk to the ground, pulling her legs up to her chin. She buried her face in her knees and stifled a cry.

He gets more of her than me and Ach get.

It was as if the sun was blazing inside of her then, burning a hole in her chest. She wanted to run away, but she also wanted to charge into her mother's bedroom and push the man away. The confusion bound her arms and legs. All she could move was her head. She shook it, sucking in her snot. Then she licked the salty tears that coated her lips.

Things were supposed to be better now that they didn't live on the beach anymore. Their corrugated tin roof shack was, after all, a step up from the ratty tent. It should have kept the three of them together and happy.

But nothing had really changed. It was still her and her little brother Acharya. Their mother remained, for the most part, absent.

An engine out front rumbled, then roared. Rasa whipped her head up. She crept around the side of the shack and saw Paul in his lifted truck. A couple of seconds later he peeled out.

Rasa swept her hands over her face and wiped away all the traces of her grief. She took a deep breath, then walked to the window of the room she and Ach shared. She snuck a look. Thankfully all the noise hadn't made Ach wake up from his nap.

Rasa went to the front door and stepped into the tiny living room/kitchen. Her mother stood there wearing nothing more than a satisfied look as she counted some money.

"Eighty," Kalindi said, her voice brimming with pride. "Thank you, Paul baby," she whispered to herself. She looked over at Rasa. Tucking a long brown curl behind her ear she said, "Here's ten for the 7-11."

The thought of food made Rasa's mouth water, big time.

Her disgust at Paul and concern about her mother mutated into something more tangible—hunger. She and Ach had shared a hodge-podge of snacks for dinner last night—some crackers, a package of dry ramen, a banana, and a splash of Pog.

There wasn't anything left for breakfast. And earlier this morning there hadn't been any money to buy food.

Rasa's face crumpled.

Paul was here with Mom. Now she has money.

"Come on, Ras, take it." Kalindi dangled the money in front of her daughter.

Rasa snapped out of her famished daze and grabbed the ten. She sprinted to the 7-11, making a mental list of the food she'd buy for Ach and herself.

When she got back, she cooked up toast and scrambled eggs, and served them with a big glass of milk. Ach was awake by then. Rasa watched him as he gobbled up every last morsel. He pushed his empty plate away with one hand and patted his belly with the other.

An intoxicating bliss spread through Rasa's body, like a drug.

Ach squirmed off his chair and waddled over to her. He poked her arm.

Rasa knelt down. They were eye level now.

Ach smiled. He leaned over and cupped her ear. "Love you, Wasa," he whispered.

Rasa overdosed. She stood up and put her arm around him. She tousled his hair as they walked out the front door and into the day.

BUT i LiKE PARO

"Oh Jaya, isn't Shah Rukh Khan so handsome?" Jayshree Mehta asked her young daughter.

Jaya didn't say anything. She was completely taken in by the drama, serenading, and dancing on their new big-screen TV.

"Jaya betta!" Jayshree sung out.

"Yeah," Jaya said pulling her eyes away from *Devdas*, the Bollywood film they'd spent the last three hours relishing. She glanced around the living room of their tiny Niu Valley house—a speck of a place on the southeast side of Oahu. All eyes—her mother's, her father's, Chander fua's, and Neela foi's—were on her.

"SRK is handsome, right, betta?" her mother asked again, twirling the forest green chunni that draped her right shoulder.

Jaya didn't know how to answer. She examined her mother and Neela foi as they sat on the loveseat across the room, waiting for her response. Her mother looked extra lovely tonight. She was wearing the splendid gold crepe silk salwar kameez that Neela foi had gifted her.

And Neela foi was dressed in an elegant black embroidered

cotton salwar kameez. Her arms, neck, and ears were adorned in twenty-four-karat gold jewelry.

Jaya looked down at the pink and green silk salwar kameez she had on. She wasn't wearing it by choice. Her mother said it would be rude not to since it was also a present from Neela foi. She wished Neela foi had gotten her a burgundy and gold dhoti-kurta like the one SRK wore in the film *Paheli.*

Jaya sighed.

Neela foi and Chander fua were staying with them for a week. Each night so far, the five of them had watched a different SRK film together. Her mother and Neela foi swooned practically every time SRK was in a scene. Jaya waited for herself to feel the same giddiness. She figured every girl should get it. In fact she even tried to will sighs of adoration at each SRK sighting.

But Jaya had a different take on SRK. It went back to the first film of his that she'd seen—*Pardes.* She felt connected to him, as if he were the older brother she didn't have. Only, she wasn't the younger sister. She was the younger brother.

Jaya stared at the orange shag carpet. She'd wanted to watch the film sprawled out on her back, the way her parents let her when they didn't have company.

Jayshree searched her daughter's small face. "Come on, Jaya? What do you think?"

Jaya slipped her left hand under her thigh and crossed her fingers. "Yeah, he's handsome," she lied.

Jayshree grinned and nodded, her expression saying, *See my daughter has good taste.*

Sanjay was sitting next to Jaya. "I better start looking for your

SRK now, Jaya. Someone like that will be hard to find." He chuckled as he elbowed her.

Chander fua threw his head back in laughter. Since he was Sanjay's older cousin, it was acceptable that he join in on the matchmaking. "I'll help. I have lots of connections," he said, raising his eyebrow at Sanjay.

"Yaar," Sanjay laughed. He pointed to Chander fua with an open palm, then slapped his back.

"Well, Jaya, I hope we find you someone as handsome and kind as your father. My parents did an excellent job arranging our marriage," Jayshree said, eyeing Sanjay.

Neela foi covered her mouth and giggled. In a syrupy Gujarati accent, she said, "Jaya, you are so beautiful, like your mother. Someday you will get many offers from good-looking men."

Jaya shifted in place on her end of the sofa.

"A toast," Sanjay called out, holding up his crystal glass of guava juice.

The adults raised their glasses.

"Jaya?" Sanjay asked. He motioned for her to lift her glass high in the air.

Sanjay switched to Gujarati. "Chander and Neela, it's been so nice having you visit us. Thank you for letting me run your store all these years. Because of your generosity, I've been able to provide Jaya with a better life than I had growing up." He paused. He grinned at Jaya, then at Jayshree.

Jaya thought about the bedtime stories her father still told her each night. Real-life stories about growing up poor in Gujarat. Stories mixed with happy childhood escapades and difficult times of hunger and backbreaking work. She felt grateful for her life on Oahu. For her loving parents. For her father's hard work. For her mother's homemaking expertise.

For all the years in this old house.

Jaya loved everything about it. The single pane walls. The peeling white paint. The dusty louver windows. The small kitchen that let her mother cook the most delicious Gujarati meals. Their time together. Eating. Talking. Watching Bollywood.

Sanjay continued. "And now I've made more than enough money to build Jayshree's dream house in Kahala, buy a brand-new BMW, and pay for Jaya's entire education at Manoa Preparatory Academy. And last but not least, I'll break ground on my first luxury condo development. Life is good. Cheers!"

Everyone cheered. Everyone except Jaya. She didn't want to move away to Kahala.

Sanjay switched back to English. "We will be very rich, Jaya betta." He stroked her head. "And I will find you a boy even more rich. You will never have to struggle." He paused and kissed her forehead. Then he whispered, "Yes, yes. A rich, nice, handsome boy for my pretty Jaya."

Jaya winced.

Pretty and beautiful should be for mum-mee.

Or Paro. Aishwarya Rai played Paro, SRK's love interest, in *Devdas*. Whenever the stunning Paro graced the screen, Jaya felt a flutter in her heart. She had to squash a deep urge to sweep Paro off her feet with romantic gestures like the ones she'd seen SRK do.

Would her father ever let her marry a girl like Paro?

SISTER-MOTHER

It was a calm day in Hau'ula, a rare thing. The flat ocean sparkled a kaleidoscope of blue. The slight breeze kept the temperature mild. Locals flooded the 7-11 to fill their beach bags with snacks and their coolers with ice and beer. The pristine roadside beach would soon be packed with happy people munching and chugging.

Rasa, Ach, and Nitya waited for their mother outside the store. For a long time, it'd only been Rasa and Ach. But then their mother had a little girl, Nitya. And four months ago, after Rasa turned ten, their mother had the baby girl, Shanti.

Ach clutched his stomach with one hand and tugged at Rasa's shirt with the other. "Where's Mom?" he asked. "I'm hungry."

"She'll be out soon." She looked at Nitya. "Bet you can't wait for that manapua."

Nitya didn't say anything.

A minute later two guys almost tripped over each other trying to be the one to hold the door open. The taller, thicker guy won. He leaned against the open door with his arms crossed, flashing a wide grin. Rasa knew right away who he was smiling at—their mother. She strolled out with baby Shanti propped on one hip. She gave the guy a big smile back. She did a subtle catwalk to her children.

Rasa frowned at the way the guy stared at her mother's bottom. She shook her head then looked at her mother. The only thing Kalindi was carrying was their sister. "Where's the food?" Rasa asked.

"They didn't let me get any on credit," Kalindi said. She switched Shanti to her other hip.

"What are we going to do? We haven't eaten all day."

Kalindi smiled at Rasa. "Don't worry. I'll think of something."

Right then Kalindi spotted two policemen approaching the 7-11. She held Shanti out to Rasa. "Here, take her. I think I just figured it out," she said. "Take the kids to the beach. I'll meet you back at the house in a few hours. I'll have money then."

"But Mom—"

"It's ok. I nursed Shanti half an hour ago and there's formula at home if you need it."

"But—"

Kalindi was already sashaying over to the policemen.

"Is she going to ask them to borrow money?" Ach asked.

"Something like that," Rasa said.

They watched their mother greet the policemen with cheek kisses. Kalindi stood facing them with one hand on her hip. One of the policemen slid his sunglasses onto his head. The other tucked his onto his uniform. Kalindi shifted, adjusting the front of her dress to free her cleavage. She licked her lips, then leaned over to whisper something to one of them in his ear. He smiled and then turned and said something to the other one. Now they were both smiling as they nodded at Kalindi.

"What's she doing?" Ach asked.

"I don't know."

Kalindi walked away with the policemen, her hand on one of the men's shoulder.

Ach groaned. "Where are they going?"

Rasa changed baby Shanti to a football hold with one arm. "She'll be back in a couple of hours and then we'll get to eat."

Ach didn't seem convinced. "What if she forgets about us?"

"Oh Ach, don't worry. She won't."

Ach's eyes filled with tears. "That's what you said last time."

He was right. Last time their mother said she'd be back later in the day, she was gone a week.

Rasa blinked. "Hey, I've got an idea! Let's go to the library and get some books, ok?"

Lucky for them their bus passes hadn't expired yet. They took the next bus to Kahuku Public Library.

Ach and Nitya ran right to the children's section. Rasa sat down and rocked baby Shanti. She thought about their mother—Kalindi, the Tupi-Portuguese-African woman who moved to Hau'ula from Rio de Janeiro, with stops in Miami and San Diego along the way.

Kalindi was always moving. Transforming. No one could tie her down. No one could hold onto her. Not even her children.

Rasa stroked Shanti's patchy straw-colored hair.

A decade and a half before, Kalindi had once told Rasa, she had changed her name—Julie Santos—because she didn't think it captured the goddess-like beauty and power she knew she possessed. She thought she required a singular name. One name. Like Madonna. Or Prince. But also something more sacred. From an ancient language. Rasa thought that the Sanskrit name her mother chose—Kalindi—suited her well. It meant "sun." She was hot and fiery alright. The name also referred to a holy river in India, Kalindi said. And like that river, she flowed. Her locks. Her curves. Her guile.

But Kalindi's attention to her children didn't flow—it trickled. Her maternal instincts percolated only in the time she took to give them strong Sanskrit names and provide them with basic care as infants. Once her children could walk, she left them on their own, preferring to spend her time either in the company of men or in the solitude of the Hau'ula mountains.

So it was Rasa who took care of Ach and Nitya. And sometimes Shanti. She prepared their meals. She made sure they bathed and brushed their teeth. She took them to school most days. She splashed in the waves and built sand castles with them at the beach.

The beach.

Rasa remembered the books on free diving she wanted to check out. She'd heard Kalindi talking to Paul about it. Rasa was curious. At one time the ocean was their literal backyard—and babysitter. Though they had a bit of a further walk to the beach nowadays, Rasa, Ach, and Nitya were in the waves more than they were in their shack. Why not make the most of it? Plus free diving was exactly that—free. And money wasn't something they had much of.

"We're done," Ach said, holding out a stack of picture books. Nitya stood next to him with a couple of board books in each hand. "Ok, my little hobbits, follow me. I wanna get a few books," Rasa said. She cradled Shanti tight in her arms as she stood up.

An hour later they got off the bus and ambled down the dirt road to their shack. Inside, Rasa went to Kalindi's room to lay sleeping baby Shanti in her crib.

Rasa did a quick check of the shack. Their mother wasn't back yet. Rasa headed outside again. She surveyed the neighbors' house. Their car was gone. They didn't appear to be in their house either. She crept into their yard and picked two papayas from their short tree. She crouched down a bit, her eyes darting around to make sure no one saw her. Relieved, she slunk out of the yard with the yellow-orange booty.

She burst into the kitchen where Ach and Nitya stood biting their nails. "Lunch is served," Rasa said. She held out the ripe fruit.

Ach dropped his hand and bit his lip instead. Nitya half smiled.

Rasa cut both ripe fruit in half. She scooped out the shiny black seeds. She found a half dry lemon wedge in the refrigerator and squeezed the remaining tart drops onto the papaya halves. "This will make it sweeter," she said. The three of them ate their halves in silence, chewing slow to relish every bite. Rasa finished scraping her half clean first. She cut the remaining half in two. She pushed the plate towards Ach and Nitya. "Have a little more."

They hesitated but then took their extra serving.

Rasa got up to wash her plate. Looking over her shoulder she asked, "How about I read you two a couple of your new books before naptime?"

"Uh-huh," Ach mumbled mid-chew.

Nitya nodded.

Just then baby Shanti started crying. Loud. Louder.

Rasa got the powder formula from the cupboard. She smiled at Ach and Nitya. "Wait for me in our room, I'll be in after I feed Shanti."

She prepared Shanti's bottle and brought it to Kalindi's room. Shanti sucked it down fast. Rasa burped her, then changed her. Baby Shanti started in on some cute babbling. Rasa giggled. She kissed her sister's little nose.

She carried Shanti to their bedroom. She sat cross-legged on the floor and propped Shanti on her lap. She motioned for Ach and Nitya to scoot to either side of her.

"Give me one of your books, Ach," Rasa said.

Ach examined the spines and selected one. He handed it to Rasa. She flipped it open and started reading aloud. Her siblings were fast asleep by the time Rasa got to page six, their heads on either of her knees. She laid Shanti on the floor in front of her and then wriggled out from her under her siblings' heads. She carried Ach first, then Nitya, to the bed they all shared.

As was her custom, Rasa confirmed that their little chests were rising and falling before she let herself do her own thing. Satisfied they were okay, she laid down next to Shanti. She picked up one of the books she'd borrowed—*How to Free-Dive.*

Shanti squealed, waving her arms and kicking her feet.

Rasa caressed her baby sister's arm and turned to page one.

PRONOUNS

A purple-and-white taffeta dress hung on the door to Jaya's bathroom. She hated it! Despite her mother's demand that she wear it to their formal housewarming party that evening, she was not about to let it touch her body. She'd find a way out. Maybe some spilled fruit punch? Jaya giggled to herself at the thought.

She shifted her eyes from the dress to the wall mirror. She studied the reflection of her naked nine-year-old body.

Chestnut brown skin. Wide brown eyes. Coarse, shoulder-length black hair. Gujarati Indian girl. Gujarati Indian girl? Why not a Gujarati Indian boy?

Back when they lived in Niu Valley, Jaya always wore clothes selected by her mother, even though Jaya thought those dresses, skirts, blouses, and Indian outfits her mother preferred were too girly, too dainty.

But Jaya wanted to please her mother.

The move to the Kahala mansion changed everything abruptly. Jaya and her parents spent much less time together. In Niu Valley, Sanjay was home every evening. These days, he rarely came home at night. And Jayshree seemed fixed on her husband and his whereabouts. Her attention to her daughter waned. As for Jaya, she didn't feel like she had to do what her mother wanted so much anymore.

She studied the gaudy dress. It reminded her of a straight jacket.

I'm not wearing it!

Her mother—and everyone for that matter—wanted Jaya to be so very feminine. It was too much, she didn't want to be like that.

I don't want to wear that dress!

Jaya shook her head.

Why can't I wear a button-down shirt and long pants to the party? Because it makes me look like a boy? Well, guess what, people? Maybe I am!

Jaya tugged on her hair, then her skin. Her belly. Her cheeks. Her flesh stretched a bit but didn't come off. She pounded her fists onto her breast buds and started crying.

She turned on the shower. When it was warm enough, she stepped into the tub. She let the rush of water comfort her for a few minutes. The tears stopped. She started to wash her hair.

Maybe I am a boy.

She squeezed her eyes tight to rinse out the shampoo. She pictured two children who resembled her. One was dressed in a polo shirt and chino shorts, his hair short and spiky. So cool. The other had on the purple-and-white dress. Her hair was in two braids down her back. They were standing in front of a door. Jaya the boy hugged Jaya the girl and wished her well. She stepped into the doorway, turned, and waved. Then she closed the door behind her and disappeared.

Jaya reached for the bar of soap and lathered up.

A big smile spread across her face.

Her face? No, *his face*. Yes, now it was his face.

DANGEROUS ARACHNIDS

Soon after Shanti turned three, Kalindi began to go AWOL more and more. Often without leaving her four children money.

Rasa tried to make ends meet. She borrowed. Accepted handouts. Earned. But as soon as employers found out she was only twelve, they let her go. Not that a minimum wage job would cut it anyway.

Weeks went by. Whatever food she got, she gave to her siblings first. There was usually very little left for her. Rasa's dresses began to look more like ponchos as she got thinner and thinner.

She'd drag herself through days and lay awake at night. Staring into the darkness, she knew something had to give. But what?

Rasa couldn't figure it out.

So she and her siblings spent more of their waking hours on the beach. Anything to forget their rumbling tummies and hankering for Kalindi. It was late in the afternoon one such day of sweltering sun, shore, and sea when they staggered back into their shack. Rasa tucked her siblings in, then lay down next to Shanti. She shut her eyes, visualizing her short free-dive. Short because her run-down body couldn't hold its breath more than twenty seconds these days. Still, she'd been suspended in the quiet of the thick turquoise water...

She drifted off. A minute later the loud bark of their neighbor's dog startled her awake. She shot up, practically panting. She got her bearings, then glanced at her siblings. They were still asleep.

Wide awake, she rolled off the bed. She sank to the floor and stretched out prone. She examined the covers of the six library books she and her siblings had borrowed yesterday. The close-up of a shiny black spider captured her attention. As did its title— *Dangerous Arachnids*.

She turned to the first chapter on black widows. There was a photo of a female black widow spider eating its mate. Its thick, black legs angled and hovered over a light brown mass of crumpled legs. Her eyes shifted to the paragraph below. She read about the defining red hourglass shape on the abdomen of females, their power over males, and how they sometimes killed and ate the males.

Rasa stared at the eerie yet awe-inspiring female predator. Ach's nasal breathing became a lullabye. Her mind slowed. The book slipped out of her hands as her eyelids drifted down. Her head drooped onto the floor. She fell into a dream.

A woman with long brown curls took Paul's hand. She led the way and they glided through a shadowy passageway. Her head turned back in slow motion. The light from the dagger-shaped red candle in her hand illuminated her face. Kalindi. The black walls ebbed and flowed like the tide and then turned into dense strands of white silk. Suddenly Kalindi and the floor vanished. Paul fell into a dark void. The wind swooshed by making his blond hair stand straight up. Below, someone saw the blur of his limbs pedaling the air. It was a woman whose face was cloaked by darkness. Her body flickered like an almost burned-out lightbulb. Then she was gone. In her place was a glossy black spider. The eight eyes on her head looked up at Paul's falling body. In an instant her head changed—into Kalindi's.

Rasa was lost in her dream, so lost she didn't hear the knock at the door. Her eyes jerked open when the knock became a constant pounding.

The dream. Kalindi.

She was groggy as she hopped up and stumbled to see who it was. Maybe it was her mother. But why would Kalindi knock?

It was Paul.

"Kalindi's not home, huh?" he asked as if he already knew the answer.

Rasa shook her head. "No. I thought she might've been with you. I'll tell her that you..."

Paul cut her off. "And the kids?"

"They're napping."

A devilish grin spread across his face. "Looks like you need company."

Before Rasa could say anything, he forced a plastic CD jacket into her hands. It had an image of a naked baby in a pool. "It's for you," he said. "But we have to go to Kalindi's room to listen to it." He wrapped his arm around Rasa and led her to her mother's bedroom.

Rasa pried apart the CD jacket. She was counting the blue squiggles on the shiny disc when Paul fished it out of her hands.

"It's an oldie, but you're gonna love this," he promised. He dropped the disc into Kalindi's boombox, then pressed play. "Better than your mom's hippie music," he said, winking.

Rasa wasn't so sure. The word "Nirvana" printed over the squiggles sounded pretty hippie dippie to her.

But then an intriguing guitar melody floated out of the speakers. Five seconds later a barrage of harsh bass and drums blasted through the room. Rasa had never heard anything like it before.

"Nirvana is one of my favorite bands," Paul bellowed. He turned the volume down. "Wouldn't want to wake the kids."

His half smile creeped Rasa out a little, but she nodded and smiled back. "What's this song?" she asked, tapping her foot to the beat.

"*Smells Like Teen Spirit*," he said with a weird look on his face. He walked to the bed. He plopped down, then leaned back on his elbows. "I got the CD for you."

"Thanks."

He nodded. "You're welcome."

"I like this song."

"Cool..." He paused, then said, "Hey Rasa, you look tense."

She shrugged.

He patted the bed next to him. "Come here."

Rasa parked herself next to him.

"You're so stiff. Loosen up, girl. I've got an idea. Lemme give you a massage." He reached behind her and put his hands on her shoulders. He began kneading. "I've been told I'm pretty good," he said with a chuckle. "Does it feel good?"

Rasa nodded.

One of his hands meandered down her back. "Stand up for a second," he said.

Rasa stood.

"Face me," he whispered.

She did.

He gripped her small wrists and pulled her onto his lap.

And though she didn't say yes, she didn't say no.

She didn't resist when he peeled her clothes off. She didn't reject the advances of his rough fingers and cracked lips on her soft body. And though the pain was sharp, like the stab of a knife, she mimicked her mother and melted into his body. Like caramel and vanilla soft-serve in slow motion.

After, while Kurt Cobain screamed the lyrics to *Stay Away*, Paul stood up. Facing the wall he pulled up his pants. He buckled his belt then reached into his pocket for his wallet. He thumbed through the bills and plucked one out. He turned to Rasa. "Bet you're hungry," he said. He put the cash on her bare thigh.

She didn't hear him or notice the money. Her eyes were fixed on his glistening sculpted torso. She was sticky with sweat herself. She ran her hand over her tummy and inspected the clear fluid on her fingers.

"The money's for you," Paul said. He was pointing at her thigh. "You're hungry, right?"

She looked where he was pointing—a crisp hundred-dollar bill.

Something clicked in Rasa's mind. Her hungry eyes danced in visions of plate lunches. The thought of watching her siblings enjoy the kalbi and mac salad she planned to buy made her forget the piercing pain down below. She grinned. "Starving," she said, licking her lips.

"Oh, and here's twenty more," Paul said. He motioned with his chin to the bright red blood stain on the beige fitted sheet. "You're gonna need new sheets before Kalindi gets back."

Kalindi.

Rasa nodded without looking. This was more money than Kalindi ever got.

That evening Rasa let her siblings eat their fill first. Only after they'd finished did she dig in. She closed her eyes to more fully enjoy each slow chew of tender meat. She breathed deeply the way she'd seen Kalindi do during meditation.

The dream from that afternoon popped into Rasa's mind.

Kalindi, the black widow spider.

Rasa took a sip of passion fruit juice. As the sugary liquid went down, she connected the sweet and tangy dots.

Maybe I can do what Kalindi does too.

That would make life easier for Ach, Nitya, and Shanti. Rasa pictured them with overflowing takeout containers. Ample school supplies. New clothes. New slippers. Maybe even shoes.

It wasn't long before Rasa, who at twelve looked sixteen, transformed her hunger and her worry for her siblings into hustle.

She discovered that Kalindi's black widow prowess was also part of her own DNA.

And so Rasa became the junior black widow of Hau'ula. She preyed on older men. High school boys who tried to crawl onto her web with their ten or twenty bucks didn't cut it.

PURGiNG & STRUMMiNG

Sanjay and Jayshree were at it again. Their angry voices shot around the mansion, bursting into Jaya's bedroom.

Jaya stopped fingerpicking and listened. More shouting. He laid his guitar on his bed.

Why were they fighting on his birthday? Had he done something wrong? What was going on with them this time?

Jaya counted back in his head. It was their fifth fight in the six months they'd lived in Kahala. He never heard them fight in Niu Valley—that old house was so small that his parents couldn't pee without him hearing it.

Jaya wondered if bigger houses meant bigger problems for grown-ups. He thought about this as he crept quietly downstairs.

The shouting was coming from the kitchen. Jaya ducked behind a nearby wall. He poked his head out and spied.

His father was finally home. He'd been gone since last night. Jaya studied his mother.

Jayshree's chest expanded like a tire being inflated as she took a slow inhale. She let go of her breath, spitting out words. "Third time, Sanjay! Third time this month you don't come home!"

Sanjay gripped the counter. "So?"

"So?" Jayshree shrieked. "Did you forget what today is?"

Sanjay's right eye twitched.

"It's your daughter's tenth birthday!"

"I'm here, aren't I?"

Jayshree crossed her arms. She scowled and shook her head, marching over to him. She lifted the collar of his white dress shirt. "What's this? Lipstick?"

Sanjay flung her hand away. He pushed his tongue around in his mouth.

Jayshree leaned in. She took a whiff of his breath. "Dharu," she said in the voice of an investigator at a crime scene.

"Shut up, Jayshree!" Sanjay said. "I give you everything. You should be happy." He whisked around but swayed. He regained his balance, then stomped out of the kitchen.

Jaya waited for his mother to storm after him. That's what she'd done the last couple of fights. But she didn't move. Her shoulders dropped. Her chin fell. She reminded Jaya of a sad Gumby. And her sadness scared Jaya. Sadness was something he thought only he felt. Something only he should feel.

His mother buried her head in her hands, whimpering.

Jaya pressed his forehead into the wall. His mind raced with ways he could help her.

Give her a hug. Tell her everything will be okay. Fix her a glass of juice. Ask if she's hungry.

He took a step towards her but stopped when she began darting around the kitchen. She rushed over to the pantry first, yanking the doors open and pulling out bags of chips and cookies. She tossed them onto the counter. Then she raced to the refrigerator. She stuck her head in to do a quick survey of each shelf. She settled on the German chocolate cake. Jaya's German chocolate cake. The one she'd bought from his favorite bakery in Manoa for his birthday gathering that evening. She'd invited their new, rich adult acquaintances since Jaya hadn't made any friends at Manoa Prep yet.

Jayshree eyed the bottle of red wine at the end of the counter. She grabbed it and twisted off the cap.

Jaya stared in disbelief as she took a long gulp. She slammed the bottle down. She tore open all the packages of food. She opened a drawer and picked out a serving spoon. One deep breath later, she began gorging. She shoveled big bites of cake into her mouth until she'd devoured the entire thing. It wasn't that big of a cake but still... Next she took a couple swigs of wine. Then she started in on the chips and cookies. More wine in between.

Ten or fifteen minutes later only crumbs were left.

Jayshree leaned on the counter. She scrunched her face and clutched her bloated stomach, groaning. Right when Jaya edged out from behind the wall, Jayshree turned away in a daze. She headed to the bathroom. Jaya followed her.

He watched his mother kneel down in front of the toilet.

Jaya held his breath as he inched forward and to the side to keep a better eye on his mother.

Jayshree lifted the cover and the seat. Then she did something he'd never have imagined—she stuck her finger way back in her mouth and gagged.

The loud sound along with his mother's violently heaving chest terrified Jaya. He smashed his balled-up fist onto his lips. How had things come to this?

Money.

Everything changed when they got money. He remembered what he'd heard his father say that first morning when he walked into their master bedroom suite, a vast expanse the same size as the living and dining rooms combined in their Niu Valley house. His parents were lying on their king-size bed, under their Egyptian cotton sateen 1020 thread count ivory sheets and matching duvet.

"Jayshree," Sanjay was telling his wife, "now we have money. We will employ a nanny for Jaya, a cook, and a couple of housekeepers. Like the rich Americans."

Jaya's mother had sat up and wrinkled her forehead. "But Sanjay, we are not like these Americans."

Sanjay yawned. He caressed her back. "We are now."

Then Jayshree sighed. She noticed Jaya standing in the doorway. "Jaya, betta, what do you think of having your own nanny?"

Jaya shrugged.

Within a week, his parents had hired all the help. That left Jayshree with little to do. Meanwhile Sanjay took on more luxury condo development projects. And though he was hardly home, he and Jayshree fought more when he was.

In Kahala it seemed the only times his parents talked as if they liked each other was at the grand parties they hosted once a month. Jayshree would be the perfect hostess. Exquisitely dressed. Witty. Holding hands with Sanjay. Acting like the Bollywood heroines she worshipped. The parties became an obsession for her. One of the only things she looked forward to.

The only thing Jaya looked forward to any more was time with his nineteen-year-old Venezuelan nanny, Milagros. He called her Millie.

Earlier today, Millie had played the beautiful melody of *Spanish Romance* for him on her guitar. The haunting notes soothed him.

Jaya adored everything about Millie. Her long, wavy brown hair. Her smell. Like gardenia and vanilla. His heart pounded every time she smiled at him. Or when her fingers accidentally brushed his arm.

He'd already daydreamed their wedding—Millie in her form-fitting white lacy dress and Jaya in a perfectly tailored black tux. Dancing. Jaya leading.

Jaya loved Millie.

And to love Millie was to also love guitar. Her guitar was her third arm. She brought it with her every day. She played for him every day. On top of that, she insisted he learn.

Guitar lessons had to be daily, she said. After school on weekdays. Midday on weekends. And always after a relaxing swim in the oceanfront pool. Millie would call Jaya to the lounge chairs. Handing him a towel, she'd say some version of, "Time to get in touch with true beauty."

Jaya would blush when she said that. The only true beauty he knew was Millie, but he didn't think he could touch her.

The lessons started the same way. First she'd demonstrate the song she wanted to teach him. She'd play it, then sing it. Jaya tried to focus on the music, but mostly he was in tune with Millie's barely there bikini.

Then Millie would break the song down for him. Chords. Strumming. Fingerpicking. Eager to impress his future wife, Jaya paid close attention and tried his best during lessons. He even practiced at night on his own guitar.

Today, she'd whispered words that nearly undid him. "Jaya, you're a natural. You learn quick." He'd been working on *Spanish Romance* since she left. It was what he was practicing when his parents started today's battle.

The terrible sound of retching and splashing dragged Jaya out of his Millie contemplation. He blinked hard and concentrated on his mother again. He watched in horror as she threw up the chips, the cookies, the cake, and the wine.

Jaya's thoughts spun.

Why is this happening? If I was the daughter they wanted, maybe they wouldn't fight. And Mom wouldn't eat so much and then throw up. Is this my fault?

Suddenly Jaya wanted to disappear.

DRUGS BEFORE FAMILY

The early morning drizzle ceased just as the sun peaked above the cloudy horizon. Kalindi sat up in bed.

She yawned and stretched her arms. Then she called her children to her room. They stumbled in, just waking themselves. She patted the worn quilt on her bed. Rasa, Ach, Nitya, and Shanti hopped on, their eager eyes glued to Kalindi.

Kalindi smiled. "Today, I'm taking you to the beach. Then if you're good, 'otai after," she whispered. She straightened her back and crossed her arms, as if she was a ruler who'd made a generous decree to her unworthy subjects.

And this was exactly how the kids took it. The prospect of a day with their mother caused them to overflow with a quiet zeal. Their eyes shifted from Kalindi to each other and then back to Kalindi. None of them could remember the last time their mother had spent the day with them.

Nitya gazed up and to the left, her expression curious. Ach dropped his head to hide a smile. Rasa, wearing a cautious grin, looked straight at Kalindi. But Shanti couldn't contain herself. She giggled as she jumped up and down on the bed, her sticky fingers brushing aside the strands of hair that fell in her face. With a soft touch, Rasa coaxed Shanti to sit still.

Rasa delighted in the possibility the day held—she wouldn't have to be Mommy. There was a glimmer in her eye as she saw herself sheathed by the warm ocean for minutes at a time.

Slinking out of bed, Kalindi stood up and turned her naked body towards the open window. She inhaled deeply, tilting her head back. She let her fingers get lost in her luscious dark brown spiral locks. Her red silk robe lay in wait on a nearby chair. She wrapped it around herself and tied the black belt in a neat bow on the side. She rolled her hips to the nightstand then pressed play on her CD boombox. The watery sound of sitar flowed out of the speakers like a gentle bubbling brook. Next she opened the drawer. She took out a package of sandalwood incense and a book of matches. Seconds later thin wisps of smoke coiled up as a woody smell filled the room.

"Breakfast time," Rasa said to her siblings. She sprung up from the bed and headed to the kitchen. She wasn't quite sure if they had enough food for all of them. She'd spent the last of her junior black widow earnings on katsu curry and rice for last night's dinner. But Rasa remained optimistic. After all, Kalindi had already surprised them with a promise of her time. Rasa smiled to herself and began searching for anything edible in the fridge and pantry.

Ach went to the tattered cloth sofa in the living room, settling in low with his head against the wall. Nitya and Shanti sat on the floor near his feet to play pat-a-cake.

"Toast and peanut butter coming up," Rasa called out like a short-order cook. She stacked the last four slices of bread on a plate.

Then someone knocked on the door.

Rasa winced as she dropped two slices into the toaster. She pushed down on the lever and gritted her teeth.

Kalindi's promise was about to be broken. Rasa felt it.

Maybe it was nothing that would spoil their plans.

Another knock, this time louder. Rasa answered the door. It was Tod, Kalindi's pakalolo dealer. And boy toy. Tod, a twenty-something guy with scraggly blond hair and a crooked nose, always had a skateboard under one arm and a dusty backpack slung on his shoulder.

"Mornin' m'lady," he bellowed, looking past Rasa. The whites of his eyes were red and he wreaked of dank, musty herb.

"Tod, dahling." Kalindi strolled into the living room. She sat on the arm of the sofa, one hand on her hip. The other hand drifted up to her hair and she twirled it. "What brings you here?" she asked, tucking some locks behind her ear.

Tod kicked off his slippers and slithered through the door to Kalindi. He kissed her on the cheek, then put a baggie of mossy green in her hand.

"Why didn't you say so?" Kalindi breathed.

Ach's eyes open-fired rage like a machine gun. "What about the beach?" he demanded.

Rasa glanced at her sisters. Nitya's slumped shoulders and Shanti's drooped head told her that they knew plans had changed.

Rasa closed the front door, squeezing the knob with all her might so she wouldn't slam it. She looked back at Kalindi, waiting for an answer.

Tod was already taking his shirt off when Kalindi finally opened her mouth. "Not today," she said. She stroked Tod's tan arm. "Maybe another day," she added. She caressed Tod's smooth back, then nudged him into the bedroom. She headed in behind him and shut the door.

SECRETS

Jaya was holed up in his room, strumming and singing Nirvana's cover of *Where Did You Sleep Last Night*. Lost in the sad melody, he forgot to eat breakfast. He only remembered when his stomach growled. He went downstairs to the kitchen, his mind still on Nirvana.

It all started yesterday. The day Tower Records in Kahala Mall closed its doors forever.

Tower Records was his favorite store. It was also his library. The place he spent hours reading CD covers. Listening to the latest and greatest. Learning about music and musicians.

Yesterday he was there all day. He flipped through each row of CDs. Six hours later, he got to the last aisle. The image of a naked baby in a pool, being baited by a dollar bill on a hook, drew him in like a spaceship tractor beam. The album cover reminded him of how almost everyone around him acted—as if money mattered above all else. Whether it was his parents. Their friends. His father's colleagues. Even his classmates at Manoa Prep. Jaya squinted as he thought about this private school he was expected to graduate from.

It was the most elite and expensive one on the islands. He pictured his classmates in a pool, swimming towards money. Trying to get to the cash first no matter what. Even if it meant drowning others.

Jaya's neck was tense. He relaxed. He lifted the CD jacket to read both sides of it. It turned out to be Nirvana's *Nevermind* CD. Of course Jaya had heard Nirvana songs here and there. Everyone had. But honestly he was skeptical of the whole grunge thing, preferring good old-fashioned hard rock. Still the CD cover lured him in. He listened to it in its entirety, from *Smells Like Teen Spirit* to *Something In The Way*. When the last song ended, he stood frozen with his hands gripping the headphones. Ten seconds later he was about to slide the headphones off but then a hidden track started. Jaya's eyebrows rose at the heavy drums, distorted guitar, and screamed lyrics.

And that was all it took. One honest listen to the CD. After a brief pause, he listened to it again, and then a third time.

Yesterday was a day he'd never forget. Not only because his beloved store closed, but also because he converted to Nirvana's unique Seattle grunge sound. He connected deeply with Nirvana's music and lyrics. Way more than he ever had with his guitar heros Hendrix and Page.

Jaya's fingers twitched and his mind reeled as the simultaneous despair, hope, and resistance in Nirvana's songs won his allegiance.

It occurred to Jaya that he had another reason to dedicate himself to Nirvana.

Millie.

She'd moved back to Caracas not long after she'd started teaching Jaya guitar.

"I'm getting married," she'd told ten-year-old Jaya with a sparkle in her eye. "You'd like him, Jaya. He's the lead guitarist in a Nirvana tribute band."

Jaya's heart had shattered. It took him months and months to heal. He mourned the loss through his fingers as they worked his guitar strings and transformed his hurt into gloomy melodies. His guitar skills grew as fast as nutgrass. If he couldn't have Millie, maybe someday another girl would be impressed by his ability to shred.

Jaya pushed the play button and listened to the Nirvana CD a fourth time. The thought of being forsaken by Millie poked and prodded at him as if it was yesterday, not two years ago. He imagined being shoved to the edge of an abyss. He flailed his arms to keep his balance. To keep from plunging into an oblivion of melancholy...

But then a slow smile spread across Jaya's face as a new idea saved him from the depths of despair. Maybe someday he could start his own Nirvana cover band. Maybe then he would get the girl. It might not be Millie, but maybe someone as amazing as her.

That night Jaya began a scholarly quest. His goal—to become an expert on all things Nirvana. Particularly all things Kurt Cobain. What Jaya ended up discovering in Kurt was the mentor he never knew he'd been searching for. Jaya admired Kurt's nonconformity, humbleness, and humor. Maybe Kurt wasn't the best technical guitar player, but he did his own thing and produced massive, insane, primal sounds. Sounds that were way more appealing to Jaya than fancy jazz chords or fast scales. The guy was also an incredible songwriter. Plus he played guitar left-handed, like Jaya.

Jaya decided that Kurt was more than someone to look up to.

Kurt was like another older brother. Now he had SRK and Kurt. And Nirvana could be his nirvana. His way to escape and find bliss when his parents were screaming at each other. He made a vow to learn how to play and sing every Nirvana song. He started with *Where Did You Sleep Last Night*. It seemed like the easiest.

Jaya reached the bottom step and his tummy rumbled again. He headed to the kitchen, but before he got there he heard Sanjay's hushed voice from the den. Curious, Jaya tiptoed past the kitchen. He peeked in on his father.

Sanjay was facing away. The telephone headset was pressed against his ear.

Jaya strained to hear what his father was whispering. Though he couldn't decipher the words, Jaya got a whiff of a womanizing conversation. The secret words drifted like the scent of the orange, cinnamon, patchouli, and vetiver root in his father's John Varvatos cologne.

But then his father's voice rose a notch. He sounded angry.

Jaya slunk back to the kitchen. He picked up the other telephone and held the receiver to his ear. He heard two voices—Sanjay's and a woman's. The woman wasn't Jayshree.

"Sanjay, I had to tell you. His birthday was yesterday. He turned two," the woman said in a business-like voice.

"Are you sure he's mine?" Sanjay asked.

"One hundred percent," she said, her tone even and steady.

Jaya couldn't have grasped the telephone any tighter. His hand tingled as it went numb.

"You can't prove it," Sanjay shot back.

Jaya caught the tremble of fear in his father's voice.

"Actually, I can. I can take you to court and get them to order genetic testing," she replied, calm as still water.

"What do you want? Is it money? Why are you telling me this now?"

Jaya couldn't listen anymore. He hung up the phone, weaving his fingers into his hair and squeezing his scalp.

Why did I pick it up?

Now he was left with information he didn't want. As if he didn't already have enough of that.

He clasped his hands on his head. The urge to run away boiled in his chest. But that scared him more than this new knowledge. Because what would happen to his mother if he weren't at home?

His appetite was gone. He hustled back to his room, slammed the door, then locked it. He collapsed on his bed and plowed his face into a pillow.

What should I do?

Probably best to ignore what he'd heard. Yes, that was it. He'd never think about it again. He'd never mention it to anyone. Especially not to his mother. Jaya figured it would break her. She was already fractured.

He rolled off his bed and stood quivering. He tried to stop thinking about the possibility that he had a half-brother. He looked at his acoustic. In a slow, hesitant motion he picked it up.

The voltage of his emotions surged and shot out of his fingers onto the strings. He played and sang *Where Did You Sleep Last Night*—over and over until his fingers were raw.

BABY BLACK WiDOW

On the eve of Rasa's thirteenth birthday, Kalindi called for her. "Sit with me, my lovely essence," she said with an enticing half-smile.

Rasa sank down onto her knees. Kalindi slid forward so that her knees touched Rasa's. The room with filled with the smell of ginger incense. The flames of tea candles tossed hazy beams from the windowsill, providing just enough sensuous light—enough that Kalindi felt no urgency to pay the past-due electricity bill to restore the shack's power.

Kalindi put her hands on Rasa's shoulders. With her chin lifted she declared, "The first rays of the morning sun tomorrow will shine brighter as you complete your thirteenth year."

Rasa stared at Kalindi.

Last year Kalindi had forgotten her birthday. Rasa held her breath, waiting to hear what her mother would say next.

Kalindi continued. "I've known your destiny from the moment I birthed you. As soon as I saw your green eyes, I knew."

Stroking Rasa's hair, Kalindi brought her face close. Her warm breath comforted Rasa, like hot cocoa on a cold night. Kalindi angled her mouth to Rasa's ear and whispered, "You and I possess something other women don't." She straightened her head and locked eyes with Rasa. "Kama. Do you know what that is?"

Rasa shook her head.

"Erotic freedom. Ancient Indian texts say kama is needed for survival. To make sure the life cycle continues. But you and I use our kama for more. You know what?"

Rasa pressed her lips together, shook her head again. *Why is she talking about all this Indian stuff?*

Kalindi cradled Rasa's face. "We use it to control men. To get what we want from them." She let go of Rasa's face to wave her hands around the room. "How do you think we got off the beach? Got this house? The car?" Kalindi paused. She sat straighter with her shoulders back and chest out. "All thanks to my kama. Did you know our green eyes represent our kama? Just like it did for my mother. And her mother before."

Rasa crossed one arm and let her chin rest on the hand of the other. She considered this new family information.

Kalindi went on. "I've watched you grow this past year. You've blossomed into a beautiful young woman. A modern day Nefertiti. And they'll crave you like opium."

Kalindi took Rasa's hands. "Remember you're a svairini. Just like me."

Rasa cocked her head to the side and made duck lips. Her eyes narrowed.

More Indian stuff? What's next? Is she gonna say we're ali'i wahine just because we live in Hawaii and we feel like queens? I bet a svairini is an Indian queen or something.

Kalindi raised an eyebrow. "Ah, you don't know what a svairini is?"

Rasa shrugged.

"A svairini is a sexually dominant woman. And you come from a long line of them." Kalindi's eyes moved up and to the left. "Sometimes I don't even want to get anything from the guys. I just like how strong I feel when I can make them want me."

"I don't know what to say."

"Don't say anything. Everything is happening exactly as it should. And tomorrow, the thirteenth anniversary of your birth, will be the day you start officially wielding your power." Kalindi's expression was serious.

Little did Kalindi know that Rasa had already started using her sexual power—though awkwardly and unconfidently at times—to get what she wanted from men: money. Money she hid and used to buy food and supplies for Ach, Nitya, and Shanti. Kalindi had no clue because she wasn't around long enough to notice these things. And Rasa wasn't about to tell her mother any of that. Especially not after tonight.

Rasa massaged her temples with her fingers.

Svairini.

Black widow.

Rasa looked at her mother. "I think of you as a black widow. Because the females dominate the males." She dropped her eyes. "I've been trying to become one myself," she mumbled.

Of course Kalindi didn't know to what extent Rasa had been trying. She caressed Rasa's hand and said, "Then we're both hoping for the same thing for you. Don't worry, you'll be certified by the end of the week."

Rasa's thirteenth birthday celebration began as a campout on the sandy crescent shore of Kahana Bay. Kalindi and her four children cavorted on the beach with a bunch of beatniks from the North Shore. Mostly men. The ironwoods provided a natural barrier between their bohemian beach camp and the road. In the distance, the Ko'olau mountains rose like an enormous nori-colored stage curtain.

Rasa didn't know where her mother had met these people. But she deduced why they'd been invited to her birthday week. At least why the men had been invited.

Under the shade of an ironwood later the first day, Kalindi explained.

Rasa listened.

"You'll begin tonight," Kalindi instructed. "With Nate."

Rasa nodded.

That night Rasa tucked her siblings into their makeshift sleeping bags. She slipped out into the pitch black. Straight into Nate's tent.

Rasa seduced a different man each night.

By the end of the week, her confidence in her sexual power over men was rock solid. She realized she didn't even have to say a word. All it took was a few seductive steps. An alluring glance. A tempting touch. That was it. They were putty in her young, capable hands.

Yet something nagged her—there hadn't been any reason to seduce men this week. Her siblings had been well-fed and safe the entire time. She'd done these things just because Kalindi told her to. And just because she could. Each of the men had desired her. But their desire alone hadn't made her feel strong the way it did for Kalindi.

The last night of her birthday week arrived. Rasa ended up in Jack's tent. Later, when he was in a soundless deep sleep, she lay wide awake. Her mind was noisy. She wiggled free of his embrace and crept out of the tent. The steady rolling of the waves outside didn't calm her as it usually did. The next thing she knew she was huddled against a fallen tree trunk. Tears pooled in her eyes. This wasn't supposed to happen. Svairini-black widows weren't supposed to cry. She squeezed her eyes shut but the tears kept coming.

She hugged her knees and rocked back and forth.

I am a svairini-black widow.

I am a svairini-black widow.

But she couldn't convince herself.

GLOCK

Jaya was used to Jayshree tossing out suicidal threats during arguments with Sanjay. Vows to jump off a building or drown herself were commonplace. But a gun to the head?

His mother had never gone this far before. He tried to still his trembling hands. Maybe he could wrestle the gun out of her hand…

Jayshree pressed the muzzle harder into her temple.

Jaya wanted to pounce, but his feet refused to budge. Only his mind moved.

What would happen if she pulled the trigger? Would her skull shatter and brain bits and blood splatter all over? Would the heat from the shot melt part of her face? Or would she look the same except for a small hole in her temple with blood trickling out?

Jaya studied his mother's face while keeping one eye on her trigger finger. She glowered at Sanjay, but Jaya saw the heartbreak in her watery eyes.

The day Sanjay bought the gun—a Glock—he'd said, "This is to protect us from those Hawaiian squatters in that empty lot down the street—when those criminals try to rob us." Pointing the gun out the window, he pretended to aim. With his chin slightly tucked and one eyebrow raised he'd gone on. "I love any country that gives me the constitutional right to bear arms."

Jaya detested his father's haughtiness. But he hated guns even more. There were many reasons. At the top of the list was his father's unjust rationale—self-serving executioner. Jaya couldn't understand why Sanjay feared being burglarized by "Hawaiian squatters." There hadn't been any burglaries in their neighborhood since they'd moved in over five years ago.

Jayshree had stopped crying. In an eerie, calm voice she said, "Sanjay, you've ruined my life." She paused then said, "I loaded it."

Jaya blinked hard. "Mom…"

Jayshree ignored Jaya and kept her eyes fixed on Sanjay.

"Stay out of this, Jaya," Sanjay growled. He glared at Jaya, poking his right cheek out with his tongue.

Meanwhile Jayshree tapped the muzzle on her temple and said, "Still think I can't leave you?"

Sanjay snickered and said, "You can't. Now give me the gun. Admit it, Jayshree. You don't have the guts to kill yourself."

Does Dad really think she's bluffing?

Jaya's eyes veered back to his mother.

Her eyes were wet again. She loosened her grip on the gun. She gave Sanjay a gapped-mouth stare. Then she whispered, "You're heartless." She dropped the gun onto the sofa and walked into the kitchen.

Jaya breathed a sigh of relief. His mother was safe. She began a binge. Jaya knew a purge would follow. But at least she was still alive.

Sanjay disappeared into his den, leaving the gun behind. Jaya sat down and picked it up. He flipped it over, examining the frame. It was heavier than he'd expected. He turned the barrel to face him and looked into the opening.

He thought about Kurt Cobain. He'd supposedly shot himself the same year Jaya was born. Jaya shuddered and lay the gun on the sofa with the barrel facing away from him. Why did Kurt do it? Had things gotten so bad in his life that music wasn't a remedy anymore?

Music was still Jaya's only medicine. It really was the best thing in his life. And on the bright side, now he had an entire separate room for his music. When he considered the cost of converting one of the spare rooms into his guitar room—walls painted a deep crimson color and lined with his equipment, including six electric guitars, three acoustic guitars, several amps, speakers, tuners, picks, straps, and a pedal board—gratitude unfolded itself like a map. It pointed Jaya away from Sanjay's intolerant, judgmental views and redirected him to Sanjay's unquestioned funding of his son's musical addiction. Well, his daughter's musical addiction, as his father saw it.

Sanjay didn't bat an eye at paying for anything related to Jaya's music. "I wish my parents had the money to let me do a hobby. I would've loved to learn sitar," he told Jaya the day the painters finished the last coat of crimson. "Now you have an entire room to play your guitars."

Jaya hugged his father. "Thanks, Dad," he said. "I don't know what to say."

Sanjay patted Jaya's back. "You don't have to say anything. I know this is a fun pastime for you." He pulled away and pointed at Jaya's hair. "Just like all this short hair nonsense is some kind of American teenage phase."

Jaya opened his mouth but then decided against trying to convince his father that his guitar playing and hair were more than temporary diversions in his life.

Sanjay would never have encouraged or funded Jaya's guitar habit if he knew that his investment indirectly allowed Jaya to donate to the Hawaii Homeless Shelter.

Jaya got the idea to help out at HHS after overhearing Sanjay at one of their parties awhile back. Whiskey in hand, Sanjay had boomed, "I want to get rid of those lazy native Hawaiians in the neighborhood. Those homeless squatters only want handouts." He'd thrown back his liquor then sneered, picking lint off his Tommy Bahama aloha shirt.

Jaya's fists clenched. His father was wrong on so many levels. For one thing, the native Hawaiian "squatters" weren't really homeless. Technically, they were houseless since they were occupying land that was originally their home. Land stolen from them by non-Hawaiians and resold over and over for profit. And Jaya didn't know what kind of "handouts" his father was talking about. As far as Jaya could tell, the native Hawaiians were making do with what they had and with what they could get from the land and ocean. Something that would've been way easier if they had access to all of their land the way they did before the arrival of James Cook.

Of course Sanjay would never see it that way.

His father's disturbing comments kept Jaya awake all night. He spent the hours thinking of a way to cancel out his father's ignorance. By morning Jaya had figured out what to do. He'd commit to performing music in Waikiki to earn money for his new cause— donating to and volunteering at the Hawaii Homeless Shelter.

And for the last six months Jaya hadn't missed a single weekly shift.

His parents had no clue about the busking or shelter work. Then again his parents basically had no concept about him at all. To them, their "daughter" was an unappreciative troublemaker who wanted to torture them by acting like a tomboy. "At least your grades are good," Jayshree muttered the last time she lectured Jaya about his hair and clothes.

His parents didn't realize that Jaya kept his grades up out of respect for how much money they spent on his tuition. Something that many of the other students at Manoa Prep didn't seem to concern themselves with. Seemed to him that most of those kids felt entitled to their expensive education whether or not they made use of the learning opportunities.

Jaya groaned. He suddenly felt spent. He thought about the Nirvana song he'd been playing earlier that day. *Drain You.* Though he'd expanded his musical repertoire to writing, playing, and singing his own music and lyrics, it was still Nirvana he turned to more than his originals. He sang the first verse to himself. Millie popped into his head.

Jaya flinched. Four years later he still felt a twinge of emptiness when he thought about Millie. She would've loved his new Martin acoustic guitar, the same kind Kurt played in Nirvana's MTV unplugged performance.

Hey, wait a second...

It occurred to Jaya to name his Martin acoustic *Millie*. It was a perfect name. Guitarists named their guitars all the time, so why couldn't he? Plus since Millie had left him to marry the lead guitarist of a Nirvana tribute band, what better name for his Nirvana tribute guitar?

He decided to go play some Nirvana on his *Millie*. But when he pushed his hands onto the sofa to get up he felt the cold polymer of the Glock. He shivered.

You don't need much of a suicide plan with a gun. It's simple— point and shoot.

Jaya had never devised a plan to take his own life. But there were many times he wished he were dead. Or that he'd never wake up. If his parents knew that, would they have hidden the gun? Would Jayshree have insisted that Sanjay lock it up? Would Sanjay have taken it upon himself to lock it away without being told?

As it was, Jaya and his mother were well aware that Sanjay kept the gun and bullets unlocked in his den. In the top left drawer of his desk.

Jaya shook his head. It was stupid to have the gun lying around in a house where both a mother and son were thinking about death. He should go toss it.

No.

He wanted to keep his options open. What if he needed a quick way out?

HAU'ULA DEVADASI

Drops of sweat beaded on Rasa's forehead. A few larger ones slid into her eyes and burned. She groaned. Buried toes to shoulder in the sand, there was nothing she could do except blink. The white hot sun in the cloudless beryl sky tried to blind her. It was already broiling her in her sand oven.

Rasa looked at her sisters.

Shanti giggled as she and Nitya kept dumping handfuls of sand over her body.

Rasa pressed her lips together to keep bits of sand from flying into her mouth, but she refused to tell them to stop even if it was nearly killing her—more important that they were happy and safe. She wanted to keep them that way as long as possible.

Rasa thought about Ach. He was a different story altogether. Last month she discovered his sketchbook under a loose floorboard in their room. She'd held her breath as she'd flipped through the pages of his drawings—penises, vaginas, and a couple of full body drawings of men with disproportionately large genitals.

Later that same afternoon, she'd approached him. "Ach," she'd whispered, holding out his sketchbook. She stroked his head.

He wouldn't look at her.

"Ach, it's ok," Rasa said, wrapping her arms around him. She pulled him close to her. "I'm here for you," she whispered.

Rasa tried to get to the bottom of it, but he clammed up.

He did, however, stop the lewd drawings. Yet he became more bitter. He acted like a jaded, vigilant hawk—not like the nine-year-old he was. Circling. Observing. Calculating Kalindi's next move. Wanting desperately to defend his sisters from their mother's actions.

Rasa knew Ach's self-appointed role as their security detail was in vain. How could he keep them out of harm's way if she, the older sister, couldn't? Worse, if their mother didn't even try?

Last night, without warning, Kalindi brought a strange man named Zeke into their shack. One look at the six-foot-two muscle man from Georgia and Ach sprung up off the sofa like a rabid dog.

"Who the fuck are you?" he snarled, trying to make his voice sound deep.

Kalindi sauntered into her bedroom. "Acharya, dahling, don't," she warned. Then she sang, "Oh Zeeeke. Come on, baby, I got something for ya."

"Be right there." His Southern drawl hung thick in the air like the smoke from his blunt. He looked at Ach and laughed. "Woah, big man. Chill." Zeke held out the fattie and raised his eyebrows, offering Ach a drag.

"Can't you see my sisters are here?" He curled his arms around Nitya and Shanti.

Rasa had been in the shower when Kalindi and Zeke came in. But she'd heard every word. She threw on her dress and stepped out of the bathroom, slamming the door behind her. Everyone looked up.

Zeke eyed her.

Ach looked back at Zeke. "Leave. Now!"

But Zeke wasn't listening. His greedy eyes were gorging on Rasa. "Is she your sister too, big man?" Zeke asked, arching a sly brow. He didn't wait for Ach to answer. He beckoned with a chin up. "Hey sis, why don't you join us in the bedroom?"

Rasa wasn't fazed. She rolled her eyes. "It's not worth it, Ach. Come on, let's eat," she said. She walked into the kitchen and rummaged for food.

But Ach had already lost it. He stormed toward Zeke.

Zeke swatted Ach away like a pesky fly. Ach stumbled back and fell.

Rasa heard the commotion. She darted into the living room to find Ach throwing punches at Zeke's gut. Nitya was crying and Shanti had covered her face with her hands. Rasa jumped in between Zeke and Ach. She threw her arms around her brother and squeezed tight. "Ach, it's ok, it's ok...let's take a walk."

But Zeke had another idea. He weaseled his hand onto Rasa's arm and tugged. "He'll be okay, I guarantee—as long as you get your pretty little ass in here with me and Kalindi."

"No!" Ach screamed.

Rasa looked straight into her brother's eyes. She stooped forward to his ear. "It's ok, Ach. Take the girls and stay at Kawika's. Bring the ramen," she whispered. "It's in the pantry." She went limp as Zeke dragged her into the bedroom.

He slammed the door shut and locked it before Ach could race in.

"Rasa! Rasa!" Ach screamed. He pounded on the door.

That was last night.

Rasa was determined to make today better for her siblings.

The tide rose and the cool, turquoise ocean engulfed Rasa's body, breaking her out of her sand prison. High tide was about to steal their beach. Rasa sprung up to grab the towels, sunscreen, and water. She directed Nitya and Shanti to the grass and then called for her brother. He trudged over with his football tucked under his arm.

They climbed the steep concrete embankment and crossed the two lanes of Kamehameha Highway. Turning left and then a sharp right at the Kim Taylor Reece Gallery, they dawdled alongside the dirt road leading to their shack.

Shanti moaned. She rubbed her eyes with her free hand. "Sleepy," she whispered.

"I know, baby girl," Rasa said, shrugging her right shoulder to hoist the heavy beach bag further up. She tightened her grip on Shanti's hand.

Nitya yawned. Rasa patted her head and said, "We'll all take naps at home, ok?"

The previous joy on Nitya's face was gone, replaced by the usual glazed expression she wore at home. Everyone knew Nitya didn't speak words, though it was hard to remember this when she was outside running around and laughing with her brother and sisters.

Rasa put her arm around Nitya's small shoulder. "Hey, you ok?"

Nothing. Nitya stared straight ahead.

Ach grunted as he tossed his football up and down. Rasa pictured his pencil sketch from this morning. She'd asked him about it.

"It's my dad," he'd reported as he shaded in the man's hair.

Sometimes Ach asked Kalindi to tell him about his father, but all she'd say was, "Hau'ula is your father."

Ach would snap back something like, "Fuck you," or "I hate you," to her hippie convictions before running out of the house.

Rasa inspected Ach's face. She caught his eye and asked, "Ach, what's up?"

"Nothing," he mumbled. He jutted his chin and looked away.

Rasa wasn't convinced.

They approached the shack and spotted Paul's new black Toyota Tundra. Next to its shiny chrome suspension and enormous grille guard, Kalindi's rusty 1970-something red Datsun looked like a toy car.

The Datsun hadn't started in over a week, but now it was parked in a different spot. Rasa and Ach exchanged glances. They knew what was going on.

Paul fixed Kalindi's Datsun.

Kalindi was "paying" Paul.

After Zeke left last night, Kalindi pulled Rasa aside and said, "Think of it this way, we're way better off than those devadasi in India. They're married to the temple and they have to sleep with whoever the priest says. We're married to Hau'ula, but we get to choose who we sleep with ourselves. And we keep the money we make." She paused and handed Rasa fifty of the one hundred and fifty Zeke had paid. When Rasa didn't say anything, Kalindi leaned in and whispered, "Anyway, why get a minimum wage job when your beauty can bring in way more money in an hour?"

Rasa folded the fifty and tucked it into her bra. She didn't bother to ask why Kalindi got to keep more of the earnings. That was just how it was. When Kalindi made the introductions, she expected

Rasa to hand over two thirds of the earnings. Rasa didn't mind because she made enough from the dates she set up herself to take care of her siblings the way she saw fit.

Last week Rasa handed her mother over two hundred dollars from three dates. Kalindi held it close to her heart and whispered, "My strong black widow-svairini. And only fourteen."

Rasa didn't feel much of anything at her mother's twisted words of affection. She kept herself focused on doing what she had to do.

Money for Ach, Nitya, and Shanti.

Sex for money was fine and dandy for Rasa. But she refused to think this type of life was good for her siblings. There were days when Rasa wished for the luxury of a carefree childhood. To go hang out with girlfriends her own age. Though she didn't have any. To go to school every day. To do nothing sometimes. These desires strengthened her resolve to make sure her siblings got as much of a happy-go-lucky childhood as possible.

Ach elbowed Rasa.

"What the fuck?" he muttered, his nostrils flaring and his eyes narrowed.

Rasa put her hand on his shoulder. She looked back at Paul's truck. Her face flushed. She was bent on shielding her siblings from a repeat of last night.

"Ach," she said, "Go to Kawika's. I'll get you later."

Ach hesitated, frowning. Rasa motioned with her head in the direction of Kawika's house.

"Ach. Please."

"Fine," he hissed before darting away.

Rasa's face relaxed as she turned to her sisters. "Ok, you

munchkins," she said pinching their cheeks playfully. "Let's go through the back. Mommy's busy." Rasa put her finger to her lips. "Shhhhhh..."

Rasa led the girls around the side. They crept like thieves, pushing away dense, overgrown foliage on their makeshift path. Rasa delighted in the way the ti leaf plants felt cool against her hot skin. The long, flat leaves brushed her arm and reminded her of being on the mountain.

They climbed the two creaky steps to the splintered back door. Rasa pushed it open. They tiptoed to their room.

Rasa nudged the girls to the bed and tucked them in. They fell asleep in no time.

Rasa wasn't tired, but she didn't want to think anymore. She pulled out her CD Walkman from under the bed. Nirvana's *Nevermind* was in. She inserted her earbuds, then cranked the volume. She skipped ahead to *Stay Away*. The hard drums followed by the guitar and bass filled her ears. Kurt's gruff voice joined in. Closing her eyes, she lip-synced.

Seconds later, Paul and her mother cried out in climatic ecstasy, so loud that it seemed to drown out Kurt's voice. Rasa heard Paul moan again.

Unwanted memories rushed in.

Kalindi's bedroom.

Kurt's voice.

Paul's moan.

Virginity stolen.

TiFFiN

Jaya watched his mother fill each of the four stainless steel compartments of the tiffin with the classic components of a Gujarati meal—shaak, dal, bhat, and rotli.

Jayshree scooped pickles into the compartment with the rotli, the finishing touch to the elaborate meal. Her downturned lips and dead eyes made Jaya feel as if his insides were being scooped out like the pickles. He pictured a penny falling in his hollow torso, plinking on its way down the empty frame of his bones and skin.

Jayshree stacked each fragrant compartment in the carrying frame. She sealed the top one with a tight-fitting lid and secured the frame's clasp.

Jaya recalled how different this lunch ritual had been in Niu Valley. Back then Jayshree whistled and flitted about as she stirred, chopped, and measured everything. It was like watching an Indian version of Disney's *Snow White*—she'd clean up the messy home of the seven dwarves, for sure, but then go above and beyond to fix a sumptuous Gujarati meal.

Not so in Kahala. Here she rarely cooked Gujarati food. At

the most it was once or twice a year. And always after Kusum foi, Sanjay's older sister, called. Jaya figured it had something to do with his mother feeling guilted into making tiffins by nosy Kusum, who had no idea what an ass her brother was. At least those were the kinds of things he'd overheard his mother mutter to herself after phone calls with Kusum foi.

Kusum foi had called this morning to congratulate them on Sanjay's new luxury condo project in Kahuku.

So today, Sanjay-the-ass would get a guilt-inspired tiffin from his wife.

Jaya followed his mother's slow, automatic movements. He tried to say something nice. "Mom, it smells so good."

Jayshree didn't look up.

Would things have been different if they lived in India? Jaya's imagination of a life in Gujarat was some form of what he'd seen in Bollywood films. Each morning before work and school, Jayshree would happily prepare tiffins for Sanjay and him. She'd fawn over them. She'd hover over him when he did his homework. As for Sanjay, he'd dutifully balance work and home life. No other shenanigans. His parents would tease each other but only because they got along so well. A loving, perfect family.

Just the thought made Jaya feel like he did when he drank a big cup of steamy chai.

In this pretend life in India, things might've been ideal. Except that even there his parents wouldn't have accepted him as their son. In their Gujarati circle, the pressure to conform to gender norms would have been more intense. He guessed roles and expectations were more defined and ingrained in Gujarat.

At least in America he got to express his gender the way he wanted, even if his parents and most of his classmates refused to acknowledge it.

The warmth in Jaya's body turned into an arctic chill.

"Jaya," Jayshree said.

"Yeah."

"Don't let the tiffin tip over in the car or the dal might leak."

"But I thought you—" In the past his mother would deliver the meal to his father.

"No, Jaya. Not anymore. I made it. You put it in his two-timing hands," she said. She didn't blink.

So that's how it was. Sanjay's cheating was an ordinary part of their life. Like showering. Or brushing your teeth. His mother despised Sanjay just enough to not want to deliver the tiffin but not enough to refuse to make it in the first place. Also not enough to leave him.

Jaya scratched his head. *So now he was the tiffin wallah?*

"Get going, Jaya," Jayshree said.

Jaya nodded. "Yeah, ok."

He set the tiffin in a small open cooler in the trunk so it wouldn't tip.

The weather was perfect—sunny and cloudless with just the right amount of breeze. He selected Nirvana's *In Utero* CD and turned it up. He drove and the music and the scenery relaxed him. By the time he reached the long gravelly road leading to the construction site, he'd reached his own nirvana.

When he stepped out of the car, the trade winds welcomed him. It occurred to him that maybe his father would want to share the tiffin with him. After all he wasn't a random tiffin wallah like in Mumbai. He was the son. Jaya flinched.

He was still a daughter to them.

The scent of cumin wafting from the tiffin took Jaya's senses on a trip. He reminisced about his family's last visit to Mumbai. Barely eight years old, Jaya had marvelled at the countless tiffin wallahs riding their bicycles through the crowded streets, maneuvering between trucks, cars, pedestrians, and the occasional cow, carrying multiple tiffins to ravenous workers throughout the huge city.

He smiled, surprising himself.

This is how Mom's supposed to feel, right?

The sun suddenly felt hotter. Stronger. The trades had disappeared. It was too quiet. He looked around. There weren't any people. No construction workers doing their thing. No engineers or architects in hard hats. Didn't the workers usually eat lunch on site?

Jaya opened the door of the trailer office. There at the far end of the trailer was Sanjay kissing someone.

Jaya froze. The tiffin slipped and crashed onto the floor. Dal leaked onto his Reeboks.

His father and the woman looked up.

Jaya was gone before they saw him. He jumped in his car and peeled out. He drove back to town shaking the steering wheel and making way-too-sharp turns.

Should he go back and call Sanjay out? Should he go home and tell Jayshree? Should he pretend like he didn't see anything?

In the end, he decided to keep quiet. The same as always.

Better to stuff it all down. Way, way down.

SAFE

The bus stop shelter near the Hau'ula Beach Park smelled of urine and sorrow. Rasa crinkled her nose at the used needles and ragged condoms that littered the area. She turned away to face the ocean. She thought about when they'd lived in a tent a few yards away. She pressed her palms together in prayer and lifted her head to the drab sky. "Thank you," she whispered, grateful for their shack. Also that her sisters had never been homeless.

The heavy clouds burst. Rain pummeled the ground. Rasa hopped over the garbage into the shelter. She stepped onto the bench under the narrow roof and hugged herself. The rain fell in thick drapes.

A cold gust of wind blew rain onto Rasa. She shivered and rubbed her bare arms. Her skin ached with chill. She tried to distract herself by counting the raindrops that landed on her slippered feet. She was at forty when a red Ferrari pulled up in front of the bus stop.

The passenger side window came down. An older man, maybe in his late thirties, called out, "Hello?"

Rasa looked up.

The man strained his neck to catch her eye. "Need a lift?"

Rasa looked left and right. No bus in sight. She sized up the man and his fancy car.

There was a stethoscope and white coat in the back seat. It reminded her of her siblings' doctors' appointments next week. She still needed three hundred dollars to cover the costs.

The library can wait.

Maybe this rich guy who might be a doctor could be useful. He couldn't be that bad if he was a doctor. He was supposed to help people, right? *Do no harm...*

She licked her lips and got to work. She made her teeth chatter. Then she leaned over so that the front of her short sundress fell away from her chest. She watched his eyes drift to her cleavage. "My savior," she said flashing her sexiest half-smile.

A flustered pink rash spread across the man's pale cheeks. His eyes widened. He gave her a closed-mouth smile. "Jump in."

He pressed a button to unlock the door.

She climbed in, breathing a sigh of relief.

"You're shaking." He reached behind her seat for a plush towel. "This will warm you up." Then he turned a dial on the center console and said, "So will this." Immediately her black leather seat began to heat up.

She cloaked herself in the towel. "Thanks." She brushed his arm with her fingers and followed his eyes following her fingers.

He shook his head quickly and adjusted the volume on the stereo. "The Police," he said, smiling to himself.

"Oh, I love them," she replied. She let her finger graze his leg.

Don't Stand So Close to Me came on. He revved the engine. "Ready?"

Rasa nodded.

Kamehameha Highway was empty but wet. Despite the slickness of the road, he floored it.

Rasa spread her fingers out and gently gripped his leg. The faster he went, the higher her hand moved up his thigh. And the bigger his smile grew.

Rasa got lost in the sounds. The swishing of the windshield wipers. Sting's pleading voice. The Ferrari's racecar engine. The exhale he tried to hide.

In no time they were on the North Shore. He pulled the car makai through a gate onto a short driveway. Rasa stepped out. The gray sky turned black. Thunder crashed. She ran ahead of...

That's when she realized she didn't know his name.

And he didn't know hers.

Oh well. Like it really matters. Like I'll ever see this guy again.

She stood trembling near the front door and peeked through the glass panels on either side. The living room resembled one of those hipster repurposed warehouses in Chinatown complete with sparse furnishing and a few massive works of modern art on the walls.

He caught up, then unlocked the door. Pushing it open, he moved to the side to let her in first. She slid her feet out of her slippers before she entered. He closed the door behind them. The sounds of the wild weather were muted. The quiet was a relief. Rasa walked to the glass double doors that overlooked the Pacific. The wild tossing waves hypnotized her. She pressed her forehead and fingertips onto the glass and pretended they were on a cruise ship. Below deck in their large suite she watched the storm, safe from it.

Safe.

Drowsiness overcame her. She forgot she was a black widow. She forgot about the money-making scheme she'd planned with this guy whose name she didn't know.

Instead she wanted to curl up on the dark brown suede couch and cover herself in the fuzzy white throw that lay neatly folded on one end. She wanted him to tuck the edges of the blanket under her. She wanted him to stroke her forehead and say, "Go to sleep." Then let her drift off into secure slumber.

Safe from the weather.

Safe from people.

Safe from him.

She turned around, determined to lie down on the couch for a solo nap.

But he was standing in front of it. Naked.

WORLDS APART

No one at school had ever rocked liberty spikes. Jaya thought he was the perfect person to introduce his classmates to this classic punk hairstyle. He was a misunderstood outsider anyway, why not be true to himself? He walked a brisk pace through the Manoa Prep campus with his head held high and his hair even higher.

He'd made it through the busy morning parking lot without any negative attention. Maybe his classmates would leave him alone today. Maybe they'd respect him for making a bold fashion statement.

Yeah, maybe.

His luck ran out as he approached the track.

"What's with the Mohawk? You're not that kind of Indian, you dumbass."

It was one of the three haole boys from Hawaii Kai, juniors just like Jaya, who bullied him at least once a week. He and his co-tormentors sprung up from the sidewalk and surrounded Jaya.

Jaya touched his scalp and looked away.

"We know you're gay, Jaya. Good thing, because no guy would ever hit that," the freckled one said with a slight one-handed shove.

Jaya took a step forward, hoping to escape their insults. But they tightened their circle. Jaya was trapped. And they turned their derision on, full blast.

"Curry-eating carpet-muncher."

"Go with me. Betcha I can turn you straight."

A minute later, someone pushed through the circle and stood next to Jaya. It was Alika Keahi. "What's going on?" he wanted to know, crossing his arms. He looked the shorter haole boys up and down, right and left. Jaya couldn't help but think of that Herb Kane painting in the school library—*Warrior Chief.* Alika was the chief thrusting his leiomano and saying, "Really? You've got no chance. Run along now, little white invaders."

Jaya stifled a laugh when the Hawaii Kai boys did just that. They left.

"Thanks, Alika," Jaya said. He extended his hand.

"No problem." Alika gave him a double-handed handshake.

Alika Keahi was more than fifty-percent Native Hawaiian with some Chinese and Portuguese. He was from Waianae. Unlike many of his classmates and their families, he and his family weren't well-off. They certainly couldn't afford Manoa Prep's tuition.

But Alika was the top wideout in the state, a talent that awarded him a full scholarship.

He was also brilliant. And ruggedly handsome—a full beard, koa skin, and light brown eyes. He had thick, wiry below-the-shoulder black hair that he always tied up in a small bun. He was the envy of his football teammates.

Not only that, but Alika was the humblest and nicest guy anyone could ever hope to meet. Just a week ago recruiters from several college football teams had come specifically to watch him play. They'd expressed strong interest in him. But it's not as if he bragged about it.

Jaya smiled and thanked Alika again. He wished he had Alika's strong, firm handshake. He also wished he had Alika's height and weight—6'3" and 190 pounds of lean muscle. There was no denying it: at only sixteen Alika was a bonafide stud. A bonafide stud who was also openly gay.

Jaya wanted to come out as trans at school. But if his own parents didn't get it, he figured there was no way classmates would. He was convinced that if he came out, no one would see him as a "real" guy anyway. They'd continue to focus on gay vs. straight like the Hawaii Kai dumbasses. They'd keep mislabeling him as a confused lesbian. In his experience, people seemed more able to wrap their heads around gayness than around being trans. Not that they necessarily were accepting of gay people, but they could discuss it. People seemed scared of the word transgender. They didn't get it and they didn't want to be near it.

But here stood Alika. Someone who not only didn't say ignorant, hurtful things to him but had also helped him out.

Jaya steepled his fingers. Maybe things could get better.

And they did. Because that was the day his friendship with Alika began. Alika not only became Jaya's best friend, he also doubled as Jaya's personal bodyguard.

MOTHER BEAR

Rasa rested her head on her palm as she took a long drag of her last cigarette. She exhaled a ring of smoke, then got up from the step of their shack's front porch. There was nothing else going on for her—Nitya and Shanti were napping and Ach said he was going over to Kawika's—and she hated being out of smokes. Her Camel Lights were one thing she could count on to make her feel better. She decided she might as well head to the 7-11 for another pack of her beloved cigarettes.

She had an appointment later at the Kahuku Women's Health Clinic to get refills of the two other packs she hated being without these days—packs of birth control pills and condoms. A few months ago, she'd had this intense burning whenever she peed. It was so bad, she took the bus to the clinic. The nurse practitioner gave her an antibiotic injection and sent her home with birth control pills and condoms. She'd asked Rasa to come back every three months to restock the pills and condoms, which was fine with Rasa. After all, those packs—unlike her cigarette packs—were free and prevented pregnancy and STDS, as the nurse practitioner said. That was great, but mostly Rasa never wanted to feel that burning pain again.

Cruising down the grassy shoulder of Kamehameha Highway, she saw a group of teenage boys up ahead. They were huddled in a tight circle. She stubbed the lit end of her cigarette on a nearby telephone pole. She slid it over her right ear for later.

She reached the edge of the circle. The first boy she recognized was David, a lanky, pimple-faced local boy. He was holding up his clenched fist and yelling.

"Hey, bastard. Lemme have that five dollars."

Rasa didn't know the boy who spoke up next. He was heavy-set with a head of thick black curls and a harelip. He cracked his knuckles and said, "Yeah, we know your mom's a ho. We know she gets paid!"

Oh no.

Rasa craned her neck. She spotted Ach in the middle. His back was to her and his hands were shoved into the pockets of his faded gym shorts. He was staring at the ground.

Then the runt among the bullies jumped forward. He shoved Ach. Her brother lost his balance and fell. A cloud of red dirt flew up where he landed. He scooted back on his okole out of the circle.

Rasa puffed out her chest. She grabbed Ach's arm. With one swift tug, she pulled him up. The boys snickered. Rasa towed her brother. "Quick! Walk. Don't look back," she whispered.

They headed straight home. The boys didn't follow them but the insults they shouted did.

"I'll leave him alone if you suck me off."

"Come on, Rasa, I taste good."

Rasa tuned them out. She took Ach's hand in hers and squeezed. They ran towards home in silence.

When they approached the Kim Taylor Reece Gallery, Rasa quick-looked at her brother. His eyes were narrowed to crinkled slits. His jaw was clenched. But it was his tears that really got to her. Her fists balled up. She snarled, low and deep. She felt an overwhelming urge to run back and beat the living shit out of those boys.

ANGER TURNED iNWARD

"Chee, Jaya. What is this hair?" Jayshree pointed to Jaya's revamped hairstyle with her open palm—liberty spikes still graced the center but he'd shaved the sides.

Jayshree shook her head. "You're so lucky my mother is dead. Because if she saw this, it would kill her!"

With her Gujju accent, the "kill" sounded like "keel." It crossed Jaya's mind to make some wiseass comment like, "She's not a ship."

"You don't look like a high school girl. You look like one of those crazy American college boys!"

Sanjay put his fork down and pushed his chair back. He stood up. "What have we done wrong, Jaya?" His wide, easy smile was now a frown.

The only reason the three of them were eating dinner together was because Sanjay had landed a huge contract for more condos. This time in Waimanalo. And he wanted to pre-party. But Jaya knew Sanjay's real party would happen later—when his father went out that night.

Sanjay paced. "When I was your age, I never disobeyed. I worked on the farm..."

Jaya let his head fall. He stopped listening. He'd heard this a hundred times before. This was his father's version of *back in my day I walked three miles in the snow to school...*

These stories weren't the bedtime stories of his father's youth, the ones he told back in Niu Valley. His father used these stories to slap Jaya in the face.

"Why do you punish us with this, Jaya?" Sanjay didn't give Jaya a chance to answer. "I know why. You're not making friends with the right kids at school." He clasped his wrists behind his back and continued to pace. "Didn't I tell you those Manoa Prep kids will be your connections in the future? Why else would I spend so much money sending you there? It's not just for the education. You have to meet the right kids. I work with their parents. Those kids don't have wild hair like this. They don't play loud music on the guitar. And those girls look like girls."

Jaya's face twisted. If his parents knew what the other kids did, they'd think Jaya was a saint. He stared at his plate. It was the same shit, different day.

Sanjay stopped. He leaned his elbows on his chair. Then he shook his head and sat back down. "You should be friends with Jennifer and Karen. Their fathers are rich investment bankers." He picked up his fork.

They ate in silence.

Sanjay opened his mouth again. "You know, Jaya," he said in a matter-of-fact way, "hanging out—as you say—with Alika will get you nowhere. He's from Waianae. His family is low-level. That's like if I'd stayed in Gujarat and played all time with Dev. Where would I've ended up? I'll tell you where—peeling dried cow dung off the streets."

Jaya squinted his eyes shut hard. He wondered what they'd say if they knew Alika was gay.

Sanjay kept lecturing, but Jaya couldn't hear a word.

We're wealthy. I don't have to struggle. I'm a spoiled brat whining about my gender rights when really I have nothing serious to complain about.

He dropped his fork and rubbed his temples.

I don't deserve anything. I'm a useless complainer. I don't want to be here. Put me out of my misery! I just want to die.

He buried his face in his hands.

How can I want to die when my life isn't a quarter as bad as other people's?

Like Roland. Roland Cruz was a thirty-four-year-old man who'd lived on the streets for over five years.

Jaya had run into him just today at the homeless shelter. It was his day to serve lunch. Roland had been the last in line. Jaya filled a plate with rice and beef stew on top. He smiled big as he slid the tray of food to Roland.

"Tanks, eh, Jaya," he said with a gummy smile.

"Sure thing, Roland." Half of Roland's left foot was wrapped in a dirty bandage. He hobbled to one of the tables, set his tray down and limped back towards Jaya. He reached the counter and leaned on it, searching Jaya's face for a minute. "Hmmmm. Yes."

Jaya scanned Roland's prune-colored face. Deep wrinkles carved the skin around his yellow eyes and cracked lips. Jaya wondered what hardships had turned this young man's face so old so quick. Roland's face didn't match the strong body it was connected to. Or the soft, optimistic gaze coming from his eyes.

"You need something else?" Jaya raised his eyebrows.

"No, no. I jus want to tell you somethin'." Roland paused and inhaled deeply. "You remind me of my son, Reuben," he whispered.

Fifteen-year-old Reuben had been killed six years ago in a hit-and-run.

"Reuben was a good boy. Always helping people. You li'dat too, Jaya." Roland stopped. He put his weathered left hand on top of Jaya's smooth right hand. His fingers felt like coarse sandpaper. "No worries, Jaya. Everyting's gonna be ok."

CRACKED HEART

Ach stared hard at Rasa. "I saw Micah coming out. Wh-why was he here?" he fumed.

Rasa knew Ach already knew why. She scratched her neck and shrugged. "He was looking for Mom." The lie slipped out easily, like a kid running barefoot on the large, wet rocks of Ka Iwi's shore.

"Bullshit!" Ach cracked his knuckles and huffed. "Ras, that fucker is like thirty. I'm gonna kick his ass."

Ach's protectiveness still surprised her. "Don't, Ach. Everything's cool" She studied his angry expression. "I'm ok." She stepped forward and grabbed his fists. She squeezed.

Ach ripped his hands away. "Nothing's ok. And it's all Mom's fault." His face contorted in pain. "How come she doesn't care about what happens to us?" he whispered. His eyes glistened with tears. "And now you?"

She bowed her head. She felt her heart crack.

Ach gave her a pleading look. "Ras...you don't get it."

"Get what?" She was having trouble meeting his gaze.

He rubbed his eyes. "Nothing."

Rasa looked up. "No, Ach. Come on. Tell me." His expression filled her with panic. "What are you talking about?"

"Nothing, Ras. It's nothing."

"Ach. I know it's not nothing. What is it?"

"My notebook…"

"Your notebook, yeah, tell me. What about it?"

"My drawings…"

Rasa waited. "Yeah I remember. Tell me what you're thinking. Please!"

Tears streaked Ach's face and snot bubbled out of his nose. He opened his mouth, but nothing came out. He pressed his lips together and looked away.

With her shaking hands, Rasa wiped away a couple of tears that dangled on Ach's jaw.

Memories of the genital drawings in his notebook flashed through her mind. She always thought he'd done them because he'd walked in on Kalindi and some guy. Maybe he'd seen them fully naked. Or having sex.

She stroked his head. "Tell me."

"No!" he blurted. Then without warning he whisked around and darted away.

"Ach!" she called out.

But he kept running.

PERFECT GUJJU DAUGHTER

Jaya admired the soft colors of dusk. The pinks, corals, and baby blues of the horizon beckoned like a bejeweled girl in a Bollywood film. He wished he could stay out on the deck all night.

Nature was safe.

People, on the other hand...

He snapped a mental photo of the sublime—harmless—scene and went back inside.

The Pacific seascape had taken care of the outside. His mother had made sure the inside was beautiful as well—candles, white ginger bouquets, dim lights, jasmine incense.

His parents' party was in full swing. Fifty or so people mingled in small groups. Jazz poured out of the speakers at just the right volume. The room was filled with the sound of drunken laughter and superficial toasts.

Jaya had been a witness to enough of these gatherings to know the whispers of wealthy entitlement that infected their merriment. He never enjoyed the festivities. His goal remained unchanged—to find food and escape back upstairs.

He spotted his father a few feet away at the long buffet table lined with shiny chafing dishes. Dodging him would not be difficult. He was surrounded by a gaggle of ladies, clearly in his element—the center of attention.

One of the ladies, dressed in a short, body-hugging black dress, touched Sanjay's arm and giggled. "Sanjay, you have such nice features." She winked. "You look like that Bollywood actor—what's his name?"

Sanjay half smiled. "I think you mean Amitabh Bachchan."

The lady grinned. "Yes, yes!"

Sanjay took a sip of his whiskey. "I get that a lot." He paused, slowly adjusting the collar of his aloha shirt. "You know, ladies," he continued, "Amitabh's first salary was three hundred rupees, which is about four-and-a-half dollars. So was mine. And look at me now!"

Jaya rolled his eyes.

The circle of women put their hands in front of their mouths. They made little cackling sounds.

Jaya felt sick. He wanted to blow chunks. He wondered if this was how his mother felt before she puked.

He made it to the chicken makhani and biriyani without being noticed.

"Jaya."

Oh no.

"Oh Ja-ya," Jayshree sang like she was Lata Mangeshkar. "Come here. I want you to meet someone." His mother's voice was way too happy.

Jaya put on a fake smile. Then he pivoted and walked towards Jayshree. She was dressed in an ornate black sari heavy with the weight of the gold thread embroidery. Her best twenty-four-karat gold and diamond jewelry sparkled on her ears, neck, and arms. Her recently dyed black hair was twisted into a tight, low bun and clung to the nape of her neck like an opihi.

Jaya was taken aback by how stunning his mother was. She reminded him of Rekha in the 80s. How could Sanjay even consider side dishes when his main entree was this exquisite?

Jaya got a load of the person she wanted him to meet—the only other Indian lady at the party. Jayshree put her arm around his shoulder and said, "Betta, this is Rita auntie. She's one of my dearest friends from school in Gujarat. She and her husband own a chain of motels in Alabama. They're vacationing here for a couple of weeks."

Jayshree's introduction of Rita auntie cued him to turn up the politeness. He extended his hand. In his most deferential voice, he said, "Nice to meet you, auntie." She was almost six inches shorter than his mother. Her hair was all gray. She was also wearing a fancy evening sari and expensive jewelry.

She shook Jaya's hand. "Ha Betta, nice to meet you too," she said in a thick Gujju accent. Her eyes wandered to his undercut. She raised her brows. "Betta, what happened to your hair?"

"She donated her beautiful long hair to this charity that makes wigs," Jayshree lied quickly. "You know, for kids who have cancer."

Jaya cringed. His hair hadn't been long since fourth grade. Denial and lies, as usual, Jaya thought.

Rita auntie tipped her head side to side in the quintessential Indian way to show approval and said, "Oh betta, you're such a kind girl." She stroked his cheek with her palm.

Jaya felt dampness in his pits. He wished he'd started testosterone therapy so her hand would've grazed hair.

Rita auntie sighed. "The other Indian girls I know are so selfish. But not you," she purred.

Jaya couldn't take much more. He needed to get away from them. He'd only come down for some freakin' food.

Jayshree chimed in before Jaya got to planning his exit. "Jaya betta, Rita auntie has a son..."

Of course.

He should've guessed. He should've expected this. Jayshree was an expert at springing this sort of thing on him.

Jaya was not about to get into a discussion of potential male suitors. "Sorry, Rita auntie, I really have to finish some homework. Big project due Monday." He gave her an ill-timed smile. "Nice to meet you though."

If his mother could lie, why couldn't he?

He did an about face and hurried to the stairs without snagging food. He heard Rita auntie's remarks to his mother. "What a generous daughter you have, Jayshree. Giving up her hair for charity. And studying when you're having such a nice party. She's going to make a fine wife someday. I hope to my Sunil."

Jaya bounded up the spiral staircase. He went straight to his guitar room, slamming the door behind him. He leaned against it, slowly sliding to a sit.

Nobody got it! None of them understood who he really was.

Not his parents.

Not their rich friends.

Not his classmates.

He couldn't even say "not my friends," because he only had one friend. When classmates looked at him, they still saw him as a girl who looked like a boy. He knew because they continued to make sure he overheard bits of their whispers at school.

Lesbian dyke.

Indian butch.

Heck, they didn't even know the uncontroversial things about him. Like how much he loved playing guitar.

The sunburst color of his vintage 1970's Univox Hi-flier Phase II caught his eye. He picked it up. He settled the strap comfortably on his right shoulder.

But then he exchanged the Univox for his Telecaster. He'd built this Tele himself. Over the past year he'd become a DIY guitar tech who modified his guitars like Kurt—stripped down, raw, and with a heavy grunge sound. The single pickup he'd installed by the bridge was a humbucker he'd reduced to the size of a single coil. He'd painted the body red. Once he'd even used piano wire for strings to get the thick sound he was going for.

Jaya plugged in, then tuned. His eyes fell on the dark scar on his right hand. A few weeks ago when he was fiddling with the Tele's electronic guts behind the pickup he'd burned his hand with the soldering gun. He smiled to himself. The pain was worth it. His Tele sounded perfect.

But the best part was the Tele's shape—a thick squarish slab of wood with one lower wing. And when Jaya played the wing seemed to emerge from his crotch. He couldn't help but imagine it was his semi hard-on.

He didn't bother warming up with something mellow like usual. He closed his eyes and pretended he was the lead guitarist/singer of a band his parents had hired for the party. Little did they or their snobby guests know that his band wasn't planning to play mellow jazz tonight...

Jaya counted in—*one two three*—then ripped into *Negative Creep*, one of Nirvana's heaviest songs. He played, screaming the crap out of the jumble of things he was feeling the way he pictured Kurt would've.

By the time he was done, sweat dripped off his body. He pursed his lips in a self-satisfied smile. He shut his eyes and dared to let himself feel better.

PiZZAZZ

Rasa managed a few more puffs until her cigarette was nothing more than a butt. She crushed it on the wooden step of their shack, then shoved it in her pocket. She took a second to compose herself before strolling in.

Sharon was there.

Sharon Kamaile was a Child Protective Services social worker. A few months ago, someone reported Kalindi to CPS for child neglect and sex trafficking of a minor, they said. Sharon had been assigned to investigate.

That first time Sharon came to their place, Kalindi hadn't been home in over four days.

"Where's your mother?" Sharon had wanted to know.

Rasa shoved her clammy hands in her dress pockets and came up with an excuse. "Oh, she's in Punaluʻu. Helping her sick hānai grandma."

Sharon narrowed her eyes. "Let's call her."

Think fast. "My mom doesn't have a cell phone. And I don't know the number in Punaluʻu."

Sharon sighed. "Rasa, is your mother making you…"

Rasa laughed a loud, unusually high-pitched laugh, cutting Sharon off. "Everything's fine," she said.

Sharon's forehead wrinkled. She stared at Rasa but then her face relaxed.

That day Sharon let it slide.

Since then Sharon stopped by every week or two. When Kalindi wasn't around, Rasa had been hard-pressed to come up with excuses. It surprised Rasa every time Sharon left without busting them.

Would their luck change today? Rasa scanned the room. Everyone was home. Her siblings. Their mother. And no guys.

"Hi, Sharon," Rasa said, grinning.

"Hello, Rasa. Howzit going?"

Rasa fake-coughed. "Everything's good." She took a quick look at Kalindi. Her eyes were red.

Uh-oh. Is she stoned again?

Rasa moved over to block Sharon's view of Kalindi.

"Rasa!" Shanti cried, limping over. "Look! Look at my foot! Still hurts."

Earlier in the morning at the beach Shanti had stepped barefoot on a kiawe branch buried just under the surface of the sand.

Rasa turned to Shanti and blew her a kiss. "I'll take a good look after auntie Sharon leaves, ok?"

"Okie dokie, artichokie," Shanti giggled.

Rasa glanced at Nitya and Ach. Nitya had her nose in a book. Ach was drawing. She looked back at Sharon.

"Well, Rasa, I was just talking to your mother before you got here," Sharon said. She stopped and tilted her head to the side to look at Kalindi. Then she brought her attention back to Rasa. "Listen, I know something's up. I'm going to get to the bottom of it."

Rasa jumped in. "Nothing's up. We're just trying to get by."

Sharon frowned. "That's not what I heard. A little birdie told me about a couple of guys..."

Rasa interrupted. "What can my mom do, Sharon? She's a single mom and she needs help sometimes. Fixing things," Rasa lied with a straight face. "You know, manly stuff," she added with a wink.

Kalindi chimed in. "That's right. The toilet's been acting up again." She gave Rasa a subtle nod.

Rasa knew what her mother meant.

Operation pizzazz.

Operation pizzazz was one of the lessons Kalindi had taught Rasa. *Use your good looks and pizzazz to get out of any situation, no matter how sticky.*

Rasa sashayed over to Sharon. She held Sharon's gaze as she angled her head to the side and batted her bright green eyes. "Don't worry, Sharon. We're ok," she said with the right amount of sweetness.

As predicted Sharon eased up. She smiled, put her free hand on her hip, and shook her head. "Until next time," she said. She reached into her purse. She pulled out a business card for Rasa.

"Thank you so much," Rasa said. She took the card.

"Ok." Sharon turned and headed outside. The screen door slammed shut.

Rasa tossed the business card onto the coffee table. "You ok?" she asked Kalindi.

Kalindi smiled. "Nicely done," she said, springing up from the sofa and gliding to the full-length mirror.

Rasa watched Kalindi fix herself up.

Seriously? She's going out right after Sharon left?

Nothing, nobody, not even Sharon from CPS, could make Kalindi change her ways. Black widows survived in extreme conditions. They were born to persevere.

And so was Kalindi. She'd told Rasa bits and pieces of her complicated past. Kalindi grew up in Rio de Janeiro's Rocinha favela. Her father was killed in a bloody gang-related shootout when she was three. Her mother disappeared when she was thirteen. Kalindi lived with various relatives until she turned fifteen. By then, according to what she'd told Rasa, she looked like an eighteen-year-old Brazilian supermodel. One summer evening, she met a handsome European postgraduate student while walking on Ipanema beach. She left Rio de Janeiro with him the next day.

Kalindi took one final look in the mirror. She waltzed to the door. "I'll be with John," she said without looking back. And she was gone.

Rasa turned to Shanti. "Let me see your boo-boo," she said in a baby voice.

"See!" Shanti stuck out her foot.

Rasa inspected the wound then kissed Shanti's hand. "You're so strong, it's better already!"

Shanti smiled a shy smile.

Rasa checked the clock. 1:30 p.m. "Lunch time?" She looked at her siblings.

Shanti and Nitya nodded. Ach remained silent.

"I'll make saimin for us," Rasa said, heading to the kitchen.

"Rasa!" Shanti called.

Rasa looked over her shoulder.

"Mommy left us again," Shanti said, blinking tears away.

Rasa turned around to find Nitya crying, her book on the ground. Ach snapped his pencil in half and flung the two broken pieces across the room. Then he slammed his fist into the wall. It left a small dent.

Rasa went into mother overdrive. "Everything's gonna be ok. I won't leave."

Rasa squatted down in front of her siblings. She spread her arms. Shanti and Nitya leaned in for a hug. Ach didn't move. When Rasa let go of her sisters, Ach grunted. He glared at her with tears in his eyes.

Rasa caressed his head, but he didn't move or speak. She examined his face. Ach resembled photos of a young Che Guevara. His skin tone was light, his eyes penetrating and dark, his hair thick and black.

Rasa looked at her sisters. They were both striking in their own way. Shanti's thin, light brown hair, narrow brown eyes, and caramel skin matched her rough and tumble personality. Nitya with her blond hair, blue eyes, and fair skin looked more like a little Swedish girl ready to dance around a maypole.

Rasa looked the most like Kalindi.

She ran her knuckle down Ach's cheek. Then she stood up and went back to the kitchen.

This time it was Ach's booming voice that made her stop. "I hate her," he blurted in a deep voice. "And you, too."

Rasa turned around.

Ach's eyes, smoldering with sadness, were glued to the wall. "Why do you protect her?"

Rasa sank onto the sofa next to him. "Because I don't want Sharon to separate us. She'd send us to a foster home. Maybe different ones," she whispered. She rubbed his back. "Talk to me," she said.

He shook his head and turned away.

Clearly this wasn't a situation for operation pizzazz. There was nothing she could do to make Ach feel better. That was something only his real mother could've done. Should've done.

PARTY POOPER

Jaya scoffed at all the Benzes, Beamers, and Lexuses lining the top street of Pu'uikena Drive's gated community. He turned to Alika. "Why'd I let you talk me into this?" he grumbled.

They climbed the marble steps to Samuel's house. Samuel was Manoa Prep's quarterback. And from one of the wealthiest families on the island. But a decent guy according to Alika.

Alika smirked. "Because I have to show face. That means so does my best friend." He snickered. "Plus it's the first big party of our senior year."

"Trust me," Jaya said. "I've been to enough of my parents' fake-ass rich-people parties for a lifetime."

"That's true." Alika laughed. "But you never know. This party might be fun. Maybe you'll meet a girl."

They got to the front double doors. Loud, thumping electronic music battered from the inside.

"I highly doubt both possibilities." Jaya shook his head, cramming his hands into the pockets of his cargo shorts. "So. I have your word. It's only to show face—then we're out?"

"Yup." Alika opened one of the doors. They stepped into the low-lit foyer.

Jaya scanned the living room. Empty beer and vodka bottles scattered the floor and end tables. From one corner, a cloud of smoke encircled several guys and girls like a cannabis forcefield. Classmates stumbled around, drunk or high. Or both. Couples were making out on the couches.

But the thing that Jaya couldn't take his eyes away from was the big glass bowl on the coffee table. Ten or so of his classmates sat around it. They were taking turns grabbing fistfuls of what was inside—pills. Pills of all different shapes, sizes, and colors. Grab, swallow, chase with a shot.

Jaya elbowed Alika. "The most expensive school on the island churns out a bunch of dipshits."

Alika chuckled. "Yeah. Let's keep walking."

They entered the kitchen.

Samuel called out, "Hey! Alika! What's up, bro?"

Alika and Samuel fistbumped.

"Beer?" Samuel held out a couple of bottles.

"Sure, why not." Alika twisted off the cap and took a sip.

Samuel looked at Jaya.

"Um, I'm ok, thanks. Driving."

Samuel shrugged. He turned to Alika. "Glad you could make it out, bro."

Jaya wandered away from the kitchen into the living room. Maybe he could kill time by exploring. None of his intoxicated classmates noticed him. Not that he wanted them to. Jaya frowned and headed towards a long hallway. At the end were some stairs.

He parked on the third step. He checked his watch. 11:30 p.m. At midnight, he'd suggest they head out.

He rested his head on the wall and closed his eyes. He almost dozed off, but a loud cry startled him. He sat up, trying to pinpoint where it was coming from. He listened. A couple of seconds later, he heard it again. Someone was yelling and it sounded like trouble.

He bounded up the steps. A few dim ceiling lights helped guide him through the narrow hallway, but each door he passed was closed. By then he could tell the shrieking was coming from the end of the hall. It grew more high-pitched as he approached the last door.

It was open a crack. Jaya looked in. The room was dark except for a small nightlight in the corner. Jaya's eyes adjusted. He focused on the bed.

A naked girl lay on it. He recognized her from school.

Julie.

She was struggling to escape a beefy, naked guy who was on top of her. He had her pinned down. Jaya didn't know who he was. He looked older than a high schooler. He was fumbling with his junk.

"No!" Julie cried. "Stop!"

Without giving it a second thought, Jaya charged into the room. He shoved the guy with all his might.

"What the fuck?" the guy yelled from the far edge of the king-size bed. He shot up and lumbered towards Jaya. "What the hell are you doing, dude?" he shouted, shoving Jaya hard.

Jaya flew backwards through the open door and hit the wall. He rushed at the guy and threw a punch. It landed it on the guy's right cheek. "Aww!" Jaya bellowed, clutching his sore fist.

The guy stood still for a second with his hand on his cheek. Then he growled, "Fuck. You. You. Little. Piece. Of. Shit." He took one big step forward and delivered a powerful uppercut.

Jaya dropped to the floor. He couldn't move his body. His eyelids fluttered. The last thing he saw was Alika and Samuel running down the hall towards him.

BODY FOR BOARD

Rasa swam back to the Hau'ula shore after her longest freedive yet—almost four minutes. She waded out of the water and collapsed on the sand. She rested her head on her knees. She caught her breath. Her heartbeat slowed. She tried to swallow but her mouth was dry. She chided herself for forgetting her water bottle.

When she felt better, she stood up. She brushed the sand off her bottom and surveyed the swell. The winds were offshore making conditions perfect for surfing.

Wish I had my own board.

She'd surfed plenty of times on borrowed boards. She looked up and down the beach. There were some families but no surfers with extra boards lying around. She sighed.

Then she caught sight of Landon. He was paddling in from a surf session.

Landon was older. Rasa happened to know that he was impressed by her. She was, after all, one of the few girls in Hau'ula who paddled in rough conditions. She could hold her breath underwater for minutes. As buff as he might be, Rasa figured he probably couldn't hold his breath underwater much longer than a minute.

When he reached the shore, he jumped up with his surfboard tucked under his right arm. He saw Rasa and waved.

She waved back.

Landon walked towards her, his eyes drifting from her gorgeous smile down to her body that was in nothing more than a red Brazilian bikini. When he was next to her, he tried to play it cool.

"Hey, Rasa," he said. He had to strain to keep his face blank. "What's up?" He laid his board on the sand.

Rasa slicked back her long wet hair. "Just finished a dive."

"Cool. You been surfing at all? Killer swell this week."

"Yeah, I've been keeping an eye on the waves," she said. "But, no, shit, I don't have a board."

They both stared at the waves. Then Landon spoke up. "I've got an extra longboard..." He cocked his head to the side.

Rasa studied his tan face. He had a bunch of sunspots on his cheeks. Water dripped from his shoulder-length blond hair. She followed a drop as it glided down his broad, bare chest and over his rock hard abs. It disappeared under the waistband of his board shorts. Quickly she brought her eyes back to his.

A smile dangled on the corner of Landon's lips. "You can borrow it anytime," he said.

Rasa licked her lips. She put her right hand on her hip and stuck it out a bit. Then she flashed him a seductive smile. She combed her hair slowly with her left fingers. "Really?"

Landon stood straighter. He adjusted his board shorts. "Oh yeah," he blurted. He relaxed his stance. Then he squinted his eyes at her. "Why don't you come over to my place and get it yourself."

He raised his left eyebrow, adding, "Maybe you can keep it."

"Well, well," Rasa said. "It is my birthday soon…"

She didn't tell him that it was only number seventeen.

GENTLEMAN

"Look who's here," Alika said with a chin up and a half-smile. "The hero." He started a slow clap.

Jaya shook his head as he slid into the booth opposite Alika at McCully Zippy's.

"Ha ha," Jaya fake-laughed. Then he touched the deep purple bruise on his left jaw and cheek. "Yeah, the hero who needed two big dudes to rescue him."

"That was nothing, brah." Alika's expression became serious. "You know you saved Julie, right?"

"I guess."

"He would've raped her."

"But you and Samuel got rid of him."

A waitress stopped by the table. "You boys know what you want?" she asked in a bored voice.

Alika looked up. "A chili omelette, please."

"Same," Jaya said.

"Anything to drink?"

"Coffee, black," Jaya requested.

Alika held up his full glass. "Water's good."

Jaya waited until the waitress walked away before he spoke. "Who was that asshole anyway?"

"Some guy who graduated from 'I'iwi Academy two years ago." Alika's lip curled. "What a loser—going to a high school party."

"Right? F'in predator."

The waitress brought Jaya's coffee.

Alika gulped a third of his water then burped. "What'd your parents think?" he asked pointing to Jaya's bruise.

Jaya laid his hand on his jaw and opened and closed it slowly. "I told my mom I fell. My dad hasn't seen it yet."

Alika frowned. "Why not tell 'em the truth? I think they'd be proud of you."

Jaya chuckled. "Yay. You'd think."

"What'dya mean?"

"My parents still think I'm a girl so they'd be like..." Jaya stopped. He looked up at Alika. He switched to a heavy Gujarati accent. "Jaya, why did you do that? Now who will want to marry you? Chee. I bet that girl, what was her name? Ju-hi? I bet she drank too much. That's what happens when girls drink too much."

Alika winced. "Oh man."

"Yeah. They're so clueless. It's actually kinda funny because *they* drink too much," Jaya said in his normal voice. "Both of them."

The waitress arrived with their omelettes.

Jaya shoveled a big bite of cheesy chili omelette into his mouth. *Owww!* When he tried to chew it, a sharp pain radiated through the left side of his face. He dropped his fork and brought his hand to his cheek. He gradually worked the bite down. By the time he swallowed, Alika had inhaled half his plate.

"I don't get it," Jaya said. "How is it that so many guys think they can do whatever they want? My dad totally does whatever the fuck he wants. Maybe he doesn't rape my mom—well I don't think so anyway—but he freakin' cheats on her all the time. And treats her like shit."

"That's messed up," Alika sympathized, shaking his head.

"You know I've been all sad over my parents fighting and stuff. But after seeing that 'I'iwi jackass in action last night, I'm kinda over feeling sorry for myself."

Alika swallowed a bite. "I never thought you felt sorry for yourself."

"I guess what I mean is that even though my parents aren't so nice, I'm not so bad. I don't think I'd cheat on a girlfriend. And I definitely wouldn't rape anyone. That all seems so obvious, huh?"

"Yeah."

They finished the rest of their meal in silence.

Jaya stared out the window as he took the last couple of sips of his coffee. He put the cup down then muttered, "If I ever get a girlfriend, I'm gonna be such a gentleman."

GONE FOR GOOD

Rasa watched Kalindi apply makeup with artistic precision. Black liquid liner painted in perfect cat eye style on her upper eyelids. Black mascara lengthened and thickened the lashes around her bright green eyes. Her skin, free of blemish, didn't require any foundation or powder, just a bit of bronzer to accentuate her high cheekbones. She glossed aubergine lipstick over her full lips and pressed them together to spread the color evenly. She inspected her face in the mirror. Satisfied, she smiled.

Rasa smiled too, admiring her mother's transformation. Still, Rasa thought her mother was most lovely without makeup.

Kalindi stepped back from the mirror. She adjusted the front of her long, burgundy dress to reveal more of her cleavage.

Wait a second. Her mother was wearing the dress she'd supposedly been saving for a "special occasion."

"I'll be with Steve," Kalindi announced. Her eyes met Rasa's in the mirror. She winked and smiled so big that her top and bottom front teeth were in plain sight. Then Kalindi started humming.

Humming? Rasa scrunched her face. Kalindi was acting weird.

Not silent or crafty like her usual black widow self. Rasa examined the reflection of her mother's face more closely and swore she saw sheer joy emanating. It seemed to surround Kalindi just like the aura around the Buddha's face on the painting that hung beside the mirror.

Rasa blew out her cheeks, then rested her chin on her hand.

Kalindi looked in her direction. "Come on, Ras," she said. She pumped some argan oil onto her palm and rubbed her hands together. She ran her hands through her dark curls. "You know it's the only way we can stay in this house."

Rasa opened her mouth to say something, but just then Shanti tapped her arm. Tucking a few strands of Shanti's thin hair behind her right ear, Rasa asked, "Who's in the mood for banana pancakes?"

Shanti jumped up and down, squealing, "Me, me! With lots of syrup!" She grabbed Rasa's hand and flipped it over. She mashed her lips onto her big sister's palm and made a kissing noise. Then she jerked her head up to Kalindi and stuck out her tongue.

Kalindi kept humming. Shanti pivoted and skipped away chanting, "Pancakes! Pancakes! Banana-nana pancakes!" She reached the front door, flung it open and trotted out. The door slammed shut behind her.

Kalindi checked herself in the mirror one more time. She turned to face Rasa. "I'll be back in a week or so." She slung her tote bag over her shoulder. She looked around and walked out the door.

Rasa shrugged. Her day-to-day duties didn't change much with or without Kalindi's presence.

But days passed without their mother's return. Her siblings didn't ask where their mother was. Shanti dragged her blanket through the house. Nitya walked around hunched over. And Ach stormed about with his eyes in an angry squint.

Another week and still no Kalindi.

One more week after that and Rasa understood that, this time, Kalindi was gone for good.

PU'U MANAMANA

Jaya's parents fought longer than usual that night. Probably because of the scantily dressed woman who showed up at the door earlier, asking for Sanjay.

Jayshree went bezerk and Sanjay went into full-on defense.

But the sleepless night that followed hadn't been a complete waste for Jaya. Thanks to *Millie*. He played her through the long, dark hours of his parents' drunken tirade. He even wrote a new song that he planned to open up with at his next Waikiki gig.

When the sun burst over the horizon in Kahala, there was finally silence. He crept out of his room and checked on his parents. As expected, they were sleeping it off. Jaya knew he should also try to sleep but he wasn't tired anymore. He decided he needed sunlight and fresh air.

He jumped into his Beamer and headed east then north, not knowing if he had a final destination or if it was only a drive. He blasted Nirvana's *Territorial Pissings*. The screaming lyrics and cacophonous music put him at ease.

An hour or so later, he passed Crouching Lion. He remembered that the Pu'u Manamana trailhead was nearby. According to Alika it was one of the most dangerous hikes on Oahu. It also happened to be one of Alika's favorites. He told Jaya he'd done it couple of times with his cousins. The elevation gain was almost 2,000 feet!

Before he could think himself out of it, Jaya swerved his car off Kamehameha Highway and parked on the grassy shoulder. He walked for a bit before he found the trail's entrance.

He began the steep ascent. In front of him the intense blue sky tumbled into the vivid green mountains. Soon the trail became narrower. The sides sloped down to valleys. From what Alika had said, the worst was yet to come.

He stepped up his pace and very soon he reached a small lookout. He took a break. The air was still. The light sweat covering his body felt thicker the longer he stood. He scanned the breathtaking view of the crystal blue and turquoise waters of Kahana Bay. He couldn't help but smile. It occurred to him that he'd forgotten about his parents' fight until that second.

He got back on the path and hauled ass. In a little while the trail had become less than a foot wide. Alika hadn't exaggerated. He kept his eyes focused in front of his feet. One misstep could mean slipping down the sheer drop on either side to a sure death. The ascent gave way to another safe spot. He rested again. Reaching into his pocket he pulled out the old, flattened Clif bar and half empty bottle of water he'd found in his car. He wolfed down the stale bar and took a few gulps of warm water.

He felt recharged as he started again. He reached several large jagged boulders with slippery-looking, almost vertical faces. They stood like unrelenting protestors on the path, their splotches of white, green, and orange lichen like hazard signs. His heart galloped as he studied the rocks. He wondered why there weren't any ropes.

What the hell am I doing here alone?

Jaya sucked it up. He settled on what seemed like the safest way over. Like a spider, he inched up using his fingers and the fronts of his sneakered feet. One wrong move and...

Keeping his breath steady, he made it over the rocks. All the concentration put him in the zone. He moved swiftly now despite the precarious nature of the path. When he reached the top, he stopped. He took a big swig of water. He finished off the bottle and held the last sip in his mouth. That's when he got a load of mountains, ocean, and valley all the way to Laie. The surprise of the spectacular view made him spew out the water. Wiping his lips, he coughed, then got ahold of himself. He soaked in the marvelous shades of green and blue.

Green is my new favorite color.

Here he was. Jaya Mehta. Alone on one of the highest mountains on Oahu. He spread his arms wide and tilted his head back. An abrupt gust of wind tried to push him over the edge, but he planted his feet firmer and resisted its force.

Ha, he thought. I will survive.

DONUT HOLES

Rasa paced in the kitchen. She was starving. She opened the refrigerator and stuck her head inside. The cold shelves were bare except for Nitya's unfinished dinner—half a Spam musubi. Rasa had skipped dinner so her siblings could eat what little food they had left. Now they were fast asleep, but hunger kept Rasa wide awake.

The salty slice of canned meat and rice wrapped in nori taunted her. Maybe one nibble...

No!

It was Nitya's. Rasa grabbed onto the refrigerator handle with both hands. She screamed a silent scream into her arm as she squeezed with all her might. She let go, then kicked the door shut. She swallowed the saliva that had pooled in her mouth.

She whipped around to face the pantry. She already knew what was in it—a snack-size box of crackers and a can of Vienna Sausage, two items she was also saving for her siblings' breakfast. But maybe there was some candy or cookies that she'd missed. She stood with her feet hip-width apart and her hands by her side. She wiggled her fingers like she was a Western gunslinger. Quick on the draw she yanked the doors open. A two-inch cockroach with brown translucent wings scurried away into a crevice at the back. Rasa wasn't grossed out. Instead, she was irritated as she envisioned a large network of the lucky bastards behind the pantry feasting on crumbs.

There was nothing to do but resume her march back and forth in the kitchen. Her head felt like it was going to explode and litter the kitchen with shrapnel of the cake, brownies, and muffins she was imagining. At the same time she felt weak and sort of dizzy.

She went outside. She inspected the neighbor's fruit trees by the light of the endless Hau'ula stars and full moon. *Nothing.* She'd eaten the last swiped banana and papaya yesterday. She fussed at herself for anticipating some sort of fruit miracle. Her frantic legs found their second wind and made her leap up the steps back into the house.

She scanned the living room with frenzied eyes. Then, as if someone fired a starter pistol at a track meet, she dashed around the shack in search of any loose change. When she was done it was as if a tornado had swept through. Drawers emptied. Sofa cushions on the floor. Furniture pushed aside. She managed to find four one-dollar bills and a bunch of loose change. She smoothed out the bills and grouped the coins. She counted $7.40 in all. Enough for a gallon of milk and a loaf of bread. And if there was a sale on those staples, then maybe also a musubi for her. She tilted her head back. "Yes!"

She put the money in a small plastic bag. She decided the kids would be fine if she made a quick trip to the 7-11.

She stepped out into the cool night, whistling. Things were looking up. Because in less than fifteen minutes she'd be indulging in milk and bread with enough left over to share in the morning. The night sky lit her way.

At the 7-11, she strolled down every aisle, savoring the options. She stopped in front of the ice cream. So many varieties. If only she had a spoon...

She felt a tap on her shoulder. She turned her head and saw Sharon.

Shit.

"Hi Rasa," Sharon said, smiling. "How are you?"

"Fine," Rasa blurted, wringing her hands.

Sharon's expression turned serious. "Look, Rasa, I know Kalindi's gone."

Rasa didn't have enough energy to commence operation pizzazz. She held her breath and waited.

"I was going to tell you this in the morning but since you're here..."

Panic jolted her into speaking. "But we're fine," she began.

Shaking her head, Sharon said, "No, Rasa. CPS is stepping in. You'll all be going to good foster homes. Tomorrow, actually."

Rasa's knees buckled. Her eyes filled with tears. "What do you mean, foster homes? Can't we go to the same one?"

Sharon shook her head. "No, I'm afraid not. You'll be with a nice couple in Waikiki and Ach, Nitya, and Shanti will be with a good family in Waialua," she said. Then she smiled big and added, "You'll be able to visit them on weekends."

There was no use arguing.

Sharon took out a twenty-dollar bill and handed it to Rasa. "For snacks tonight," she said.

Rasa took the money. "Thank you," she whispered.

"I'll see you at 8 a.m. sharp," Sharon said. She put her hand on Rasa's shoulder. "Don't worry, everything's going to be ok."

Rasa stood there staring at the twenty in her hand.

Ice cream bar? *Musubi*? *Hot dog*? *Nachos*?

Another shoulder tap. "Rasa?"

She looked over her shoulder. Tad stood a few feet away. Rasa zeroed in on his basket full of chips, soda, beer, and microwavable burritos. She crammed the twenty into her pocket and forgot about Sharon and foster care.

"Hey, Uncle Tad," she said. She called him Uncle Tad because he was one of her mother's "friends."

"Hey," he said. "Late night munchies?" His eyes followed the invisible line from Rasa's eyes to his basket of groceries.

"Yeah," she said, wiping her mouth.

"Where's Kalindi?"

"I don't know." Her stomach growled in impatient fury.

Tad heard it and raised an eyebrow. "Lemme buy you some food," he offered.

Rasa avoided his eyes. She felt warmth in her cheeks. She heard herself say, "Ok, thanks."

Ten minutes later they left the 7-11. Tad carried the big brown paper bag of groceries in one arm as he walked her home. When they got to the front door of the shack, Rasa said, "Thanks, Uncle Tad." She stretched her arms out for the bag. All she could think about was gobbling up the sugary donut holes and chugging the milk straight from the carton.

"It's heavy. Let me help you inside," he suggested.

They entered. Tad followed her to the kitchen. He set the bag down on the small breakfast table. Rasa gave him a grateful smile as she pulled out the box of donut holes. She slit the seal with her nail. She snatched up two of the perfect white spheres and shoved them in her mouth. "So good," she mumbled, white powder dusting her lips. Then she pushed another one into her mouth.

She was so focused on the delicious sweet softness of the donut holes, she didn't care that Tad's arms snaked around her from behind. She was about to open the milk when he spun her around to face him. A split second later he was on his knees, kissing her. She pulled her lips away and turned her head back to eye the milk.

"There's more where that came from," he whispered, "if..."

Hunger was a tricky manipulator. It made Rasa forget about the new reality morning would bring. It made her forget about the twenty dollars from Sharon. It seemed to be in cahoots with Kalindi because her mother's words rung.

Use your power to get what you want. What you need.

Kalindi had been gone a month. Rasa was in charge. She'd spent the last of her earnings on the electricity bill. There was no other option. This was work.

Rasa brought her head back to Tad and their eyes met.

NiCE GiRLS DON'T LiKE NiCE GUYS

The Ala Moana Foot Locker was like the high school *it* spot that Saturday afternoon. So when Jaya and Alika strolled in, they immediately recognized a couple of Manoa Prep athletes among the bustle of teenagers. Jaya was relieved that Alika didn't bother to stop for a chat. The two of them headed straight to the back where the most expensive shoes were displayed like rare artifacts.

"I've been waiting to get my hands on these Jordans," Alika said. His eyes were ecstatic as he lifted one of the black-and-varsity-red Q Flights. He flipped it over in his hands "Geez."

"What?"

"One hundred and thirty bucks?"

Jaya shook his head. "That ain't right." But he made a mental note. *Birthday present for my bro.* "Hey, let's grab some food. I'm starving," he said.

"Wait, not yet," Alika whispered.

"Why are you whispering?"

"Don't look, but there's a girl checking you out."

"Whatever," Jaya said, rolling his eyes. "Can we go now?" That kind of positive attention from a girl happened to Jaya about as often as a full solar eclipse that was visible from Oahu. Less than that actually, because it'd never happened.

"No brah, I'm serious. She's with a couple of friends. Count to ten and look behind you." He picked up some Jordan iDs and pretended to inspect them.

Jaya waited the obligatory ten seconds then turned around. Sure enough a pretty girl with long reddish-brown hair was eyeing him. She smiled, then dropped her head. Jaya whisked back to Alika. "Holy crap! What do I do? Let's just get out of here."

"No, no, no. We will do no such thing," Alika said with authority. "You, my friend, are going to get your ass over there and talk to her."

"No way. There is no way. Come on, we're leaving," he insisted.

"Not leaving until you talk to her."

Jaya began to sweat. "Alika, don't do this. I wanna go."

"You can't get a girlfriend if you don't talk to girls," Alika said. "Now get your shit together, you gentleman you. Come on."

"Fine," Jaya mumbled.

"Fine what?"

"I'll do it. But it's your fault if I crash and burn," Jaya said, wagging his finger.

"You won't. Now go."

Jaya took a deep breath. He kept swallowing as he walked, his eyes shifting from the girl to the floor and back to the girl.

The girl and her friends saw him approaching and ducked their heads, giggling.

Jaya forced himself to keep going. He was almost there when he saw William and Cole enter. Jaya considered them to be two of the biggest fuckboys at Manoa Prep. He cringed, hoping they would go straight to the shoe altars at the back.

No such luck. They strutted over to the girls. Jaya veered right, faking like he was going to a shirt rack nearby. He grunted to himself as he pushed hangers back and forth. He wasn't sure if the fuckboys knew the girls or if they'd just cock-blocked him on purpose. He peeked over at them. The girl who'd actually shown some interest in him was now gazing all dreamy-eyed at Cole. She touched his shoulder. When she threw her head back in laughter, Jaya felt himself deflate like a punctured balloon.

Fuckboy beats transboy.

ALASTAR

The loud ringtone of her cell startled Rasa awake. Without moving her body she dangled her arm and felt around on the floor. Her fingertips found what they were looking for and brought it close to her face. She checked the screen. Alastar. 4:50 p.m.

Shit!

She was late. She bolted up, fully alert. In her panic, she didn't answer the call. She slammed her bedroom window shut and gathered her things. She ran out of the apartment to the elevator. When she got outside she sprinted towards Kapahulu Avenue.

The late afternoon air was heavy and sticky. She took a quick look at the dense clouds. They crowded together in an angry jumble. Any second they could unleash their wet fury.

Rasa ran faster. As she wove through people on the sidewalk, she thought about how much her life had changed over the past six months.

For one thing she lived with her foster parents, Sam and Ann. They were in their mid-thirties. They'd been taking care of foster children, one or two at a time, for over five years. They seemed nice enough. And Sharon had vouched for them. They didn't talk to Rasa much, but they were good providers. They gave her a room of her own, hot meals, and school supplies.

Rasa went to a nearby public school, Kaimuki High. It was the first time in her life she'd maintained perfect attendance. She even asked her teachers for extra help with the things she couldn't figure out on her own. One of her teachers, admiring her dedication, tutored her almost every day for an hour after school. All the hard work paid off. She maintained a 4.0 GPA.

Ach, Nitya, and Shanti were with a foster family in Waialua, just like Sharon said. The family turned out to be perfect. Also like Sharon had promised. They had three young children of their own so her siblings had playmates to distract them from the reality of the unwanted changes in their lives.

Still the separation from them was brutal for Rasa. She counted the days between visits. So far she'd seen them once a week.

A month ago Sam and Ann introduced her to Alastar, their thirty-something friend originally from New York City. He used to work for CPS, they said, and had lots of experience working with teenage girls. "He'll take good care of you," Sam had said. "Especially since Ann and I have been really busy at our jobs recently and haven't been able to spend much time with you. Think of Alastar like an uncle."

And he was. He became like the long-lost uncle she never had.

He talked to her. He listened. Rasa welcomed his attention. Plus he seemed kind. He gave her rides to school, took her out to eat and bought her clothes.

She ran faster down Kapahulu.

Her cell rang again. This time she answered it.

"Rasa, where the hell are you? It's five!" Alastar boomed.

Was it that big a deal?

She was only ten or so minutes late. And it's not like she'd been late before. Besides they were only going to dinner.

"I'm so sorry. I'll be there soon."

"You better be," he snarled.

She tried to picture him mad, but she couldn't.

The sky turned murky gray. A second later the dank clouds sprinkled a few thick raindrops.

Then thunder rumbled. The sky became an ominous black. The drizzle turned into a shower.

There was a red light when she reached the corner of Kapahulu and Kalakaua. She pressed the crosswalk button and tapped her foot. The rain wasn't letting up. When the light changed, she dashed across the street. She turned right and raced down Kalakaua.

She got near the Duke Kahanamoku statue. She saw Alastar standing under one of the concrete oceanfront pavilions. He was wearing a sleek gray suit with a soft white shirt, top buttons open.

She reached him and stopped. She was close enough to see the throbbing veins on his neck. "Sorry," she said in between shallow breaths. She brushed the rain from her face and slicked back her hair.

Alastar grabbed her arms tight. It hurt. He squinted and his eyebrows slanted towards his nose. "Don't ever be late again! Where the hell were you?"

"I was taking a nap, sorry I—"

He cut her off. "From now on, be on time!" he yelled. He squeezed her arms tighter.

"Yeah. Okay."

Alastar switched all of sudden. He released his grip and took a step closer. His face softened. His smile became ethereal.

Rasa held her breath. Her heart hammered in her chest. Conflicting emotions hung over her like blinking Christmas lights. The white of relief flickered, alternating with the red of uncertainty. Why was he acting like this?

With one hand, he stroked her damp hair. With the other he lifted her chin.

He kissed her lips.

Rasa froze.

He pulled her close and the familiar feeling of being pressed up against a man's strong chest coaxed her inner black widow to crawl out. Months in hibernation, it was ready for fresh male prey. Her body relaxed the same way it had always done with men when she was in the zone. She closed her eyes and opened her mouth. She welcomed his warm, sweet tongue. His hands slid down to the small of her back. Then lower.

He pulled away. "Time to go shopping."

Rasa examined Alastar's face. Maybe she'd been wrong about him after all. He had never shown this kind of interest before.

The first time he took her to dinner, he'd given her the lowdown about his connection to Sam and Ann. "I met them my freshman year at Colorado State. They were juniors. We were all majoring in psychology and they kinda took me under their wing. After college, they got jobs with CPS on Oahu. I was so jealous. Who wouldn't want to be in Hawaii, right?" He winked and chuckled. "Anyway, when I graduated, they gave me a heads up on a CPS position that had opened up here. I applied and got it."

"That's so cool," Rasa said. "Why'd you all stop working for CPS?"

"I think we were all just ready for a change. But we vowed to continue helping teens even if it was just by volunteering."

"So where do you work now?"

"I do some private contracting."

Rasa was going to ask what that meant, but their dessert arrived and her question got lost in the anticipation of tasting the warm chocolate molten cake in front of her.

Alastar ran his hand forward over his red Caeser-cut hair. "You know, sometimes bad things happen to pretty girls in state custody. That's why Sam and Ann became foster parents. They wanted to give teens a safe place to live. After they got you, they called me sort of freaked out. Sam was like, 'Oh my gosh, Alastar, Rasa's so beautiful. We gotta keep an eye on her!' See, Rasa, if a teen acts out in their foster care home, she gets moved around to a different one. And not every foster home is good news."

Rasa nodded. It seemed legit to her. More than anything she felt protected and lucky.

"Ok. Time to get you home. School tomorrow."

But today was different. And now they were strolling down Kalakaua as if they were newlyweds on their Waikiki honeymoon. The sun shoved all the clouds west. Out of sight. The skies radiated a majestic blue. The day warmed up and so did Alastar. He smiled at Rasa, letting go of her hand and putting his arm around her shoulder instead.

Rasa smiled back. "Where are we going?"

"I'm thinking Chanel for my little Rasa," he whispered.

Rasa rarely ventured to the high-end part of Waikiki. She tried not to get excited. But she couldn't help it. No man had ever bought her expensive clothes before. She guessed everything inside Chanel would cost at least $500.

They sauntered into the Chanel store as if they were regulars.

"Look around," he said. "See what you like."

Rasa walked to the nearest dress rack cupping her mouth, as if someone just announced she'd won a million bucks. She pushed the hangers along and examined each dress. She was about to select a refined black dress with short sleeves. It's top was form-fitting. It had a high waist. The bottom was like an upside umbrella. An elegant upside-down umbrella. It reminded her of something Audrey Hepburn would wear.

But then she heard Alastar. "Here, this one," he said, as if that was the only one she should try.

She put the black dress back on the rack. When she turned around, he was holding up a tiny dress. It had black-on-white swirly designs on top and black spaghetti straps. The bottom was all black and looked like an ultra short sarong.

It fit perfectly. Alastar was waiting outside the dressing room with a pair of shiny black heels hooked on his right index finger.

"These."

The heels were over six inches. *How would she ever walk in them?*

Alastar paid for the dress and shoes. Close to $3,500! He slung the garment bag and shoe bag over his shoulder. He offered Rasa his elbow. She wove her arm through it. They stepped out of the store and made their way up Kalakaua.

Their pace was brisk. *Where were they heading now?*

Alastar seemed to read her mind. "We're going to my next surprise for you," he said. He was grinning big. Like the Chesire Cat in *Alice in Wonderland*.

"Cool." she said. She couldn't get over how much he'd spent on her in the Chanel Store.

They arrived at the Waikiki Parc Hotel. They stopped in the lobby and he embraced her.

She felt his lips graze her ear as he whispered, "I got a room for us. Ocean view."

GOD HATES GAYS

Jaya carted his gig gear to his usual Waikiki spot—the corner of Seaside and Kalakaua. Flocks of tourists passed by as he set up for his one-man unplugged show.

He scooted into a comfortable perch on his stool. The index finger of his left hand traced the letters M-I-L-L-I-E he'd carved on the soundboard of his Martin acoustic. He dug into his pocket for a pick. Then he adjusted his hands—his right on the fretboard and his left over the soundhole.

He scanned the bustling sidewalk for anyone familiar, classmates in particular.

All clear.

Here in the streets of Waikiki, Jaya was secure in being unknown. His bottom rung social status at school didn't matter.

Earlier today his classmates had reminded him that he was anything but anonymous on campus. Alika wasn't around so they'd used the opportunity to up their passive-aggressive torment. When an unsuspicious Jaya walked past them in the cafeteria with his sandwich and chips, they threw him contemptuous glances, followed by whispered taunts just loud enough to be heard. Then they scurried away, holding their noses as if Jaya exuded the foulest stench.

He glanced around one more time. Only tourists swarmed by on their way to dinner or debauchery or both.

He opened the set with one of his originals, but he wasn't relaxed playing it. Not like when he played Nirvana songs. So he dove into familiar waters for the rest of the gig starting with *Come As You Are*.

Playing and singing Nirvana songs was always comfortable. It made him calm and confident. Tourists began to pause or stop to enjoy the free grunge show. Soon Jaya was lost in his performance.

Fans tossed bills into his open guitar case—usually a one, sometimes a five. A few stopped for several songs in a row, perhaps the true Nirvana devotees, and dropped in a ten or twenty.

By the time Jaya was close to wrapping up his set, a sizeable crowd had gathered in a semicircle around him. He finished playing *All Apologies*, then grabbed a sip of water. Out of the corner of his eye he saw money piled up in his case. He began *Pennyroyal Tea*, pleased to be raking in the bucks for HHS.

When he dove into his final song for the evening—*Lake of Fire*— Hana, Leila, and Kylee, three of the most popular senior girls at Manoa Prep, happened to stroll by with some military guys.

"Hey," Hana said, prodding Leila with her elbow. "Isn't that Jaya?"

Leila nodded, brushing her bangs out of her eyes. She turned and whispered to Kylee, "Don't look now, but your girlfriend's here."

Kylee giggled. Then she stared at Jaya and exclaimed, "WTF? As if that lezzie needs more money!" She rolled her blue eyes.

"Right?" Hana agreed. "Watch this."

The girls and their G.I. Joes pushed through the head-nodding crowd. They made it to the front and pretended to listen for a minute.

Jaya didn't notice them until Hana and her Semper Fi man took a step forward.

Hana caught Jaya's eye. In a loud, caustic voice, she said, "Damn, the trash makes noise in Waiks now."

Her jarhead put his arm around her and snickered.

Jaya ignored them. There was not much else he could do. Alika wasn't here to prevent what he knew was about to go down. But in his head Jaya shot back, "And the privileged white pigeon shit speaks." He looked away, satisfied with himself. As he continued to play and sing *Lake of Fire*, the lyrics took on new meaning for him. He sung with more gusto. Full-on Kurt style.

Disappointed that she hadn't thrown Jaya off, Hana took it further. She shook her head. Crossing her arms she said, "Hey, Jaya, God hates gays."

Always-faithful boy jumped in. He pointed at Jaya's head and in a serious voice said, "An inch off that hair and we'll be bros. You could even enlist. What'dya say, bro?" He lowered his finger and directed it at Jaya's crotch, adding, "Don't worry, my lips are sealed."

Jaya refused to meet their eyes. He also resisted the urge to give this guy a lesson on the illegality of Don't Ask, Don't Tell.

Hana guffawed. She kept it going. "It's all good, Jaya. We know it's not your fault you're a lesbo."

A few people in the crowd frowned.

But Hana went in for the kill anyway. "Being a lezzie is a mental disorder."

Jaya kept his eyes focused above the crowd and on the passing Kalakaua traffic.

So is being a stuck-up nympho who needs to be the center of attention.

He pressed his lips together for a second so the words wouldn't spill out. No one noticed that he skipped a line in the song. When he opened his mouth he sang the rest of the lyrics without missing a word.

By then Leila, Kylee, and the two other dudes were standing next to Hana and her guy. Hana blew her cheeks out before she kicked Jaya's guitar case. Some of the bills flew out, landing on the sidewalk. Then the six of them stalked off, high-fiving each other.

Jaya finished the last chord of the song. He set his guitar on the portable stand. The audience clapped and whistled.

"Thank you," Jaya said, taking a slight bow.

The crowd dispersed. Jaya retrieved the bills off the sidewalk before the trades blew them away. He returned them to the case, then took a moment to stretch. He grabbed his water bottle. As he took a swig, he heard a familiar voice.

X MARKS THE SPOT

The first thing Rasa saw when she woke up was Alastar.

Alastar!

She shot up. The second thing she saw was a million-dollar ocean view. She looked back at Alastar. He was sleeping, naked. Crisp white sheets and a down comforter lay twisted and tangled on the floor. She glanced down at herself. Fully nude.

Everything came rushing back. Being late. Alastar's anger. Alastar's kiss. Chanel dress and shoes. The surprise room at the Parc…

She tried to push herself off the bed with her hands but a sharp pain in her wrists made her stop. That's when she remembered the rest…

Alastar had gripped her wrists, his strong legs pressing down on hers. In a hard, unflinching voice, he'd said, "You will call me Xander. Not Alastar. Xander. Got it?"

He'd growled, "What's my name?"

"Xander," she'd whispered.

"Louder." He'd squeezed her wrists.

"Xander." Regular volume.

"I can't hear you."

"Xander!"

Rasa spotted a fuzzy white robe hanging in the closet. She slid off the bed and got the robe. She wrapped it around herself. She tied the belt as she went to the window. She rested her forehead on the glass. She sighed and got lost in the vastness of the ocean...

But Xander's voice cajoled her back to the real world.

"Rasa baby, come here," he said.

He sounded sweet. Nothing like...

Her fingers brushed her wrist.

"Oh Rasa..." he sang.

She turned around, caressing her other wrist.

Xander was sitting up against the headboard. His arms were open and he was smiling.

Rasa was perplexed, but she went with it. She smiled back and crawled into his embrace.

"I got another surprise for you," he said. One of his hands glided down her back, the other tugged at her robe's belt. "But first..."

An hour later they were in his Benz driving on H-2.

"Where are we going?"

"You'll see." He rested one hand on her thigh.

When Rasa saw the sign for Waialua she figured it out. She smiled.

Soon enough they pulled into the driveway. Rasa's heart skipped a beat as she saw her siblings on their foster family's large, grassy front yard. There was a nice spread of food on a picnic table behind them.

Xander introduced himself to the foster parents. As he shook hands with the foster dad, he leaned in and said in a hushed voice, "I used to work at CPS. What these kids had to go through..."

The foster dad nodded. The mom put her hand on her heart and sighed. Then they rounded up their three children and went inside.

Xander walked back to his Benz and let Rasa enjoy lunch and a quiet chat with Ach, Nitya, and Shanti.

But way too fast, he decided Rasa's visit with her siblings was over.

"Time to go," he called out. He was leaning against his car, his hands shoved in his pockets. The North Shore sun sat directly overhead and the clouds that had covered half of it drifted away. Xander peeled off his polo shirt.

"Rasa! Time to go. I'm sweating balls out here."

Ach crinkled his face. "Who is this guy again?"

"A friend of my foster parents…"

"Rasa!"

"I'm coming!" She extended her arms to her siblings. "Come here, my little opihis."

They crowded in and suctioned themselves onto her. She hugged them tight.

"I miss you already," Shanti whispered. Her small brown eyes were extra wide.

Rasa stroked her hair and smiled. "I miss you already too." Then she looked at Nitya and Ach. "Both of you, too."

Nitya was staring at the ground, biting her finger. As usual, she didn't say a word. Ach was glowering.

"Rasa! Get over here!" Xander hollered.

"No," Ach muttered under his breath, shaking his head.

Rasa put her arm around him again. "It's ok, Ach."

"No!" Then he ducked out from Rasa's arm and marched towards Xander. "Leave my sister alone," he shouted.

Rasa chased her brother. "Wait, Ach!"

But Xander already had Ach in a headlock. He struggled to get out. Xander took out a knife. The knife looked more like a dagger. Its black and silver handle was carved in a Celtic knot design. Xander brought the tip of the knife to Ach's throat.

"Calm down, little man," Xander said, "or I'll cut you."

Ach stopped squirming. Rasa inched forward until she was standing next to her brother.

"Xander," Rasa said in a calm voice. "Xander, boo, come on. I'm ready to go."

"Li'l man needs to be taught a lesson."

"I'm sorry, Xander. Here, let me talk to him. I'll take care of it," Rasa put her hands on Ach's shoulders. "Please let him go," Rasa whispered. "I'll make it up to you."

Xander appeared to loosen his hold on Ach but suddenly firmed up the headlock and nicked the side of Ach's ear with the tip of the blade. Ach yelped from the sting. A small line of bright red blood appeared like magic water paint.

Rasa blinked hard. "You can teach me the lesson, Xander. Please let him go," she said.

Xander smiled an eerie smile. He pushed Ach away and yanked Rasa's arm. "Hold still," he commanded. He slashed two lines in the fleshy part of her forearm. She screamed. It was only after she wiped off the blood that she realized it was the letter X. Just like the one Xander had tattooed in the exact same spot on his arm.

GENDER iN MOTiON

"Jaya!"

Jaya turned his head to see Nohea sashaying towards him.

"Eh, Jaya!" she said, waving.

Jaya threw up a shaka. He first met Nohea last summer after one of his Waikiki gigs. She'd introduced herself as "a proud Hawaiian mahu." She'd been working at a nearby convenience store for years and claimed to know everything that happened on this Waikiki block.

Later Jaya learned that Nohea's name was like his—it could be for a man or woman. But Nohea slid along the gender line according to how she felt at any given time, though she gave special time to her feminine side.

Nohea had told Jaya that she'd spent her twenties in San Francisco. She'd joined the gay rights movement there after hearing Harvey Milk speak. Jaya was impressed that she'd signed up for Milk's door-to-door education campaign about California Prop 6. If passed into law, it would've banned gay or lesbian people—and possibly anyone who supported gay rights—from working in the state's public schools. Thanks to Harvey Milk and volunteers like Nohea, it was squashed.

But what Jaya most admired about Nohea was that she didn't assume things about people or focus on labels.

Nohea stood in front of Jaya and took her cigarette out of her mouth. She put one hand on Jaya's shoulder. "Oh Jaya honey, don't you listen to those small-minded imperialists," she said in her thick, sugary voice.

Jaya chuckled. "No worries, Nohea. I've heard worse." Nohea was like the awesome auntie he always wanted. "You working?"

"Yeah. But Coco Cove is supa slow tonight so I took my smoke break early." She let her cigarette dangle from her lips. Then she twisted her long gray and black hair into a bun.

Jaya liked the sound of her wide Hawaiian bracelets clanking as she fixed her hair.

"Cool," he said.

Nohea adjusted her mu'umu'u and continued. "Those girls, they so off. Bet they got no clue that you one modern-day Robin Hood. Earnin' from da tourists and givin' to the poor." She gave a closed mouth smile. "You still holdin' it down at HHS?" She held her cigarette and took a long drag.

"You know it," Jaya replied.

Nohea exhaled a couple of smoke rings. She peeked into his open guitar case. There were enough crumpled bills to cover the entire bottom. "Cha-ching! I see you made some big bucks fo' dem."

He looked at the cash and smiled. "Yep." Then he looked back at Nohea and smiled bigger.

"What, little bro?"

"I finally figured out the tat I'm gonna get."

"Do tell," Nohea raised her left eyebrow.

"Tritiya-prakriti."

Nohea's forehead wrinkled. "Treat-your-pecker-ity?"

"No. Tri-ti-ya pra-kri-ti," Jaya sounded out. "Sanskrit words that will remind me that I'm not a weirdo just because my parents and classmates don't accept me as I am."

"Damn straight!"

"I'm gonna get it right here," Jaya pointed to his right inner wrist.

"Fabulous!" Nohea took Jaya's hand and squeezed. "You have to go see my friend Kalani at his shop on Ena Road. He's the best in town."

"Hey, is his shop called Kākau by any chance?"

"Yeah, how'd you know?"

"I never told you that's Alika's cousin's place?"

Nohea shook her head.

"Well, it is and I already got me the hook up!"

"Fo' real?"

Jaya nodded then yawned. He checked his watch. 11:15 p.m. "It was a shitty day, until now. Thanks for making it better."

MAGNETISM

Hau'ula was the opposite of Waikiki. It was on the northeast of
Oahu, Waikiki was southeast. It was uncongested country, Waikiki
was crowded city. It was forested mountains, Waikiki was concrete
highrises. It was natural shoreline, Waikiki was imported sand.

Hau'ula was Rasa's sweet past with her siblings, Waikiki was her
bitter present alone.

Rasa missed Hau'ula almost as much as she missed her siblings.
She visited as often as possible. She was headed there today.

She slipped on her sunglasses to cut the brilliant lemon sunrays
pouring in through the bus window. She adjusted the frames. The
intense green of Mokoli'i caught her eye. The pointed rock islet in
Kane'ohe Bay was typically blackish-brown. But last week's rainfall
had transformed it into a gigantic moss-covered shark fin.

Her eyes skimmed the surface of the sparkling turquoise water.
She thought about free-diving. How she used to push the limits of
her breath each time. She closed her eyes and imagined herself
suspended in the deep silence of the ocean, then ascending through
the glorious rays of sunlight that hung in the depths like crystal
string curtains.

The bus hugged the twists and turns of the narrow road winding along the island's eastern coast. She rested her head against the window and opened her eyes. Kualoa Ranch passed on the left. The bus moved a little faster along a straight part of Kamehameha Highway.

Her fingers traced the X-shaped scar on her arm. It'd been five months since Xander had turned her out. He'd made his role in her life clear. He wasn't an uncle. He wasn't a boyfriend. He wasn't a lover. He certainly wasn't a friend. He was her boss. A Romeo pimp who kept her guessing with alternating and unpredictable displays of intense affection and brutal expectations. His bottom line was clear—turn tricks for him or her siblings would get hurt.

Fatigue from last night's "date" with some bigwig foreign dignitary set in. Rasa's eyelids drifted down. She fell into a dream. She darted this way and that on a mountain trail in hopes of catching up with a mysterious person. Just as she caught sight of the person's face, the bus wheels hurdled over a bunch of potholes. Her eyes jerked open.

The dream...

Kalindi?

She shook her head and scanned the bus. The other passengers reminded her of wax figures. Molded into set poses. Subtle smiles. Gazing at nothing in particular.

The bus slowed down and stopped near Hau'ula Beach Park. Rasa hurried to the front. The second she set foot on the ground she felt it. The feeling of home. Warm familiarity. The balmy Hau'ula air nuzzled her. She thought about yesterday morning's visit with her siblings. She woke up today weighed down by how much she longed to be with them.

Rasa was desperate to find the comfort of the past. Everything and everyone was predictable back then. But now she could only see her siblings when their foster family had time. And the word on the street was that Kalindi had been killed by some pimp who'd moved her to Los Angeles. Rasa didn't believe it because she knew her mother always worked solo. Kalindi would never let a man control her.

Of course that's what Astrid had thought about her mother, Ingrid, in Janet Fitch's novel *White Oleander*, a book that Rasa was currently halfway through.

Rasa hoped maybe she could channel her mother today. Balance out her uncertain life by recapturing Kalindi's spirit.

The glimmering Pacific was right in front of her. She walked around the bus stop shelter to the grassy area in front of the beach. The waves advanced and receded on the thin strip of coarse sand. She watched children splashing about on the shore.

Further out, a few surfers rode the choppy waves, fanatic in their dedication to paddle out into the swells no matter what. Rasa sighed. She could relate. She wondered what had happened to the longboard Landon "gave" her. CPS hadn't allowed her to take it to Sam and Ann's. Plus there was no room to store much of anything in their cramped apartment.

Out of nowhere the trades stopped. The hot air strangled her. For a second it was hard to breathe.

When a kid squealed in delight on the shore, Rasa realized she was holding her breath. She let it go. The breeze returned and soothed her. She inhaled the smell of salt and coconut long and slow, like a cold 'otai at noon. She closed her eyes and tried to invoke her mother.

No luck.

She turned around and faced the mountains. Kalindi used to spend more time in the Hau'ula mountains than with her own children.

These mountains probably know more about Kalindi than I do.

Probably the best chance of capturing her mother's spirit required a bit of a trek.

Rasa walked carefully across the grass and the parking lot in her slippers, avoiding the scatter of broken beer bottles and a few used syringes. She waited at the edge of the crosswalk for an approaching pickup truck to pass. Then she jogged across Kam Highway.

The brisk trades returned with a vengeance and tried to strongarm her dress up. She caught it in time but a second gust harassed her, this time with a handful of smells and memories. She stood still and closed her eyes.

Huli huli chicken.

Plumeria.

Mock orange.

Ach, Nitya, and Shanti giggling in the gentle surf.

The cracking of twigs underfoot in the mountains.

Sweet and tart liliko'i.

She squeezed her eyelids.

Incense. Hands. Lips.

Still no Kalindi though.

A grizzled biker on a Harley Fatboy raced by. The roar of the engine broke her trance. She turned her head and watched it disappear around the bend on the deserted highway. Then she looked back up at the mountains.

Several cars were parked on the shoulder by the 7-11. She walked past them. A cloud of smoke floated inside one of them, tempting her with promises of hazy relaxation. Her fist balled up gently. Her knuckles approached the rolled-up driver's side window. Rasa knew all she'd have to do was knock and bat her eyelids and they'd let her join in. She took a step forward but stepped on a kiawe branch. One of the sharp spikes punctured through her slipper. Scowling, she stumbled back. She steadied herself and took it as a sign from the universe—*sorry, mary jane, can't hang with you today.* Anyway she wasn't looking for an afternoon of elusive liberation. She was looking for Kalindi's ghost.

Family before drugs.

Kalindi would have taken spliff over daughter. But Rasa refused to let herself go there.

She stopped by the 7-11 and bought the cheapest bottle of water and a pack of Camel Lights for later. Then she stepped up her pace all the way to Hau'ula Homestead Road. Turning right, she followed it straight back through the peaceful neighborhood. Dogs in fenced yards broke the quiet with their vigilant barks. She got to the access road. Immediately the air cooled off. The lush, thick trees near the hunter and hiker check-in station kept the sun's heat at bay. A proud rooster with a multi-colored comb strutted by, reminding Rasa of waking up to loud crowing on chilly Hau'ula mornings.

A local woman approached from the opposite side of the check-in station's wooden podium. Maybe twenty, she hustled down the road with her hands deep in her jeans' pockets. The hood of her oversized black sweatshirt was pulled over her head and strands of her long, stringy hair tumbled out like dark seaweed. As they crossed paths, Rasa noticed the woman's eyes. Vacant, but shifting back and forth. She tugged at her hood, drawing it further over her splotchy face. She tucked her chin and walked faster. But not before Rasa made out her edgy, nervous expression.

From the time Rasa had stepped off the bus, the clues were everywhere. Beer bottles. Dope needles. Pakalolo smoke. And now a meth head. Even in the loveliest places, it seemed people needed to escape their lives.

She came upon the graffiti wall—a retaining wall that local kids used as a canvas for ever-changing throw-ups and tags. She slowed her pace and admired the colorful designs. One piece depicted a large, angry, muscled Hawaiian warrior with a leiomano in one hand and a kahili in the other. He stood, seething, before a background of a massive Hawaiian flag. The intensity of it made the surrounding pieces seem like child's play.

She continued on the road to a small, faded sign for the Ma'akua Ridge Trail. The path beckoned. She stepped onto the dirt and that's when she felt it. The powerful presence of her mother.

Kalindi's essence enveloped her like misty clouds swallowing mountain tops. The feeling absorbed her.

She blinked hard and didn't let the tears flow.

Everything seemed to be imbued with her mother's spirit, especially the vibrant green foliage. In no time she began the switchbacks. She pictured herself following Kalindi's springing curls over the rocks, roots, and Norfolk pine needles. Just like she'd done countless times as a child.

She paused at the lava rock overhang. It appeared different today. She moved to the left to view it from another angle and it struck her—it resembled the giant head of a warrior similar to the one depicted on the graffiti wall. Rasa decided this was a good place for a quick smoke break and a drink of water.

But then she caught the faint sweet fragrance of liliko'i. She followed the perfume to the other side of the trail.

She took a step forward and felt something mushy under her slipper. She looked down. There were at least twenty overripe liliko'i littering the ground.

She looked up. The sight of a lone orange-yellow liliko'i made her eyes widen. It glowed in the tangle of overgrown green and brown vines, leaves, and branches. Its delicate scent invited Rasa again. She stretched her arm up, but the heavenly fruit was just out of reach. She jumped and grabbed it.

"Gotcha!" She beheld the soft jewel. Ten or more tiny black ants scattered from the top. She brushed them away and pulled off the stem. She took a few steps back and sat under the shade of the rock overhang. She examined the liliko'i again, this time with more care, like a scientist discovering a new plant species. She brought her eyes closer. Slowly she flipped it over and over. She was sure it was the most perfect liliko'i she'd ever picked.

She drew the liliko'i to her nose, closed her eyes, and inhaled deeply. Then she opened her eyes and wrapped both sets of fingers around it. In one swift motion she made an even, longitudinal incision in its flesh with her thumbs. The seedy pulp burst out. She slurped both sides clean. The texture and taste were pure luxury. She smacked her lips at the sugary, slightly sharp, deliciousness of the fruit. Immediately she wanted more.

Her eyes followed one last ant as it scurried down the fruit's outer skin onto her finger. She could understand why ants frantically tried to get at its lusciousness, kind of like all the men who tried to get a piece of Kalindi's fruit.

She searched the vines for more edible treasures. There were plenty. In the middle of the mess of branches, she found a single purple-and-white striped liliko'i flower. It dangled upside down, swaying in the trades. If Kalindi was the prized fruit, then was she the enchanting flower? Waiting patiently to transform?

One of Kalindi's mantras echoed in her mind. *Rasa, you and I are something to be desired. Something to be shared with the world. Something golden.*

Rasa's gut dropped—she was nothing more than a trampled, forgotten flower.

All those years in Hau'ula.

Rasa hurled the liliko'i carcass into the dense labyrinth of the forest. She was Xander's property! Where was her mother? She needed her so much.

She sprang up and paced back and forth on the trail, trying to push the yearning for Kalindi aside.

She stood in front of the dozen or so liliko'i still waiting to be picked. Working quickly, almost in a hypnotic state, she grabbed all the lovely fruit. She balanced them in a pile on her arms, wishing she had a bag. She glanced to her left.

Woah.

She did a double take.

There on the trail was a girl. An Indian girl with short, spiky black hair.

The girl's magnetic androgyny made Rasa curious. The

temperate air seemed to thicken. It tightened around Rasa like the liliko'i vines that snaked around the tree branches.

Time stood still. She forgot about the liliko'i in her arms, about Kalindi, about Xander, and the kids.

THE GODDESS

A little after midnight Jaya finished unloading his gear in the garage. He trudged into the quiet house with *Millie*. In the living room, he propped *Millie* against the coffee table then plopped onto the sofa. He closed his eyes and thought about his tat. He interlaced his fingers behind his head, smiling to himself. He closed his eyes and nodded off.

The next thing he knew his mother's drunken voice rang out like an alarm.

"Who the fuck is Nicole?" Jayshree slurred.

Jaya's eyes shot open and landed directly on his mother's contorted face. She was standing in the bright kitchen staring at Sanjay. The rest of the downstairs was dark. It was as if Jaya were watching a play on stage.

Jayshree downed the rest of her wine. She stomped to where Sanjay stood. There was an open bottle of cabernet next to him. She grabbed it and filled her glass to the rim. "Who the fuck is Nicole?" she demanded again. Her voice was creepy and low this time. She took a big gulp of wine.

Sanjay ignored her. He pushed his tongue against his inner cheek, moving it around in his mouth. Then he turned around and reached for the Scotch.

Jayshree must've taken Sanjay's silence as some sort of confession because all of a sudden she splashed the remainder of her wine on Sanjay's back. A second later she flung the empty glass across the kitchen. Miraculously it didn't shatter. She ran into the bathroom, leaving the door open. Jaya heard the violent splashing in the toilet.

Sanjay didn't seem to notice that his white shirt was drenched in cabernet. He poured a cup half full of whiskey and downed it. He smashed the cup down and headed into his den.

Jaya sighed. It was going to be another night of babysitting his angry, drunk parents. He wished he could escape. He'd rather be hanging out with Alika or Nohea. But as much as Jaya despised the way his parents brawled, he couldn't get himself to ignore them. Especially after what he'd heard this week at school. One of his classmate's father passed away of alcohol poisoning. They found him dead in their four-car garage.

Leaving the house when they were fighting wasn't an option for Jaya. For now all he had to do was stay awake. He didn't have to actually spy on them again until they'd finished drinking and their fight was over. Getting in the middle of the fight wouldn't change a thing. They'd ignore him. All that would happen was a ramp-up in his worry, frustration, and sadness.

Jaya scooted to the edge of the sofa. There appeared to be a lull in their battle. A perfect time to make his getaway upstairs to wait it out. Jaya lifted himself and *Millie*. He snuck to his guitar room.

Though he'd already spent hours strumming Nirvana songs in

Waikiki, it hadn't been for him. It was for HHS. Right now what he needed was his own nirvana.

His parents resumed their yelling. He tuned up and started with *Dumb*. In between each Nirvana song he played, it seemed his parents' vicious fight intensified. When he started in on *Something In The Way*, he thought about how the lonely guitar intro and then the sad drums, bass, cello, and lyrics in Nirvana's CD version were an accurate musical description of his life—that something was always in the way of feeling good.

Was that how Kurt felt?

Hours later, as the sun lifted its sleepy head over the horizon, his parents managed to stumble upstairs into their bedroom. Jaya waited a half hour to make sure that this was indeed a ceasefire before he tiptoed in.

Sanjay was sprawled across the bedroom floor on his back. Jayshree was passed out on their bed. Jaya went to his mother first. He squatted near the bed and brought his finger near her nose. The light puff of her breath warmed his skin. *Good.*

Then he sank down next to Sanjay. He leaned all the way to the floor so that he had a horizontal view of his father's chest. It rose up and down slowly.

It was safe to get away.

He hopped into his Beamer. When he rounded the corner of Kalanianaole, the glare of the sun blinded him. He retrieved his shades from the sun visor and put them on.

Better.

He kept driving. Soon Kalanianaole tapered, curving this way and that.

Jaya's eyes feasted on the incredible view that surrounded the road—the unending dark blue ocean on one side and towering green mountains on the other.

By the time he reached Kane'ohe Bay, he felt better. He glanced out the passenger side window at Mokoli'i. It was entirely green. It reminded him of a giant green guitar pick. A guitar would have to be huge for a pick that size—a super-size guitar that would drown out his parents' rage. That would've come in handy last night.

He turned off the AC and opened all the windows. The trades blew a fresh, cool resolve into him. He put his Iphone playlist on shuffle. The opening drum hits of Bob Marley's *Three Little Birds* resounded. He loved it! He imagined Bob and the Wailers walking in the jungle of the lush mountains to his left with little birds chirping at them.

Jaya remembered the exhilaration of being at the top of Pu'u Manamana just last month. He could use some of that today.

Pulling over to the side of the road, he looked at his Oahu map book. His eyes honed in on the Hau'ula Loop Trail and Ma'akua Ridge Trail. Both trailheads were in close proximity to each other on the access road off Hau'ula Homestead Road. He'd never done either.

He settled on Ma'akua Ridge Trail. It wouldn't be crowded. It wasn't exactly a first choice for tourists.

He got back onto the road, driving with purpose, looking forward to being alone, being quiet.

He reached Hau'ula Homestead Road and parked between two rusty, broken-down cars. Abandoned, by the looks of it.

No one was around. He passed the small sign for the Hau'ula

Loop Trail on his right. A narrow trail behind it led uphill. A couple of hundred feet later there was a long wall drenched in vibrant graffiti. He slowed down, staring. Then he started his search for the Ma'akua Ridge Trail sign. It took him ten minutes of walking back and forth, but he finally found the partially hidden sign among some foliage on his left and set out on the dirt path.

It was as if the soaring trees and dense plants and creepers inhaled him, then blew him out in some other deep forest in another time and place. The Amazon, pre-Western contact, maybe. He caught the faint scent of liliko'i. He shivered but shook it off.

Halfway up the trail, already soaked in sweat, he saw someone ahead. He stopped, paralyzed.

There was a beautiful girl about ten yards in front of him.

He rubbed his eyes. She was still there.

He could only see the girl's profile, but there was no denying she was a goddess. She had a pile of liliko'i in her hands. She was scanning the overhead vines for more of the wild fruit.

I must be dreaming.

Jaya blinked hard. When he looked again there she was in the same spot. This brown-skinned girl. This girl could've been the love child of Aishwarya Rai and Adriana Lima. That was her league. The big league. This was a girl who belonged in the stadium's extravagant VIP suite. Not in the cheap bleacher seats. Not anywhere near someone like Jaya, an awkward transgender boy.

The girl's long brown-black hair, like satin strands, flowed down the middle of her back. A short, red dress with Om print and spaghetti straps covered her body but the silhouette of her plentiful curves teased Jaya anyway. An orange amber crystal dangled from a black cord around her neck. Her left nostril was pierced by a tiny glistening diamond stud.

Ah! There was a large tattoo of a black spider on the girl's right inner arm. Something was on its abdomen. He squinted at it.

A red hourglass!

Killer.

Oahu was full of incredible-looking girls of mixed ethnicity. So many hotties that were part this and part that. But this girl was different. Unique in a way Jaya couldn't figure out. An intriguing blend of east, west...and south. Yeah, definitely something south.

Jaya Mehta, who saw himself as a boring full-blooded Gujarati boy, stood without moving. Silently he thanked the temple of the gods that had sent him this girl.

She didn't attend Manoa Prep. He knew that. Maybe she wouldn't be totally repulsed by him. He crossed his fingers.

The light blue sky was cloudless. Maybe the bhagavans were watching him? Rooting for him? Smiling down from the heavens while sipping cups of steaming chai? Maybe they'd directed his finger to Hau'ula on the map.

A few beads of perspiration slid down his forehead but he couldn't move to wipe them off. He swallowed hard. The sweat kept coming. He opened his mouth and started to say something, but then it occurred to him that maybe the bhagavans were playing a joke on him. Setting him up for sure failure. Huddled around up there watching and waiting for Jaya to make A. For this girl to laugh in his face. Or worse, taunt him. Or even worse, to be puzzled, then sickened by him. Jaya's sweat glands froze. His skin sucked back all the perspiration. Suddenly he was dry as a bone.

He ducked his head and prepared to pass her by. But she turned in his direction. He peered up. He caught a glimpse of her eyes. Their bright green color shocked him. His knees buckled.

Then she smiled. She actually smiled at him. "Hey, I didn't see you there." She held out her cupped hands. They were overflowing with wild liliko'i. "Do you have any room in your pockets for these?"

THiS iS MY LiFE

"Allow me," Xander insisted. He took the copper kettle from Rasa and refilled her small ceramic cup with the cold sake.

Rasa had stopped counting after the fifth pour. She concentrated on Xander's lips to try to understand his words. Her attention strayed though, taking in bits and pieces of the commotion at Nobu—the constant drone of English and Japanese interrupted by bursts of laughter.

"Kanpai," Xander cheered, holding up his cup.

Rasa's eyes landed back on him, but she thought of Jaya.

Fuck this. Throw the sake in Xander's face and get outta here. Find Jaya.

But then she thought of her sisters and brother.

She took another sip.

"Drink up, girl," Xander commanded. He set his cup down without drinking and eyed her.

Rasa needed a game plan. And more sake seemed to be the perfect strategy. She tipped her head back and guzzled, then slammed the cup down on the table.

She was wasted. He refilled her cup.

She was going to get so blitzed that she couldn't spend the evening obsessing over how much she despised Xander for constantly threatening her siblings. And for taking her away from her sweet thoughts of that girl.

Jaya.

The butch girl standing there in the mountains of Hau'ula. The girl whose masculinity sparked an intense desire in Rasa. From the moment she'd laid eyes on Jaya, nothing else was the same.

Rasa downed the new pour of sake. She stared at the empty cup. Then she shook her head and sighed. She set the cup down gently this time and pushed it away. She tried to bury her thoughts of Jaya. She had to concentrate on her job. She couldn't risk being lost in her resentment of Xander or pining over Jaya.

"You look gorgeous in that dress," Xander said, kissing his fingertips and tossing them away. Rasa felt his wily eyes drift down her neckline to her cleavage. "Totally worth it," he whispered.

Rasa got a grip. She resumed her "business" role by turning up the seduction. She flashed Xander a sultry look, then winked. Keeping her voice steady but breathy, she said, "Me? Oh, I know."

Xander raised his eyebrow and half-smiled. He stroked his recently grown full beard of red hair.

"Oh yeah. You," he said, nodding. "You rock your uniform."

Xander liked to pretend that the fancy dresses he bought her were her "uniform." Tonight's uniform was short and black with thin shoulder straps. Tight-fitting with subtle patches of sheer material alternating with areas of sequiny lace. Feathery tassels at the bottom. A plunging neckline. Xander loved plunging necklines. Especially on his Rasa.

He dressed Rasa in haute couture. His fat cat clients more than covered the thousands of dollars he spent on her outfits. Politicians, attorneys, businessmen, and the occasional doctor handed Xander rolls of cash as soon as they caught a glimpse of her. Tonight's dress and shoes were the most expensive so far. For good reason. Tonight would prove to be different. And lucrative beyond anything Xander had thus far arranged.

Rasa had no idea about her job tonight. She knew better than to ask too many questions.

"How do the stilettos feel?" he asked with genuine concern. "There might be dancing."

She peeked at her black Jimmy Choo's. When she lifted her head back up to face Xander, her brain reeled as if she'd just stepped off a spinning teacup ride at the amusement park. "Like I've got nothing on," she managed to say.

"Good," Xander said. He checked his Rolex Submariner. Then he glanced at the bill and laid a bunch of cash on the table. He pushed his chair back. "Ready to go?"

"I was born ready," she slurred. She pushed her chair back slowly to keep her balance.

Xander rushed over. "Here," he offered, taking her hand. He helped Rasa up and they walked out of the restaurant arm-in-arm. Xander held his head high, but Rasa glued her eyes to her feet. Tripping would be disastrous. She dreaded what Xander would do if she injured herself and couldn't work.

Xander let go of her hand so that he could wrap his arm around her shoulder. He drew her close and caressed her bare upper arm. She inhaled the L'Eau d'Issey cologne he'd splashed on earlier that evening. She caught another whiff when he leaned in to kiss the top of her head. The complex mix of yuzu, sandalwood, and bergamot tickled her olfactory nerves. Her body tingled. When she witnessed Xander's tender and sexy side, she almost believed he cared for her.

But then reality broke through like a jackhammer. She remembered what he'd said an hour ago on the way to Nobu. He reminded her that he "owned" her. "Don't think about running away or telling anyone, Rasa." He paused and pulled out his knife. "Your brother and sisters..." He used the tip of his blade to draw a slow line across his left cheek.

The hum of an engine shook Rasa out of her thoughts.

"Here you are, sir," a valet said, stepping out of Xander's spotless black Benz.

"Miss," another valet said, holding the passenger door open for Rasa. She realized she was stroking the scar on her forearm. "X" for the Xanax she wished she had right about now. She dropped her arms to her side and climbed in, blocking out Xander's cruelty and instead evoking all her black widow skills.

Xander tipped each valet ten bucks, slid into the driver seat, and peeled out.

Rasa fiddled with the tuning buttons on his satellite radio, setting it to her favorite station—90's grunge. She cranked the volume. Nirvana's *Breed* blared out of the speakers. She squealed in delight. "One of my favs," she blurted. She shot Xander a sultry look. "Kinda puts me in the mood, if you know what I mean," she said in a voice like Marilyn Monroe. Then she giggled.

Xander grasped Rasa's thigh. He sped down Kalakaua. In

no time they were on the top floor of a packed ten-story parking structure. He turned off the ignition. "Open the glove," he ordered.

Rasa opened it. There was a small glass vial with white powder. Coke.

Since Xander had introduced her to nose candy a few months ago, she was always game. Especially because it was free.

But she didn't want that kind of high right now. She wanted a different kind of high. A natural high.

Jaya.

She pictured Jaya's brown eyes. Piercing, but gentle. Not like the scary brown eyes and matching scary ways of that tattooed Yakuza goon from a week ago. He'd been so rough.

"Hurry up," Xander ordered.

Rasa hesitated, frozen with apprehension. Xander groaned and grabbed the coke, the small square mirror, and the razor blade from the glove compartment. He cut two lines and motioned with his impatient eyes for her to do it.

Rasa plugged one of her nostrils with her index finger and snorted a line. She tilted her head back and inhaled sharply. She snorted the other. She wet her finger, swept up the bits of coke left on the mirror, and rubbed them on her gums.

"Ah yeah, that's the stuff that dreams are made out of," she said, reclining the passenger seat and laying back. She lifted her arms over her head. She closed her eyes as the coke hit her brain. Exhilaration flooded her.

"No time for rest, Rasa," Xander said. "Come here, sit up."

He adjusted the lever so the seat sprung back to upright. By then Rasa was so jittery that she couldn't keep still. She ran her amped hands over her body because she didn't know what else to do with them. Her eyes whizzed about in alert anticipation. They landed on Xander.

Without warning he took her face in his strong hands and pressed his open mouth onto hers. His tongue found hers and took it hostage. Rasa couldn't be sure how long their mouths and tongues were locked. When he finally pried himself away, he whispered, "Damn, you're fine." His hands still framed her face. He held her gaze. His eyes penetrated into the depths of her soul.

At least that's what it felt like coked up and all.

Damn, you're fine.

Rasa thought about Xander's words. Words she was used to hearing from other guys. She pictured Kalindi. She imagined her saying, "Rasa, use your beauty. It's your power. It's my gift to you. He'll think you're giving him all of you, but you're taking what you want from him."

Then she heard a little version of herself counter with, "That's bull, Rasa. Xander's your pimp. Kalindi abandoned you and now you got jack."

Before Rasa had a chance to think more about that, Xander was suddenly there opening her car door. He rested his arm on top of the roof. "Back to the grind," he said, his face serious again.

Rasa shifted to find a comfortable sitting position while her mind raced. When she didn't get out of the car, Xander exhaled his anger so loud that it echoed through the parking garage. He reached in, took hold of her forearm, and yanked her out. He practically dragged her to the elevator.

They stepped out onto street level. The sign for the Waikiki

Trade Center flashed. Rasa swore it was blinking in some sort of code that was trying to warn her of imminent danger. Xander towed her to their destination. Thebes, a nightclub.

The line outside the club stretched around the corner.

They approached the line. Her head began throbbing. She pressed her peace fingers into her temple wishing she had a couple of Advil. A hour or two in line would surely turn her headache into a full-blown migraine.

But Xander walked them straight to the VIP entrance. There were two bouncers seated on either side of the roped-off area. Xander gave them a strong chin up. They responded in kind.

That was it. They were in.

"Really?" Rasa whispered to Xander, her elation masking her headache.

Xander switched back to nice. "Uh-huh. You're a star, girl. And stars don't wait." He led her through the entrance into the dark hallway.

Rasa let herself believe him. She walked a little taller.

The hallway twisted. Shiny gold-colored statues of exotic women welcomed them in with a deference that made her feel like even more of a celebrity. She clutched the railing to steady herself as they climbed the winding staircase. The pounding music grew louder with each step. And so did her excitement.

They reached the dance floor. It was packed with the gyrating bodies of mostly young women. Xander tugged her around the side towards the bar lined with hawkish guys quickly getting hammered so they could join the ladies on the dance floor. Relief flowed through Rasa because she was sure they'd get a drink first. She wasn't sober, but she didn't want to risk coming down to reality until the night was over.

No drink. Xander led her past the bar and up a couple of more stairs to the VIP lounge with huge windows facing the dance floor. He closed the door behind them, muting the music and commotion from the rest of the nightclub. He turned a knob. Soothing music trickled out from the speaker in the room like warm, fragrant massage oil on tight muscles. Rasa recognized the mix of dub, acid jazz, Middle Eastern, and electronic—Thievery Corporation. Xander's preferred seduction music. A well-lit fish tank against the far wall provided the only light in the room. A bottle of champagne chilled near one of the two large black leather couches. Xander popped the cork and filled two flutes. He handed one to Rasa. "To you."

"To me." She threw her head back and sucked it all down.

Xander didn't drink anything. He put his flute on the low glass table in front of them. He reached into his pocket. He pulled out the vial of coke. Then he dumped some of it onto the table and cut it into two lines with the tip of his knife.

"All yours, Rasa," he said, pointing.

The bubbly hit Rasa and she felt her eyelids droop slightly despite her mind being extra alert from the cain she'd snorted earlier. She stretched her eyelids. She decided she was drunk and high enough to get this job done. She didn't need additional chemical assistance. She leaned back on the couch. "I'm good. Really."

Not what Xander wanted to hear.

Without warning, he seized the back of her head and pushed it down an inch away from the lines. "Do it!"

Rasa did both lines.

Then things got weird.

Two men walked into the room wearing expensive suits and an air of entitlement. They looked to be in their forties. One of them was about six foot and bald. Despite the dark room, Rasa noticed his thick wedding band when he walked past the fish tank. The other was half a foot shorter with slicked back hair and a pathetic beard.

Drugged out and drunk, Rasa watched them creep towards her.

Watched as each of them took one of her hands and pulled her off the couch.

Watched them grind with her.

Watched them take turns kissing her mouth then her neck.

Watched them lead her to the darkest corner of the room.

Watched them unbuckle their pants.

Watched them lift up her dress.

She looked towards Xander. He was relaxed on the couch. Observing. Sipping his champagne.

Rasa felt like she was standing next to herself. She saw everything happen in slow motion to a girl that was her but wasn't.

Much later, as the sun was rising, Xander dropped Rasa off at Sam and Ann's apartment. Before she got out of the car, he clinched her hand. "Rasa," he said.

She turned her head back.

He gave her a cocky wink. "Anything you need, you let me know." Then the right side of his mouth curved up and his eyes flashed a gleam of deviltry. "I gotta keep my prize girl happy."

Rasa didn't say anything. She and her deadpan face schlepped to the elevator. She entered the apartment. She went straight to the kitchen sink. Cupping her hands under the faucet she took large gulps of water. She stumbled into her room and slept the day away.

THE DRiVE HOME

Jaya traced the seven faded numbers on his arm. Rasa's digits.

Rasa.

He sighed, then grinned, wide and easy.

One week ago today, he'd met the most beautiful girl in the world. One week ago today, he'd felt the first flicker of love.

Jaya didn't know much about love. In his younger years, it'd been wide-eyed wonder towards Millie. A flutter in his heart. A tingle on his skin. An ache in his loins. Gut reactions that eased the knot caused by his ever-present melancholy. But these sensations never matured into anything more.

Real love was a foreign concept to him. Sure, he'd seen the blaze of it acted out between couples in films. But in life itself: years ago, between his parents when they lived in Niu Valley. But now—*nada.*

Real love had been mostly elusive.

Until he met Rasa.

And maybe, just maybe, what Jaya was feeling now—an amorous high pumping through his blood vessels—was the beginning of real love. And being in the thick of love euphoria was perfectly fine with him. It was as exhilarating as ripping Nirvana's cover of *Love Buzz* on his Fender. Not just any Fender. His Olympic White '62 Jaguar reissue.

Jaya replayed their first day together.

They finished the hike. Mostly in silence. But comfortable silence. When they got to Hau'ula Homestead Road, Rasa suggested they grab some 'otai. They walked to one of the fruit stands on Kamehameha Highway. They sat at a small table and shared a spoon to scoop the sweet, soft chunks of mango and shreds of coconut. They talked in a way that to Jaya felt as natural as when he talked with Alika. Or Nohea.

Jaya started with the most popular question on Oahu. "So what high school do you go to?"

"Kaimuki," Rasa said. "What about you?"

"Manoa Prep, but..." He rolled his eyes.

"But?"

That's when Jaya noticed the dark X on Rasa's left inner arm. "What's that?"

Rasa stiffened for a second. She took her arms off the table and dropped them onto her lap. "Nothing."

An awkward lull in the conversation followed.

Jaya tucked his chin and ran his hand through his hair. *Shit! I shouldn't have asked...*

Rasa spoke up. "You were saying...about Manoa Prep?"

Jaya looked at her. She was smiling.

"It's just...well...I'd rather go to Kalani. Or to your school. Or any public school for that matter."

"Why? Seems like Manoa Prep is a great school."

"Yeah, it's pretty good. For how much it costs, it damn well should be. But, I don't know, there's this pretentiousness that hovers over everything. It's just not my thing."

"I know what you mean. I know some people who've gone there. The fathers of—" Rasa stopped, her face turning to stone. She recovered, tilted her head to one side and said, "Well, honestly, I never would've guessed you went to school there. You seem really chill."

Jaya relaxed. "By the way, what year are you?" he asked.

"A senior.".

"So you're seventeen?"

"Yup. How about you?"

"Same."

"What brought you to this side today?"

Jaya bit his lower lip. "I needed to get the f out of town. I needed to find some peace."

"Funny, same here."

"Any luck?"

"I guess so. How about you?"

"Yeah, I got the peace I predicted. And some excitement I hadn't," Jaya said, grinning.

Rasa giggled. "I used to live here—" She stopped. She bolted up. "Wh-what time is it?" She checked her phone. Her face turned pale. "Shit, I have to be in Waikiki in less than an hour. There's no way I'll make it back in time on the bus!"

"Woah, slow down. What's up?"

"I gotta meet Xander...I mean...help my Uncle Xander," she blurted.

"I'll give you a ride back. Don't worry, I'll get you back on time."

Rasa grabbed Jaya's hand. "Really? I totally owe you!"

The car ride home was a cozy thrill. Like wearing flannel pajamas on the last day of school. Rasa's outgoing personality encouraged Jaya to be more himself.

The first thing Rasa started talking about was how nice his BMW coupe was. But Jaya was completely embarrassed by the luxurious sixteenth birthday present from his parents. For him it was an unnecessary display of the privilege he had. He wished it was an old, hand-me-down, Ford pickup truck.

Rasa said she preferred riding in Beamers over Benzs.

"Dang, girl! How many other guys have given you rides?" Jaya teased. Suddenly his eyes widened. He felt warmth in his cheeks. Would she think it was weird that he said "other guys?" Since most people assumed he was a girl, he didn't know if she thought the same. They hadn't talked about it. Jaya peeked over at her.

She didn't seem to have noticed. She was busy searching through her bag for her pack of Camel Lights and trusty Zippo. She smacked the open pack against her palm until a cigarette jutted out. She offered it to Jaya. "Smoke?"

Jaya's eyebrows rose a notch. "Uh, no. I-I'm good." He'd never smoked anything and he wasn't planning on starting. But she didn't need to know all that.

Shrugging her shoulders, Rasa pulled the cigarette out of the pack, put in her mouth, and lit it.

Out of the corner of his eye, Jaya watched her take a long, slow drag. She opened the window and blew a puff of smoke outside.

Jaya opened his window too. The temperate air refreshed him. He cranked up the stereo. Stone Temple Pilot's *Sex Type Thing* came on.

Rasa made it even louder. "I love this song!"

"You do?" He never would've guessed. Reggae, Jawaiian, pop, R&B, or hip hop he could understand. But this local girl loving rock? And STP at that?

"Hey, it's better than the hippie dippie music my mom used to listen to."

Jaya laughed. "I hear ya."

"I was twelve when I first heard grunge..." She paused, took a drag, and exhaled a smoke ring out the window.

"Cool," Jaya said. About the grunge and the smoke ring. "What's your favorite band?" he asked.

Rasa didn't hesitate. "Definitely Nirvana. Their music and lyrics are freakin' genius."

"Really? What's your favorite Nirvana song?"

"*In Bloom*," Rasa said without a second thought. "I love that they're totally making fun of people."

"Wow." He pressed a button on his stereo, skipping ahead until the opening notes of *In Bloom* blasted through his system. He looked over at Rasa. A slow and sexy smile formed on her lips. Jaya's heart beat a little faster. And faster still when she began nodding her head.

Was this for real? This gorgeous girl loved the same band he worshipped. The same band that basically inspired his future goal of being a lead guitarist/singer. The same band who he would cover tonight at his Waikiki street gig.

"What's your take on Nirvana?" Rasa asked.

"They're good." He wished he had the balls to invite her to his performance. He pictured playing *In Bloom* just for her.

He changed the subject, before he exploded. "Hey, so what do you have to help your uncle with?"

"Oh. That. Yeah...I gotta help him move stuff into his new place in Waikiki."

"Need some help? We can use my car," Jaya offered.

Rasa blushed. Her second cigarette hung immobile in her mouth. "That's so sweet, thanks. But my uncle's...how can I put it? A private guy."

"Ok." He pulled up in front of her place.

Rasa rummaged through her bag. She brought out a permanent marker. She captured his right arm. Holding it firmly, she printed her digits. Jaya held his breath.

It got better.

Before Rasa jumped out of the car, she leaned over and planted a quick but warm kiss on his cheek. Then she said with a shy smile, "Let's hang out again soon."

Jaya gulped and gave her a cow-eyed stare.

That was seven days ago.

Jaya whipped out his phone. He scrolled through his recent photos. He found the one of Rasa and him under the thatch-roofed 'otai stand. He brought the phone close and stared at her penetrating green eyes. Green was even more his favorite color now.

Jaya wondered if this was how Shah Rukh Khan's character felt in *Dilwale Dulhania Le Jayenge*. His mother had been watching that SRK film on the big screen this morning. Coffee in hand, Jaya joined her. Bollywood for breakfast.

It'd been the same since Niu Valley—his mother lived vicariously through the gorgeous, coy heroines and he crushed on them.

Over the years he'd identified more and more with SRK. Of all the Bollywood actors, Jaya considered SRK to be the best with the ladies. A true loverboy. He'd convinced himself that he resembled SRK too. They both had a longish face and brown skin. Short black spiky haircut gelled in place. Brown eyes always in a slight squint. A symmetrical full nose. Plus they were both hopeless romantics.

Well, that's what Jaya wanted to be.

Jaya and Shah Rukh Khan were pretty much bros.

Unlike SRK though, Jaya's mood was crap most the time. And Jaya never got the girl.

But that was about to change.

He hoped.

He got ready to call Rasa.

Not text. Jaya didn't text. He also refused to take part in any sort of social media. Jaya considered the social media world to be fake and pompous. He already lived in a big-ass Kahala mansion and drove a BMW. Why would he want to add self-centeredness to self-indulgence? He'd given social media and texting a fair chance in the past, but each time it felt phony. Besides, nobody texted him anyway. The only person who contacted Jaya was Alika—and he wasn't much of a texter either.

Ok. I got this. Jaya unlocked the screen. He pressed Rasa's digits on the number pad. It rang. He held his breath. Maybe she'd given him a bogus number?

Someone answered. It was Rasa. Jaya exhaled.

"Hello?"

Jaya's willpower cowered in a corner. His mouth felt like it was stuffed with cotton. He couldn't get a word out.

"Hello?"

"Um, hi."

"Jaya," she said, "What's up?"

Jaya found his words. "So what are you doing today?

"Oh, nothing exciting. Just cleaning the bathroom."

"Fun," he said sarcastically, imagining Rasa scrubbing the toilet. Even goddesses do boring, ordinary things.

"How about you?"

"Just chillin a little before going to HHS."

"HHS?"

"Yeah. The Honolulu Homeless Shelter."

"You homeless all of a sudden?"

Jaya laughed. "No. I volunteer there."

"Cool!" Rasa exclaimed. "What exactly do you do?"

"Help make meals and serve. Get new clients settled. Things like that."

"No way," Rasa said. She paused.

Jaya panicked. Maybe she thought he was totally dull and nerdy.

But then Rasa spoke, softer and slower. "No one else I know does things for other people without some kind of payback."

She sounds kind of impressed. That's a good sign. But he didn't want to make a big deal out of it. So all he said was, "Hey, it's better than scrubbing the crapper."

Rasa giggled. Then her voice changed to serious. "Hold up," she said. "I've got another caller. Lemme check who it is."

A second later she said, "It's my uncle. I gotta go. Talk to you later, ok?"

"Ok."

"Bye, Jaya. Thanks for calling."

"Bye." Jaya pressed the red end call button. He jumped around his room pumping his arms over his head in victory. Then he ran downstairs and onto the deck. He waltzed to the railing. The sky merged into the gleaming water. It was a like a rainbow of blues—light blue to turquoise to bright royal to dark azure.

But all he could see was the green of Rasa's incredible eyes.

iT'S NOT ALL ABOUT HiM

Rasa never gave a second thought to guys. Guys were like the ketchup packets that came with her fries at McDonald's—she used a little, then threw the rest away. These days, they were Johns that meant nothing to her. But this girl she'd met...

Jaya.

Rasa scrolled her phone to a photo of the two of them. They were sitting at the 'otai stand. Rasa thought they looked like a cute couple. Swiping her thumb and index finger outward on the screen she enlarged Jaya's face. She was definitely attractive, but in a studly kinda way. She stared at Jaya's eyes.

That's what it is. Jaya's eyes reminded Rasa of the Guanyin bodhisattva painting that used to hang in Kalindi's bedroom. The one where the Goddess of Mercy's eyes were open. And kind.

Rasa smiled to herself. Warmth spread through her body. Suddenly she wanted answers. Were they just going to be friends? What was up with the chemistry she felt? Should she make the first move? Or wait for Jaya?

Rasa was baffled. And that didn't happen often to her when it came to people.

Jaya hadn't done anything, blatant or subtle, to express an interest beyond friendship. No sexual innuendos or cheap lines praising her beauty. No raised eyebrow glance. No "accidental" brushing of her thigh. Nothing that guys usually did to get her out of her panties.

What's more, Jaya acted like a gentleman! Or at least the way Rasa figured a gentleman would act. She thought about one of her favorite movies, *When A Man Loves A Woman*. In the last scene, Michael talked about how he should've really listened to Alice. Funny, because Jaya was the best listener Rasa had ever met. And they'd only talked a couple of times.

Not only that, but when Jaya spoke, her words were so unassuming. Then there was the chivalrous ride home from Hau'ula. And oh my god, Rasa thought, Jaya freakin' volunteers.

Was this girl for real? *Enough already. You know you wanna talk to her again. Call her*!

Rasa dialed. Today Xander couldn't interrupt—it was only 10 a.m. No dates were ever this early.

Jaya answered. It was playful banter at first. With each back and forth, Rasa accepted that she liked Jaya. Not in some bi-curious way but in an I-really-really-really-dig-her way.

And when Rasa made her mind up about something or someone, she wasn't one to beat around the bush. But she needed to calculate the odds with Jaya.

No more wasting time. I need to know. "So are you lesbian?" Rasa asked. The silence that followed made Rasa facepalm. She wished she could suck the question back in. Had Jaya hung up? Rasa held her breath.

Finally Jaya let out an anxious chuckle. "Um...no. I'm straight."

Rasa let her breath go, relieved that Jaya didn't sound insulted.

But damn. She's straight.

"Oh, I just thought that..." Her mouth went on strike. Not a usual occurrence for her.

"There's something I want to tell you. Promise you won't laugh at me though."

Numerous disheartening possibilities leapt about in Rasa's mind. "Ok."

"I am straight...but I like you," Jaya said.

Rasa tried to sound upbeat. "Yeah, me too. So...we're homies, right?"

"Yeah...no...wait."

Jaya inhaled.

"Jaya?"

"I like you like that!" Jaya spouted.

"Like what?"

"Well, see I'm..." Jaya stopped. "Look, the only person who knows about this is my friend Alika. Well, him and Nohea."

"I'm confused."

"I was too, but I'm not anymore." Another pause. "Let me give it a shot," Jaya said. "There are boys *and* girls named Jaya."

"Uh-huh."

"And I like my name. I don't want to change it. Uh...I don't know how to say this."

"It's all good. Tell me."

"Shoots, ok. You're right. I'm just gonna say it. Underneath my clothes there are girl parts. But in my heart and mind I'm all boy—" Jaya stopped. "Ugh. Nevermind," he muttered.

Rasa rested her cheek on her palm and stared at the ceiling. Her thoughts swirled. Neither of them spoke.

Finally Rasa opened her mouth. "I get it."

"Huh?"

"I get it, Jaya."

"You do?"

"I do."

Another long silence. Rasa bit her knuckle. *Maybe I have a chance.* She was about to ask, but Jaya spoke.

"Do you also get that I like you?" he asked.

Rasa felt giddy in her belly. "Uh-huh. And it's mutual." She grinned, feeling herself again. "So does this mean you might be my boyfriend soon?"

"Um..." Jaya paused. Then he whispered, "Oh. I hope so."

Their convo took off after that. An hour rushed by like a bullet train. They didn't get into anything else really personal, but they found common ground in their discussion on the Seattle sound. Jaya said he loved grunge because it was more intricate musically than punk. Rasa wasn't sure about that, but she also liked grunge more than other kinds of rock. They agreed that grunge expressed anger like metal and hardcore, but it was also full of uneasy sadness. And that made it more interesting. They agreed that Nirvana was by far the most compelling because their music, lyrics, and fashion kick started grunge's expression of frustration and indifference to society.

"Sometimes I think it's strange listening to Nirvana when it's sunny outside," Rasa said.

"Yeah. Do you think their songs sound better in gray and rainy Seattle weather?" Jaya asked.

"I think so. Plus it's colder there so you have a practical reason to be all lumberjack," Rasa laughed.

Jaya laughed too. "Yeah."

After they hung up, Rasa entered a shadowy, hazy world. Kind of like when Frodo put on the ring of power. Time dragged by, only Rasa was cloaked in infatuation instead of invisibility.

Jaya was unlike anyone she'd ever met before. He didn't seem to have any shady motives. He was genuine.

Rasa thought about the other people in her life. Their intentions ambled about in her mind like her mother's slow-drifting incense.

My mother.

Kalindi had groomed Rasa to use men. And to be the main caretaker of her siblings. Was this for Rasa's own good or for Kalindi's? Seemed like Kalindi got more out of it. Then Kalindi up and left not giving a second thought to them. What if Kalindi knew about Xander and his threats to hurt Ach, Nitya, and Shanti? Would her mother care? Worry? Rasa shook her head. Didn't matter anyway because Kalindi wasn't around. She might even be dead.

All the men. They just wanted her flesh.

Oh well. She was a black widow, right? She was in control, right? Even her first time with Paul. All she had to do was give some skin and she got dough.

Sam and Ann. Ha! Supposedly well-intentioned foster parents who wanted to keep pretty girls safe! What a load of crap! They were scum. How could Sharon not have a clue? Sam and Ann were the very type of people that CPS was supposed to protect kids from. And to think Rasa had been so appreciative to have a place to live. And that Sam and Ann introduced her to Xander.

Xander.

He was even worse. He was the pimp who held the reins of her life. He gave her expensive clothes. A little spending money. And nonstop fear.

A few weeks into being Xander's "employee," she learned that he paid a shit ton to Sam and Ann every month for her. Like high rent. She couldn't believe she bought all the BS he'd fed her about how he, Sam, and Ann wanted to help kids.

Greedy bastards.

All of them.

But with Jaya, everything was different.

DENIZEN X

"Is this what being American means to you?" Sanjay hollered, glaring at Jaya. "Is it, Jaya? Cutting your hair like a boy even though we tell you to grow it? Why do you act gay?"

"Dad, I'm not gay—"

"I hope not. Chee." He paused. Then he wagged his finger at Jaya. "No good Indian boy will marry you looking like this." He turned away and pulled out the stop from a new bottle of whiskey.

Jaya didn't bother anymore. He knew better than to argue with his father when whiskey was involved.

"Gay, chee," Sanjay muttered as he poured his first drink for the evening. Neat. He took a long sip, then exhaled. His crimson face became a more neutral color.

Jaya plodded up the stairs thinking about how whiskey was his father's self-prescribed medicine. A potent amber elixir for calming nerves and settling temper.

But there was a delicate balance for Sanjay. Without it, he gushed conceit and dogma. If medicated the right amount, he was jovial and charming. Too much unleashed his inner beast.

Jaya reached the top of the stairs. He caught his reflection in the wall mirror. He ran his fingers through his slick new haircut and grinned. He hoped Rasa would like it. They'd be hanging out in less than twenty-four hours.

He stepped into his guitar room. Here he was master. He eyed his eight shiny electric guitars and three high-end acoustics. Like a watchmaker in a small, dark one-room shop in some remote village, Jaya laid out equipment to begin his intricate work. Today's task was to service his 1965 sunburst-tone Fender Jaguar. The same year and model that Kurt Cobain often used. With quick precision, he removed the six old strings, conditioned the fretboard, and cleaned the pickups and bridge. Then he put in a new set of thick strings. Less than twenty minutes later, he hooked on a black leather strap and plugged into his pedalboard and amp.

When he reached for a pick to tune up, he noticed his notebook laying nearby. It was flipped open to a list of potential names for his future band.

Sanjay's words from earlier this morning echoed in Jaya's ears.

You will marry a boy. The two of you will take over my company. Bhus.

But Sanjay had no muscle in this room. Jaya smiled as he imagined himself at a fork in the road. He bypassed his father's money-hungry-developer footsteps on one road and took the path less travelled. The one that Millie had shown him without knowing it when she'd left him for her musician boyfriend. The one that steered him to starting his own band and being both its lead guitarist and singer.

Jaya scanned his list. He got stuck on the last band name.

"Denizen X," he said out loud. "Denizen X," he repeated. The words glissaded out of his mouth like they were on a skimboard coasting along wet, flat sand just after a wave rolled out. That was it. The perfect name for his future band. Kurt would've liked it, there was no doubt.

Jaya tuned up. Then he tested his chorus pedal with a few chords. He warmed up with one of his favorites—*Come As You Are*. He played a few notes of the intro. The grungy tune invaded the room.

Just then his cell rang. He scooped it up from the top of the amp, hoping it was Rasa. Alika's face covered the screen. He wore a silly grin. Jaya answered, a little disappointed, but still glad to hear his friend's voice.

"What's up?" Jaya greeted.

"Nothing. What's up wit' chu?"

"Music therapy."

"Cool."

"Where ya at?"

"At home, chillin'."

Jaya eyed his notebook again. "Hey, what do you think about the name 'Denizen X'? You know, for my future band?"

Alika was used to Jaya's earnestness when talking about anything related to music. "Denizen X. Like Citizen X? The movie about the Russian serial killer?"

"Yeah."

"What's the connection?"

"Ok, so a citizen has rights. A denizen may or may not have rights. Trans people are kinda like denizens. And in the movie, the X means average joe citizen. But in my band name, it represents something other than the XY boy or XX girl that people seem to be ok with."

"That's deep," Alika said in an intense voice. "Denizen X. I like it."

"Sweet." Jaya circled the name in his notebook.

"Hey, I gotta ask ya something," Alika said.

"What?"

"Is everything ok?"

"Yeah, why?"

"Seriously, Jaya, you've been acting weird at school the last couple of days."

"Weird?" Jaya asked. He went over the last few days.

"Yeah. In class you've been staring out the window. And yesterday you walked right past me. You didn't hear me when I called your name. Plus you had this idiotic smile. I was gonna catch up to you, but the bell rang."

Jaya got it. Alika had noticed his Rasa-infatuation firsthand without knowing what it was. Jaya figured no one would realize that cupid's arrow had pierced his heart. But apparently he couldn't get anything past his best friend. "Dude, I'm sorry. You know I'd never ignore you on purpose. I've been kinda distracted."

"That's an understatement," Alika chuckled. "But for reals, what's up?"

"Nothing. Everything's cool."

"Hmm. I'm not buying it."

"Really, I'm good."

"Oh yeah. You sound really good," Alika said sarcastically. "Don't front, Jaya. I know you. I know something's up. Spill it."

Jaya's body tensed. He knew he should tell Alika about Rasa. He wanted to. But he was convinced that he'd jinx his chance with her if he told anyone. Even his best friend. "No really, Alika, it's all good."

"Fine. I'll let it go." He paused. "For now."

Jaya relaxed, glad to be off the hook for a while.

"Oh shoot, my mom's calling me," Alika said, "I gotta go. Laters."

"Laters."

Jaya retrieved his pick. He closed his eyes. Then he counted himself in. He began the forlorn riff of *Come as You Are* and melted into the guitar. The lyrics drifted through his mind like fluffy clouds. But it was the song's long guitar solo that he looked forward to. It spoke to him much more than the words ever could.

He thought about his parents. His eyes opened and he rolled them. His parents would never tell him to "come as you are." They wanted him to be something he wasn't.

Forget them.

He thought about Rasa instead.

He played with more fervor. When he got to the last verse, he closed his eyes again and sang with Kurt's subtle zeal, pretending to serenade Rasa. It was strange combining the morbidness of the lyrics with his passion for Rasa. But it felt so good.

AN UNLiKELY PAiR

Tourists scuttled about loud and obnoxious on the Waikiki Beach Wall. But Rasa still nodded off. It was only the shrill cry of a baby that made her eyes jerk open. She remembered why she was waiting.

Jaya.

She cursed the fatigue that was trying to interfere with her first, non-trick date. She double-cursed Xander—her tiredness was his doing. She rubbed the sleep from her eyes and let her thoughts of Jaya energize her.

But then memories of last night put her in a chokehold.

Halfway through shoving her body into the skin-tight red Chanel "uniform," Rasa got pissed. She wanted to go home. She wanted to be in her room getting ready for bed, not getting ready for a trick that she knew would keep her awake all night. She wanted to be well-rested for her date with Jaya.

The top half of the dress hung over her hips when she marched up to Xander. "I'm going home. I'm not doing this tonight."

Xander didn't say a word. He only smirked. He wrapped his strong hands around her bare waist. Slowly, softly, he slid them up and over the sides of her rib cage. Over her chest. Around her neck. And then he squeezed. Tight. Tighter.

Rasa's eyebrows rose in desperate semicircles. She couldn't breathe or make a sound. Instinctively she clawed at his hands. But Xander didn't let up despite her sharp nails drawing blood.

Rasa felt herself fading.

"You're doing this," he growled. Then he let go.

Rasa gasped with a violence that made her chest hurt.

In the meantime, Xander retrieved a photo from his bedroom. He held it up. It was a recent one of Ach, Nitya, and Shanti. He drew his knife and pointed the tip at each of their faces in turn.

A flurry of fear and anger, more excruciating than the neck pain, made Rasa's eyes water.

Xander threw the photo down. He stepped on it as he got close to her. "Get dressed," he demanded, holding the knife to her neck. Then with scant pressure he inched the tip across her neck and said, "Now."

Rasa obeyed.

When she woke up this morning, a dark bruise circled her neck like a velvet choker necklace. Before she left the apartment she applied a layer of concealer and foundation over it.

Rasa turned her head to the flat, calm waters of Waikiki. Maybe a cigarette would help clear her mind. She reached into her bag but then stopped. Out of the corner of her eye she spotted Jaya.

She forgot about everything. Smoking. Xander. Her neck. The steady flow of tourists vanished from her sight. And just like the first time she'd seen him on the Hau'ula mountain, sounds ceased and time slowed. It was only Jaya in her sights.

He got closer. Her body prickled. She wasn't used to being skittish with a guy. It was as if she were about to step into some delicious unknown.

Soon Jaya was standing before her in the flesh. His hair was spiked and shiny. On his face, aviator sunglasses and a faint smile. A ribbed black tank top revealed his thin but toned arms. From the pocket of his black-and-white plaid cargo shorts, a thick silver wallet chain dangled. His feet tread with assurance in black Doc Martens.

Rasa had this sudden urge to fling herself onto him. Wrap her arms and legs around his lean frame. Smell his hair. Plant kisses all over the smooth brown skin of his face. She shoved her palms under her thighs and pressed down hard, willing herself to sit still.

Jaya's eyes fell on her. His timid smile turned into a grin.

He slid his sunglasses onto his head. "Hi, Rasa."

"Hey, Jaya." She smiled.

He stuffed his hands into his pockets and stooped a bit. "How you doing?"

"Good. How about you?"

"I'm good. Getting better each second. What do you wanna do?"

Rasa wasn't used to guys asking her what she wanted to do. In her experience they either hinted at or told her what they wanted to do. And their agenda always involved sex.

Rasa blushed. "Um...let's walk around Diamond Head?"

"Cool." He held out his hand to help her up.

They walked east on Kalakaua. At first neither of them spoke. Rasa glanced at Jaya. She swore she saw a faint golden glow around him. His silence spoke a language of its own to her, whispering honeyed words into her ear. Saying way more than all the flattering words spoken to her by other guys. Their jumble of words to get to the birds and the bees seemed silly compared to Jaya's mature reticence.

They passed Kaimana Beach. Still neither of them had said anything. Rasa felt more at ease. As if she and Jaya had known each other for years. She reached to touch his shoulder but stopped short.

Jaya turned his head to her and said, "I haven't walked around Diamond Head since I don't even know when."

"That's too bad. The view's always amazing, right?"

Jaya nodded.

Rasa continued, "I walk here as often as I can. To get away from the craziness of Waikiki."

"Yeah, you must miss the country. I mean Hau'ula's like a hidden gem."

"You got that right."

"Why'd you move to town?"

"I-I had to," Rasa stammered. She struggled to figure out what to say. White lies hatched from thin shells of compunction as she pondered her situation—Kalindi's abandonment and possible death, separation from her siblings, and being turned out by Xander.

Ashamed, Rasa dropped her head. "My parents died when I was twelve. I've been in foster care ever since."

"Oh no. I had no idea."

"It's okay." She was relieved that Jaya bought it.

"There's your Uncle Xander though. Any other family?"

Rasa's palms got sweaty. "Yeah, I've got a younger brother and two younger sisters. But they're with a different foster family on the North Shore." She dried her palms on her dress, glad to tell one truth.

"Geez. That must be hard. When did you last see them?"

"A week ago."

They reached the hill on Diamond Head Road. They ascended without speaking. The Pacific stretched out like an endless blue sarong.

"How about you? Any siblings?"

"No. I'm an only child."

"Oh. You live in town, right? Where?"

Jaya ran his hand down the back of his head. His mouth twisted. His eyes darted to Rasa then away again. Then he pointed and asked, "See that giant tan house with the blue roof?"

Rasa pretended to wipe sweat from her brow. "Phew!" she said. "For a second I thought you were gonna say Lani Kai!"

Jaya loosened up. He laughed.

"But for real, your parents must be loaded. What do they do?"

"My dad builds luxury condos. My mom throws parties. And I mooch off them," he said with a glimmer of mischief in his eyes. "Not exactly a rough life."

"Believe me, you don't want a rough life."

Jaya didn't know what to say.

They reached the rock wall that overlooked the distant waves. From where they stood, all the surfers looked like tiny toy action figures wanting in on the set.

"Let's sit down."

Rasa nodded. She pushed herself up backwards, taking care to keep her blue babydoll dress tucked. She swung her legs around to face the ocean.

Jaya hoisted himself onto the wall. He sat with his right knee up.

Usually when Rasa hung out here watching the surfers, she wanted to be out there with them. Especially on days like today when the winds were offshore. But she was consumed with the way the fabric of Jaya's shorts tickled her bare thigh. Their legs were almost touching. And Jaya hadn't pulled his leg away.

Rasa didn't dare move her leg. She shifted her upper body slightly to face Jaya. "You ever surfed?" she asked.

"Yeah, I tried it once. It wasn't pretty. Let's just say I don't go in the ocean anymore. Not even to cool off. How about you?"

"Yup. Been in the water my whole life, free-diving and surfing. I try to get out whenever I can." Rasa looked out at the waves and sighed. "I didn't get to bring my longboard to Waikiki though. My foster parents have no room for it."

Jaya's face lit up. He touched Rasa's arm. "You know, I've got an 8-6 Downing collecting dust in my garage. It's yours whenever you need it."

Rasa quickly towed her eyes back to Jaya's hand. Then she looked at his animated face. "Well..." Landon popped into her mind. The last time someone gave her a surfboard was in exchange for sex.

"What do you think, Rasa? Do you want it?" Jaya asked again. "I mean you can keep it at my house. I can bring it to you whenever you want."

Rasa studied him. There was eagerness shining in his eyes. Not lust. "Really?"

Jaya nodded vigorously. His fingers were still on her arm. He pulled them away quickly but not before his cheeks flushed.

"Thanks, yes." She bit the side of her lower lip.

Rasa wondered what it was going to be like getting something so valuable without having to do anything. Would she be this generous if she had plenty? Jaya certainly was charitable. She assumed his parents were also. She thought about how lucky he was to have his family.

She edged closer to Jaya. "Did your parents give you the board?"

Jaya's face became somber. He nodded slower.

"What's the matter?" she asked, alarmed that maybe she'd said something wrong.

"Nothing."

Rasa wasn't convinced. This time she laid her hand on his arm. "What just happened? You look sad. Tell me."

"I am sad. But I shouldn't be. Why should I when I've got my real family. And a freakin' mansion. And pretty much everything I could ever want."

Rasa's forehead wrinkled. "Seems like there's more to the story than that."

"Nothing more than extravagant first-world pain."

Rasa slid her hand down Jaya's forearm to his hand. She wove her fingers between his. "Pain is pain," she said. "It doesn't matter what causes it."

And so they sat. Hand-in-hand. Rasa and Jaya. An unlikely pair. Watching the waves as an honest love kindled between their fingers.

SWEET AS CAKE

The elevator doors slid apart. And Jaya's heart stopped.

Rasa.

She floated towards him like a Bollywood starlet on the red carpet. When she caught sight of him in his car, she waved. Her exquisite eyes and smile were like defibrillator paddles, shocking him back to life.

Jaya sat up straight. His armpits were suddenly wet. His heart went into a nervous and delighted spasm.

His mind played a scene from the Tarantino film *From Dusk Till Dawn*—the one where Salma Hayek appears on stage for her snake dance. The Tito & Tarantula song *After Dark* echoed in his ears as Rasa seemingly slow-walked to him. She was wearing these oh-my-god-so-sexy white high-waisted super short shorts and a matching off-the-shoulder crop top.

She hopped into the car. "I'm starving!"

He heard what she said, but he couldn't say a word. All he could do was stare.

Rasa touched his shoulder. "Jaya, do you feel like eating?"

Her fingers pressed the play button on Jaya. He pulled his eyes off her. "I could eat," he said as he started the ignition. He couldn't very well let this gift from the heavens stay hungry.

"Shoots! We go grind," she replied in full-on pidgin.

Jaya drove them to Coffee Talk for some pineapple, coconut, and mango açaí bowls—the closest thing to Hau'ula's 'otai in town. They sat at a tiny round table outside the cafe overlooking the street. Jaya's nerves cooled off a bit. Waialae Avenue was busy with traffic, but to Jaya it seemed as if they were in their own world. All he could see was Rasa. He savored every word she spoke the same way he savored the spicy bites of hamachi sashimi at Nobu. He surrendered to the pleasure of his senses that were indulging in everything Rasa.

Rasa told him more about her siblings. About growing up in Hau'ula. She didn't talk much about her mother. She never mentioned her father. Or how the two of them died.

Jaya figured it was too soon to dig deeper about her parents. So he didn't. Things were going well. Rasa seemed to be having a good time. Jaya darn sure knew he was. A couple of times he got tongue-tied trying to talk and look at her gorgeous face at the same time. Like when she asked him to tell her about being Gujarati. He stumbled on his words at first but eventually got into a comfortable rhythm with her. He told her about school, Alika, and neutral stuff about his parents.

He didn't mention anything about playing guitar because he'd decided that one of these days he'd surprise her with a serenade. After all, he finally had a chance to become the hopeless romantic he wanted to be. Just like SRK. Even if the song he chose wasn't going to be exactly a tender, mellow love song. Anyway Rasa loved Nirvana. Then again, maybe he'd write a song for her.

The day was kind and moved slowly. When the sun eventually grew tired, Rasa said she had to get going. Jaya drove her home.

"Hey, I'm getting my first tat tomorrow. Why don't you come with? Then we can get some sushi after," Jaya suggested.

"Tattoo? Sushi? I'm in!" Rasa said with big eyes and a huge smile.

"Yeah. My buddy Alika's gonna be there. You two could finally meet."

"Cool! I can't wait!" But then Rasa's face changed. All serious and a bit sad, she said, "Shoot. It's Saturday tomorrow. I gotta help my uncle with some stuff again." She gave him a weak smile. "Sorry."

Jaya crushed his urge to whine.

"It's ok. Next time." That was all he'd intended to say. But then his mouth committed treason against his brain. "I'll miss you," he blurted. He groaned as soon as the three words came out.

Alika had warned him about the rules of dating a while back. And Jaya had just broken one of them—don't say mushy things after hanging out with someone only a couple of times. You're supposed to play it cool. Not get all clingy.

But Jaya didn't have too much time to beat himself up because all of a sudden Rasa was holding his hand.

"I'll miss you too," she said. "I'd rather hang with you."

They arrived at Rasa's apartment. Jaya wished he could call Alika to strategize about the next move.

Luckily he didn't have to figure anything else out. Rasa took the lead. She leaned over and kissed his cheek. Then she pulled her head only slightly away, so that their faces were within an inch. She looked into his eyes and kissed his lips. Soft. Moist. Sweet. Like the fresh Japanese Castella Cake his mother served at their parties.

She gave him a half smile and got out.

Jaya peeked at himself in his rearview mirror to get a load of his expression. He wanted to remember everything about the day he had his first kiss.

PRiZE GiRL

It had been a wonderful morning with her family. Even Ach was excited.

"One more time, Ras!" he called, tossing his football high over Nitya and Shanti's heads.

Rasa caught it, praising her sisters on how high they'd jumped trying to intercept it.

Shanti marched in place, chanting, "More monkey in the middle! More monkey in the middle!"

Nitya smiled big and nodded.

But then they heard Xander's bark. "Rasa!" he shouted.

Rasa and her siblings didn't make a fuss. They huddled together and whispered their goodbyes. "I'll see you next week," Rasa said, as tears pooled in her eyes. "I'll...I'll..." Rasa got all choked up.

Nitya and Shanti took turns kissing her cheek.

"We'll miss you too," Shanti cried.

Ach became stolid and somber.

Rasa saw through him: he was forcing himself to be impassive because she was leaving. She stroked his cheek. But all that did was blend anger into the subtle sadness already on his face. This was the same mix Ach got every time Kalindi would leave.

He dropped his eyes. "I'm gonna tell on that scumbag..." he mumbled.

"What? What are you going to do?" Rasa asked, trying to keep her voice calm, though she felt sweat in her palms and pits.

"I'm gonna tell my foster parents about Xander. There's something wrong with him. He's not a nice person."

"Rasa!" Xander yelled again.

"Ach," Rasa said, putting her hands on his shoulders, "please don't tell them. Or anyone. He's not my favorite person, but he's ok." She lifted his chin. "I'm ok. Don't worry. I'll take care of it. The main thing is I get to see you and Nitya and Shanti, right?"

Ach frowned, but then he nodded. "Ok. I guess..."

"Thanks, Ach." Rasa kissed the top of his head. "I gotta go. I love you," she said, locking in her tears. She did an about-face and trudged to Xander's Benz. As soon as she climbed in and shut the door, she started bawling.

Xander rolled his eyes. "Stop crying, or you'll get too puffy-eyed. You still gotta work tonight."

The irritation in his voice gagged her into silence. She took a quick peek in the sun visor's mirror. Her cheeks were glossy. Like she'd painted them with a coat of clear varnish. She wiped her face. Then she looked out the rear windshield. She waved goodbye to her siblings.

Shanti was fidgeting. Nitya was a statue. But it was Ach's face that killed her. He was crying so hard that his body convulsed. His head bobbed as he tried to suck in his snot.

Rasa lost it. She buried her face in her hands and sobbed. She envisioned a cord that connected her heart to her siblings. It stretched tight as Xander backed the car onto the main road.

The cord was taut when Xander looked at her and warned, "Don't fuckin' forget their lives are on you." Then he stepped on the gas. Rasa felt the cord strain and snap.

"Knock it off!" Xander yelled.

Scaring her straight didn't work. Her tears kept coming. Her head pounded. She tried resting it on the window. She tried closing her eyes. It was no use. With each mile away, her headache and crying intensified.

Xander shook his head. "What?" he huffed. "Oh my God, Rasa. There's always something." He drove faster.

Rasa managed to shut herself up. She pictured Shanti, Nitya, and Ach. She thought about why the four of them were in this predicament in the first place. Her chest began to burn with rage at Kalindi.

She glanced at Xander. Recollections of tricks he'd made her turn converged in her mind.

Meanwhile Xander dialed up the volume of the stereo. Dave Grohl hammered the drums and a few seconds later the rest of Nirvana joined him and laid out the powerful song *Scentless Apprentice*. Kurt Cobain started screaming the lyrics. Ordinarily Rasa loved this song. Today it dragged her into a powerless abyss. Her emotions shifted from anger to fear. She started breathing fast and shallow.

Xander pretended not to notice and laid into some sweet talk.

"Rasa, you know you're my prize girl," he said in a deep, seductive voice. He paused then to deliver his news. "And because of you, I'm starting a new monthly North Shore party. Get this. Fancy, secluded beachfront house. Pumping music. Unlimited liquor and coke. And rich men willing to spend anything for a chance at some time with you. My crown jewel. There'll be other girls, of course. But you'll be the star."

He ran his hand over Rasa's head but clenched it back. Her hair was drenched with sweat. "Gross! What's up, Rasa?"

She didn't answer. She was doubled over, clutching her stomach. By now they'd reached H1.

"Pull over, Xander. I'm gonna barf."

He slowed a bit, swerved to the side of the road and slammed on the brakes.

Rasa flung the door open. She vomited clear, frothy liquid. She hung her head and waited. Nothing else came out. She sat up and shut the door. "I'm ok." But she was still woozy.

"I don't know what the hell's wrong with you, but we're going straight to my place. You can rest for a couple hours, but then it's back to work. I've got an extra important date lined up for you tonight." He grabbed the back of her neck. "Don't fuck it up." He let go. "Oh, and don't plan on seeing your bratty sisters and brother next weekend. You're gonna stay with me and work."

Rasa closed her eyes. She knew she'd get through the trick later today and the extra ones next weekend. Those things weren't bad.

What was bad was that she'd have to lie to her siblings. Again. And to Jaya. Again.

And she wouldn't be able to see any of them next weekend.

Loneliness punched her in the gut.

THREE REASONS

Jaya watched the needles of the tattoo machine puncture the skin of his right inner wrist like tiny bayonets. The scratchy, sharp pain made his eyes water, but he sucked it up. It was worth it. He leaned back in the hydraulic chair and smiled to himself.

"How you doing?" Kalani adjusted his grip on the tattoo machine.

"Good."

Kalani continued his work. After awhile he asked, "So. Everyone's got a story for their tat. What's yours?"

Jaya sat up. "Umm, it's kinda complicated."

Kalani lifted his eyes only. "Well, what does this Sanskrit lettering mean?"

"It's pronounced tritiya-prakriti."

"You're gonna have to help me out a little more."

"Basically it's my reminder that society doesn't define my gender. I do."

"And I'm guessing there's a reason you want it on your right wrist?"

"Yeah, so I can see it when I play guitar."

"Cool." Kalani shifted a bit in his chair. He turned his attention back to his work.

It was then Jaya got a better view of the traditional Hawaiian sleeve tattoo—black geometric and wave designs—that wrapped around Kalani's entire right arm.

Bad ass.

Jaya looked around the shop. The walls were plastered with photos of multi-colored tattoo designs interspersed with photos of happy newly tattooed people.

Alika pivoted back and forth on a rolling stool. He teased, "How are you really doing, Jaya? No act now." He flashed Jaya a mocking smile.

"I'm doing good, dickhead. Just like I said."

Alika snickered. He ran his fingers down the three rows of black arrows that covered his upper arm and said, "You should've seen when Kalani did this one. Old school tapping. If you'd have asked this Hawaiian how I was doing then, *good* wouldn't have been it."

This time Kalani snickered.

Jaya took his turn at a little teasing. "Ho, da moke couldn't handle a little tap tap."

Kalani chimed in. "Yeah, big 'ole baby."

Alika raised his eyebrows. "Ok, let Kalani tap your next tat. Then we'll see who can't handle."

"Shoots." Jaya held out his fist to Alika.

Alika bumped back. "Hey, I didn't know you knew Sanskrit?" He strained his neck for a closer look.

"I don't, I just did some research on this lettering. Can you believe it? Not all Indian culture thinks everyone has to be this or that." Jaya rubbed his left palm over each of his cheeks, wishing he felt stubble.

"So cool. Kinda like mahus in Hawaiian culture."

"Yeah. But if my father saw this tat he'd throw out some wise ass comment like, 'You should've gotten the Sanskrit word svairini.'"

"What's svairini?"

"I'm not totally sure because when I looked it up there were like three definitions. Get this. It can mean lesbian or prostitute or a sexually independent single woman."

"Dang. So it could mean you're Ellen DeGeneres, Air Force Amy, or Beyonce?"

Jaya cracked up. "Ha! I'm thinking my parents would mix it up a little. They'd call me 'svairini svairini,' and mean Ellen Amy, a lesbian prostitute."

Alika started to laugh but then stopped himself. He knew how much it hurt Jaya when his parents said cruel things. He muttered something as he swiveled on the stool.

"Huh?" Jaya asked.

"I was just saying how that sucks."

"Yeah, pretty much."

"I don't get why your parents are like that."

Jaya shook his head and shrugged.

"I wish they were more open-minded."

"I wish your parents would adopt me."

"They totally would."

Jaya smiled. But then he remembered what Sanjay wanted to do to the land where Alika's home sat. "What really sucks is that my dad's going to bulldoze land near your neighborhood for a new luxury condo development. It won't matter if your ancestors' bones happened to be buried nearby."

Alika frowned. "Your dad's really going to build in Waianae?"

Jaya nodded. "If you knew what my father just did on the North Shore..." He was shaking his head now.

"What did he do?"

Jaya stared at the floor. *My father bribed some state people so he could start construction on a known Hawaiian burial site.* He frowned. He couldn't get himself to say it. So he kept quiet.

"Jaya?"

Jaya looked up.

"What did he—" Alika stopped. He ran his thumb and index finger over his beard. "No worries, Jaya. My family knows you're a treati-pakeyti who despises the injustice of development without restraint."

A grateful smile surfaced on Jaya's lips. *Tritiya-prakriti*, he mouthed to himself. He loved Alika for trying.

There was a lull in the conversation. Jaya listened to the music that played softly in the background. Hoobastank's *The Reason* was on. Jaya thought about the lyrics. He thought about how he couldn't change what his parents did, but he could change himself. He could try to see his cup as half full even when he felt all empty. And it turned out that he had more than one reason to change. He had three—Alika, playing the guitar, and Rasa.

Rasa first.

TROJANS, CAMEL LiGHTS, AND COPS

Rasa sensed Xander's edginess. He yanked her hand as he towed her through Waikiki.

"Faster," he ordered.

Tonight's date was "extra important," according to him. Seems like that was what he said about all of her dates.

His unease rubbed off on her. *Nothing that a cigarette couldn't fix.* But she'd run out this morning.

They approached Coco Cove. Rasa saw her chance to snag her smokes.

"Xan-der," she sang, "can we please go in here for a sec? I wanna get some cigs."

Xander came to a dead stop, exhaled loudly, and flung her hand away. "Make it quick."

"Thanks, Xander baby." She hustled into the convenience store.

The bright lights inside somehow amplified her stress. She hunched her shoulders and hastened her steps.

The cashier was the only other person in the store. She was

standing behind the register writing in a binder. She looked up from her work and caught Rasa's eye. They exchanged quick glances.

Rasa passed the cold soda section. Why not add a nice caffeine high to the nicotine buzz she was anticipating? Pepsi would do. Or maybe the Monster...

She didn't think she was standing there that long but suddenly she felt Xander's hand grip the back of her neck.

"Just cigarettes," he ordered, squeezing. He led her by the neck straight to the cashier.

The cashier's gold bracelets clinked as she bent down to put the binder under the counter. She stood up. Rasa saw the woman's eyes widen as she looked first at Rasa's heavily made-up face, then down at her short dress. Then she looked at Xander. Her eyebrows shot up. Rasa saw suddenly what the lady was seeing: Xander still choking the back of her neck, Xander way older than her and not looking like any kind of relative, Xander with that cocky gleam in his eye, a Louis Vuitton French cuff shirt, and a big-ass Rolex. Rasa was sure it was obvious that Xander was her pimp. She figured the cashier probably saw this kind of thing all the time working in Waikiki.

The cashier quick made her face flat, without opinions.

Xander let go of Rasa's neck. "A pack of Camel Lights, uh..."—he leaned forward and inspected the cashier's name tag—"...Nohea. Oh, and where are the condoms?"

"Ova there." Nohea pointed to the middle left wall of the store.

"Rasa, go get a pack," Xander said but then changed his mind. "No. You stay here. I'll get it." He headed over.

Rasa wiped her sweaty palms on her brown suede minidress.

"No! Wait! Don't do that," Nohea reached under the counter and pulled out a paper towel roll. "Use this." She tore off a sheet.

"Thanks."

"Baby girl, you ok?" Nohea whispered "You like me call da cops?"

Rasa shook her head. "No, Auntie, everything's ok."

Nohea examined Rasa's face. "You shua?"

"Uh-huh," Rasa replied, crossing her arms and drumming the fingers of her right hand on her left arm.

"Is this guy..." Nohea stopped. Xander was back.

He tossed a pack of Trojans onto the counter. "This and the Camel Lights."

Xander slid a fifty-dollar bill across the counter.

Rasa scanned Nohea's face. Maybe this lady really could help her. She pictured herself pushing Xander away and screaming, "I changed my mind, Auntie! Call the cops!"

"Hea." Nohea handed Xander some bills and coins.

He shoved the change in his pocket and headed to the entrance. "Let's go."

Rasa took a deep breath. She turned, but Nohea grabbed her hand and mouthed, "Wait." Nohea scribbled something on a small scrap of paper. "If you change your mind," she whispered, slipping Rasa the paper.

Rasa scanned it: Nohea's name and number. She looked back at her and smiled. "Thank you," she mouthed.

"Rasa!" Xander roared from the sidewalk.

"Coming," Rasa shouted back, stuffing the paper in her bra. She put on her sexy game face and catwalked out of the store.

SOME COUNT, SOME DON'T

The trades blew over the Manoa Prep campus in irregular bursts. Vibrant red hibiscus waved about fitfully, their large petals flapping like a muleta. Jaya swallowed the last bite of his chicken wrap as he watched a jumbo bee charge into one of the showy flowers.

The bell rang. Lunch was over. He slung his messenger bag across his shoulder and dragged himself towards the library. Next period was study hall, no reason to hustle like everyone else around him. Good thing because there was no way to rush what was on his mind. His legs took slow steps as he created an unhurried Rasa fantasy.

Escape campus and drive to Rasa's place. Come As You Are *plays on the stereo. Arrive. Park. Sneak into her bedroom and...*

From out of nowhere someone shoved him. He stumbled forward but caught himself before he face-planted. He turned around to see who it was.

Ron, Steve, and Faye.

These were three seniors he'd be happy to never see again after graduation. Everyone knew they were descendents of some of the original missionaries in Hawaii. Their families were among the wealthiest in the islands. Jaya used to feel sorry for them. If his ancestry had stolen land and culture from the Native Hawaiians, he'd carry so much guilt he'd be a saint to everyone just to be able to live with himself.

But these three weren't like that. This year they'd taken a particular interest in harassing Jaya. There wasn't a good reason as far as Jaya could tell. Other than that subjugation ran in their blood.

Ron crossed his arms. "If it isn't the LGBT poster child," he said.

How do they always know when Alika's not around?

Faye stepped up to Jaya, her hands on her hips. She was chewing gum like a maniac. "Where are you going, Jaya?" She blew a huge bubble. The pink edge of it almost touched his nose. She let it pop, gathered the sticky remnants with her tongue, and started chewing the crap out of it again. "Looks like you're headed to the library."

Aren't you a genius?

By then Ron and Steve were standing next to Faye. The three musketeers all crossed their arms at the same time and stared at him. Jaya crossed his arms and stared back. He pictured them as the three wise monkeys' estranged cousins—the three stupid monkeys. He almost laughed out loud.

But then Steve spoke. "Why don't you sit with us in the library," he suggested. "We're doing research on what turns people into fags. Bet you know all about it."

Ron moved behind Jaya. "You're a fag, right?" he whispered. Suddenly he raised his voice and demanded, "Come on, Jaya. Admit it." He lifted his hands to push Jaya but stopped when he spotted Mrs. Tosh, the librarian, walking towards them.

"Oh Ron, I've got that book you requested. Come with me," she called out.

Ron hesitated.

Mrs. Tosh waved to him and said, "Come on. I've only got five minutes before my meeting."

"You're off the hook," Ron whispered to Jaya. "For now." Then he turned and followed Mrs. Tosh.

Steve and Faye went with him like faithful minions.

Jaya breathed a sigh of relief. There was no way he was going to the library now. He decided to head over to the Vat for some R+R.

He hotfooted it to the old, standalone storage building at the northernmost edge of the campus. It was his favorite place to hide out from his peers. No one was ever around up there. He made it to the thick patch of trees that formed the campus border just as the late bell rang. Pushing through low branches and foliage, he spotted the Vat's rusty front door. He tossed his bag onto a grassy patch to use as his pillow. He stretched his legs out. The tall blades tickled his calves. Gentle sun rays cascaded through the droopy tree branches and dull green leaves. He closed his eyes. He forgot about Ron, Steve, and Faye. He let his mind go where it wanted to go—to Rasa.

Rasa's slow walking to me in a gold and black lehenga choli. Choli Ke Peeche *plays in the background. Her hips roll like soft waves. She looks like a tigress on a hunt. She approaches all sinuous. Her green bedroom eyes intoxicate me. She's so close. Her hands interlace behind the back of my head.*

Then Jaya let his hand go where it wanted to go—down, down, down.

She touches my hair, caresses my head. She closes her eyes and leans in. Her lips are on mine...

Just then voices interrupted. Jaya yanked his hand up. His eyes flew open. His Rasa fantasy evaporated faster than hand sanitizer. Which he wished he had. His heart beat like a fast bass drum.

He sat up and surveyed the area. He saw them.

Again?

It was Ron, Steve, and Faye. Again. They were supposed to be in the library. Instead here they were. Standing behind some bushes to the left of him. Luckily, they hadn't seen him. He wanted to keep it that way. He didn't move his body, but his eyes followed them as they lit up a joint and passed it around.

A sweet and sweaty-smelling haze wrapped one of its tentacles around him. Bits and pieces of their conversation sailed past him like the expensive boats he knew they navigated.

Then, as if Ron whipped out a megaphone, Jaya heard seven words loud and clear.

"Some people count and some people don't," Ron said. He took a hit and then coughed.

They all laughed. Jaya wasn't sure if it was because of what he said or because he coughed. Seemed like it was probably the first. And it reminded him of something Sanjay yelled last night in his drunken rage.

"Construction's going well in Waianae," his father boasted.

Jayshree didn't say anything. She was focused on twisting off the cap on a bottle of red zin.

Before Jaya could stop himself he blurted, "I can't believe you don't give a shit about the burial grounds!"

"Jaya, the past is the past. They need to forget about it and so do you. Besides, lazy Hawaiian people don't count anymore. Only people that work hard and make money count," he slurred in his Gujju accent. His eyes flamed with his next four words. "We count. Not them."

There was so much Jaya wanted to say. Scream. Like, Hawaiian people do work hard. And it's not only hard work. What about the fact that Native Hawaiian culture had been largely eradicated by western domination? Or that out of their highly functioning cultural context, maybe Hawaiians became like fish out of water? And that it's really hard to try to function at your best if you're oppressed? Plus how could his father not have more empathy when he hated how Indians had been persecuted by the British?

But Jaya kept his mouth shut. From his experience, fighting with bullies didn't work for him or his mother. Plus he didn't have the energy to get into it with his father.

Ron laughed. "There are two kinds of losers," he said. "First, gay people because they can't get anyone of the opposite sex to like them. Kinda like Jaya. I mean who'd want to be with her? Right?"

Steve and Faye nodded and laughed.

What kind of conversation was this? Were they forming some kind of new right-wing extremist organization?

"And second, public school kids. That's obvious, huh?" Ron asked.

Steve and Faye cracked up.

Those words reminded Jaya of Rasa. *They're making fun of her*!

Jaya snapped. He pressed his hands into the grass, ready to jump up and beat the rich, white entitlement out of Ron. And Steve.

And Faye. But then the sheer hypocrisy of it all settled him down. As did his guilt. How could he be mad at them when he was the son of people who thought just like them? And he was born to a luxury of lies. Just like them. And he enjoyed the fruits of wealth. Just like them.

Rasa.

Jaya rested his head on his knees and massaged his temples. When he looked up again, Ron, Steve, and Faye were gone. A couple of minutes later, Alika showed up.

"Hey, Jaya, I knew you'd be here," Alika said, stomping over twigs and dead leaves. Alika got a load of Jaya's face. His eyebrows shot up. "What's wrong?"

Jaya traced his tattoo and thought of Rasa again. It was time he told Alika about her. "I met someone." He thumped his fist against his chest a couple of times. "She's incredible."

Alika perked up. "What? Who?"

"I met a girl."

"No way!" He gave Jaya an eye-crinkling smile and elbowed him. "Do tell."

"Her name is Rasa," Jaya said. "She's the most magnificent, sweet, and smartest girl ever. I mean *ever*. I can't believe she hangs out with me."

Alika brought his palm to his mouth and leaned forward, all ears. "Go on."

"I met her when I was hiking in Hau'ula. We've been hanging out ever since. It's not only that she's pretty much a goddess, but it's how I feel when I'm with her."

"Yes, yes, how do you feel?"

"Don't laugh."

"Come on already."

"Ok, ok. Besides you and Nohea, she's the first person I feel totally myself around. Without all the BS of my parents. Of school. But..." Jaya stopped. He smiled, fanning himself with his hand.

"But what?" Alika asked, pounding his fist on his knee.

"But with Rasa, there's also this crazy attraction. Oh. My. God," Jaya said, a little breathless.

Alika's face relaxed. "You're making her up, right?"

Jaya bit his lower lip and shook his head.

"Oh man. When can I meet this Rasa?"

THE RHYTHM & THE MELODY

Rasa crossed her arms tight, shivering as the chilly ambient air inside of Jaya's mansion enveloped her. She followed him across the spacious living room.

Jaya's parents weren't home. Neither was any evidence that they lived within these walls. There were no happy family photos. No wedding photos. No baby pictures. No photographic evidence at all of Jaya, his parents, or anyone. Nothing that Rasa imagined a normal family would have on display. On top of that, the orderliness and rare extravagance with a subtle Indian theme reminded her of a museum rather than a home.

They approached the ceiling-to-floor glass wall overlooking the ocean. Jaya pulled open the sliding door. They stepped onto the large deck. The sun had melted the clouds hours ago. The blue sky emerged before them like endless yards of a royal silk sari.

The gentle sloshing of the waves on the shore reminded Rasa of her days on Hau'ula's beaches. She took a deep breath. The clean ocean air invigorated her. She closed her eyes and when she opened them she was in a new world. One where it was only her and Jaya. Here and now. No place to go. Nothing to do but be together.

Xander wasn't a part of their here and now. And she didn't have to turn tricks.

"The view—oh Jaya, this is like a dream," Rasa whispered, grasping his shoulder. Her fingers glided down the smooth fabric of his long-sleeve rash guard. She slipped her hand into his.

Jaya squeezed it. "Right." His voice cracked.

Rasa stroked the back of his hand with her thumb.

Jaya smiled. "How about a swim?"

Rasa smiled back. "Just what I was hoping you'd ask," she said, already hoisting her dress over her head.

"I haven't been in the pool in years," Jaya said retying his guy's board shorts a little tighter. "The last time was with my nanny when I was a kid."

Rasa adjusted her bikini top. Jaya was watching her. She glanced at him. He looked nervous. Not creepy or ruttish like those older guys when they saw her half naked. Jaya's expression was more innocent. Hungry, but innocent. Like a kid in a candy store.

She took a step back. "Ready?" was all she asked.

She skipped to the pool's ledge. She looked back at Jaya and raised her eyebrows up and down a couple of times as if she were Groucho Marx. Jaya laughed. She giggled.

Then she dove in. She swam the length of the pool without coming up for air. Fifteen seconds was nothing for her.

Jaya cannonballed in. He swam over to her. Something about watching his less-than-polished strokes in the water reminded her of the time she'd taught Ach how to swim. *Ohh...*

She swam to the ledge and crossed her arms on top, resting her chin on her forearm. She let her weightless body float up behind her.

By the time Jaya reached her, Rasa's eyes were glued to the horizon, but her mind had drifted off to memories of her brother.

Jaya propped his elbows on the ledge next to her. He peeked at her from the corner of his eye. "You're deep in thought."

"Yeah."

"What's up?"

"My little sisters and brother," she answered. "And..." she stopped. She pressed her palms on the ledge, pushed herself up, and hopped out of the pool. She grabbed a towel from the stack and wrapped it around her waist. She walked over to the railing.

Jaya followed her. He took her hand. "And what?"

Rasa looked at him. There was a softness in his face, in his eyes. He seemed to read her sadness like a morse code distress message. Still she didn't say anything. She only shook her head. Her towel loosened where she'd tucked the ends together and slipped off her waist.

Jaya extracted his hand carefully from hers. He picked up the towel and draped it over her shoulders. Then he put his arm around her.

Rasa rested her head on his shoulder.

"I think I know what might make you feel better," he said, smoothing the wrinkled towel over her upper arm.

She lifted her head. "What's that?"

He slid his hand back into hers. "Come on. There's something I want you to see. And hear."

He led her back inside. They climbed the winding staircase and went down a long hallway. They stopped in front of a closed door. Jaya tightened his grip on her hand. "Ok, close your eyes."

Rasa shut her eyes. She heard the creaking of the door. Jaya pulled her forward.

"Ok, open."

They were standing in a room full of guitars. It took a second for her eyes to adjust to the low-level lighting in the room.

Jaya closed the door. "What'dya think?"

Rasa crept around the room. The rich crimson walls glowed from the recessed lights. There were a bunch of shiny guitars perched just so on their stands. She ran her fingers across the tops of several amplifiers then over some low shelves packed with guitar gear—picks, straps, tuners, pedals, and cords. When she got to the black leather sofa, she sank down.

"It's rad," she said swinging her legs onto the seat cushions.

"Cool."

Rasa got comfy on the sofa. Her towel fell open. She didn't fix it. Her immediate impulse was to give Jaya a sly smile and say, "I've got a thing for musicians." But she refrained. Instead she said, "Play something for me."

"Exactly my plan." He hooked a strap to one of his guitars. "This is a 1970's Gibson SG. A year ago, I took the liberty of painting its body light blue. Just like Kurt did in the early 90s."

"It's beautiful."

Her eyes took in the scene—Jaya and the room that was his stage. It struck her that he was doing something special for her without any expectations. He wanted to share his musical world with her. He was in his element and he wanted her there with him.

She breathed easy, glad to be hanging out with Jaya. There was no pretense. No black widow facade. And Jaya was nice. Simple as that. Oh how she dug him. Really, really dug him.

She dared to let her thoughts go further.

Is this love?

Jaya plugged in and tuned up. He warmed up with some chords. Rasa's breath quickened as she watched Jaya move with ease in the silky ambience of the room. He played a riff. Rasa immediately recognized the melody. Their eyes met. She knew what he was about to play.

Nirvana's *About a Girl.*

Rasa sat back.

With his guitar slung low, Jaya launched into the captivating guitar intro. He was totally in the zone.

Rasa couldn't look away from his brown irises. So sublime.

Then Jaya sang. A croon at first. But by the first chorus, his vocal chords delivered the lyrics with throaty power. He strode to her as he transitioned into the guitar solo. He was close. So close that Rasa could see the unevenness of the blue paint on the body of the guitar. So close that she saw the initials "R.S." carved into the body near the tone knobs.

Are those my initials?

Her heart galloped. She leaned back and studied his fingers working the strings. She was under Jaya's musical spell.

I am in love.

What came next she couldn't have stopped.

She rose from the couch and slunk behind him. She pressed the front of her body against the back of his. He turned his head so that his chin was over his shoulder. She touched her lips to his. Then she dropped her forehead onto his shoulder. She slid her arms around his waist. Her heart beat to the rhythm of the third verse.

Jaya got to the final chorus.

But he never finished.

Because as he opened his mouth to sing, Rasa's lips were on his. Barely at first. His fingers kept playing while she gave him a soft kiss.

Next thing they knew, the guitar was on the floor and they were on the sofa. Rasa straddled Jaya. Their mouths were in sync. Like Jaya was the rhythm and Rasa was the melody. Jaya moved his fingers up and down the fretboard of Rasa's back.

She sat up on Jaya. She untied her bikini top. It dropped on his face. He swept it off then gave her a subtle smile that made her tingle all over. She laid her body flat against Jaya then pulled the towel over her back. She needed to fuse with Jaya that instance. It was that or risk exploding from the mounting pressure of desire.

They were so into the new music their bodies were creating that they didn't hear the door. Rasa's eyes happened to open for a second. She caught sight of an Indian woman.

Jaya's mother?

The woman quickly left the room, closing the door behind her.

Jaya's eyes were still closed. He lifted his head so his lips could find Rasa's again. Rasa gave Jaya one more deep kiss then lifted herself off of him. She grabbed her bikini top and tied it back on.

Jaya caressed her back. "Everything ok?"

She looked over her shoulder at his smiling face. "Yay, it's all good."

She wanted everything to be all good.

So she kept her lips sealed about the woman at the door.

MARVELOUS TORTURE

Jaya touched his lips, craving the unbelievable sweetness of Rasa's mouth on his. He closed his eyes and let his fingers skim from the tip of his nose down to his chin. He smiled at what this set in motion in his mind—a blur of sensations, images, and sounds of Rasa's luscious curves set to Nirvana's *Love Buzz*.

Jaya decided that Rasa was the most marvelous torture. He'd never known this type of excitement. And when he wasn't with her all he experienced was desperate fiending.

He sighed and opened his eyes. He put his hands behind his head and leaned back on the living room sofa. He watched the blades of the ceiling fan spin. And his thoughts of Rasa spun into a fantasy.

I'm napping by the pool. I feel someone climb onto me. My eyelids flutter open. When my vision clears and adjusts to the daylight, I see Rasa. She's straddling me. Then she bites her lower lip. She slowly unties her bikini top. She drops it onto my chest. Then she lifts my hands to her...

A fever spread from Jaya's head to his feet leaving a patch of wet tingling in the middle. He closed his eyes again. His hand had no choice but to slide down the front of his shorts. When it stumbled upon female anatomy it froze, caught off guard. Disappointment almost made him retract his hand, but his intellect convinced his fingers to stay, reminding him that his female pleasure organ had practically double the nerve endings compared to the male counterpart. The egregious anatomical mistake he was born with became more tolerable.

"Jaya!"

His mother's angry voice ended his Rasa daydream all too soon. His eyes shot open as he ripped his hand out of the deep below. He sat up just as Jayshree marched into the room. She tossed a handful of 3 x 5 glossy photos onto the coffee table. "Pick one," she demanded loudly. "All good Gujju boys. From rich families. Good education."

The words rushed out of her mouth. They blasted Jaya like the jet spray of a hose. He looked at the scattered photos. His hands went numb. The paralysis spread through his body.

"Good Gujju boys," she repeated.

His mother had never taken the deal about marriage to this level. Why now?

She pointed to his hair. "No more cutting. You will grow it long," she barked. She curled her upper lip then added, "How many times do I have to tell you, Jaya? No good Gujju boy wants to marry a girl looking like a boy."

"But, Mom..."

"No buts, Jaya. If you cut your hair again, I will throw out all your guitars!"

Jaya gasped and his mouth hung open as he envisioned walking into an empty guitar room.

"Pick one. Now!" Jayshree demanded.

Jaya debated picking one of the photos just to calm his mother. Maybe then she'd forget about her threat to get rid of his guitars. But he couldn't bear the thought of betraying Rasa even if it was a ruse. So he dropped his head and stared at his feet instead.

Mount Jayshree erupted. "Fine. Don't pick one. I'll pick one for you!" She grabbed the photo closest to her and barreled towards him. When she stopped, her toes were jammed into his. She shoved the photo into his face and said, "This boy. You will marry him." She dropped the photo onto Jaya's lap.

Then, without warning, Jayshree swept her arms across the table. The violent motion sent all the other photos flying. Glaring at Jaya, she paced. She opened her mouth to say something, but changed her mind and pressed her lips together.

Jaya watched his mother continue her furious marching back and forth. Finally she shoved her hands onto her hips. "Svairini who dresses like a boy. Girl who cuts her hair like a boy. Ha! Over my dead body!" She stomped off to the kitchen.

Jaya flinched. He could deal with the marriage stuff. It was cultural. He could forgive that. But it was just plain cruel that his mother didn't think to talk to him about why he dressed the way he did or about why he cut his hair the way he did.

If Rasa was his upper, then his mother was his downer. Jayshree's harsh words blew about the living room, driving him under the dark, heavy clouds of melancholy that typically shadowed him. He rubbed his wrist and looked at his tattoo. *I'm a guy. I'm ok.*

He thought about Rasa. He tried to recapture the good feelings and understanding that only she could bring.

Relief was nowhere to be found. He stood up and charged after his mother. Maybe she'd never get that he was a boy but since she assumed he was a lesbian, why not tell her about Rasa? He was determined to do just that. And to make it clear that there was no way in hell he was ever going to marry a boy.

But the familiar sounds of Jayshree's pain stopped his truth-telling mission. Cemented in the hallway, he listened. He knew the order that the sounds would occur, like the chord arrangement of a song he'd practiced over and over on his guitar. First, the slamming of cabinets and the crinkling of packages. A muffled devouring. Gulping in between.

Jaya stiffened. He lost his resolve to assert himself to her.

And with his mother's heaves and the splashing into the toilet, he fell back into the way things were for them—his mother expelled and he absorbed. The confusing emotions. The pain. The lies.

How could Jaya think he was ok and stand up for himself when his own mother showed her disapproval of him by hurting herself?

TOM FRANZ

Tonight's trick was under the pretext of an exclusive North Shore party.

Rasa inspected her right eye in the chrome-rimmed mirror. Her cat eye makeup was perfect. She painted a symmetrical cat eye on her left upper eyelid.

The rest of her makeup was a breeze. Lashes lengthened, thickened, and curled with black mascara. Blessed with good skin like Kalindi, she didn't need foundation. Except when she had to cover up a bruise from one of Xander's assaults, which thankfully she didn't need to do tonight. She brushed a smidgen of bronzer on each cheek. The finishing touch, her aubergine lipstick. She stood back and checked her reflection. For a split second, she thought she saw Kalindi staring back at her and her siblings standing behind.

She shut her eyes. She heard their pleading voices.

Rasa...

She imagined them stuck on a life raft drifting in the middle of the Pacific. She got a sudden urge to sneak out of the immense house and hitchhike to Waialua.

If only it were that easy.

Besides Xander was standing right outside the door. Waiting for her. She wasn't going anywhere except downstairs to work.

She lifted the vial of coke that he'd slipped her earlier that evening. She flipped it between her fingers.

She cut two lines and inhaled them in a flash. Euphoria drowned her memories.

Giddy and energized, she moseyed to the full-length mirror in the corner of the large bedroom, one hand on her hip. She planted herself close to the mirror and struck a pose. Hand still on hip. Free hand behind her head. Lips in a pout.

Sexuality oozed out of her like sparkly lipgloss from a tube. Her eyes caressed the curves of the emerald green cocktail dress that clung to her body. The green of the dress matched her eyes exactly, like she'd cut some of the dress' material and covered her pupils. On her chest, the deep V neckline didn't leave much to the imagination. The dress tapered below her hips and cuffed her thighs eight inches above her knees. And her six-inch black stilettos transformed her tanned legs into long, caramel stick candy.

The pounding house music from downstairs grew louder. She felt the vibration reverberate within her thorax.

She smiled at her reflection, knowing that her black widow domination would be in full operation tonight.

That's when Xander snuck up behind her. He slid his hands around her hips. He moved them up her tummy. Over her breasts. He gripped her shoulders and whisked her around.

"The place is packed. Drunk, high, happy guys. They're gonna be on you like leeches," he whispered with a sinister smile. His hands glided down her back and seized her butt. "No less than ten G's for the night," he commanded, holding her gaze. Then he let go. "Where's the coke?" he asked.

Rasa pointed to the vanity.

He cut another two lines. "Come on," he ordered.

Rasa hesitated. She'd already done two lines. Xander's agitation sounded with each tap of his foot.

Her only option was to obey. He held her hair as she snorted the lines. Then she threw her head back and inhaled sharply, rubbing her nostrils with her thumb. Another rush of exhilaration hit her like that time she was in a barrel at Pipeline.

Xander's hands commandeered the soft skin of her upper arms. He dug his fingers into her flesh. "And Rasa, you better give me the tip. Don't try to hide it. Or else..." He glared at her. Then he flung her around and slapped her bottom. "Now get out there and make Daddy some money."

She giggled, high as the sky.

"Don't fuck this up."

Never have.

Rasa plastered an unflappable expression on her face. She opened the door. Tall and proud, she walked to the railing.

She scanned the immense open room below to familiarize herself with her hunting ground. She glided her hands along the smooth wooden top rail as she took notes. There was a soft glow downstairs from the recessed lighting in the high ceiling and walls. The side of the mansion facing the ocean was glass, all the way from the second level, where she was standing, to the floor. The innocent waves rolled on the other side. The white walls were bare. Five rectangular ivory backless sofas of varying sizes were scattered across the marble floor.

She caught familiar man scents—expensive cologne, weed, sweat. There was a DJ in the corner of the room. Hunched over his MacBook, he laid out the seductive soundtrack for the lechery underway.

Men in expensive suits of all colors prowled the indoor landscape. Getting drinks from the bar. Snorting lines of coke off the glass table. They stumbled about trying to find a mate. They ran their paws over alluringly dressed women who looked older than Rasa. Women who Rasa could tell lacked black widow aptitude. She saw abjection in their movements. And that elevated her innate drive to conquer. It pumped motivation through her veins. Her face remained serene, but her heart beat even faster as she relished the thrill of the chase.

She descended the curved marble circular stairs. Even though she was high and in stilettos, her descent was quiet and effortless. Halfway down she could see that every man in the room was staring at her. To them she was nothing more than a hot, rousing, stacked figure of aphrodisia. An object. But she didn't care. Black widows don't care about these things. She smiled. Every male jaw dropped.

She reached the bottom. The men attempted to return to their previous conversations, but she felt their eyes still on her. She hoisted a glass of Dom Perignon from one of the bikini-clad female servers and made her way to the glass wall. She sipped and gazed at the water. The outdoor lights made the tops of the waves glisten.

She was alone for about thirty seconds before several men in their late forties encircled her like flying termites to a light bulb.

They took turns introducing themselves, the eager look in their eyes giving away their pretend nonchalance. John Banson, CEO of Oahu Electric Company. Peter Hanzer, president of Bank of Oahu. Richard Hardeon, state senator.

Hardeon.

An unfortunate name, Rasa thought, cracking up inside, but keeping a subdued smile on her face. All she had to do was listen, smile, and laugh while the men put on their best show.

Let the games begin...

The men cut each other off trying to impress her. Rasa tuned out five minutes in.

Only when Dick Hardeon touched her shoulder did her ears return to the conversation. "And that's how I got my last million in an hour," he said, winking at her.

Rasa was about to make a witty comment when she felt an arm around her shoulder. She turned her head and looked up at a tall, tan, and handsome man with an eager face. He also seemed to be in his late forties.

"Ah, the lovely Rasa, I was looking for you. Excuse us, gentlemen." The words seemed to float out of his mouth like the tiny bubbles in her champagne. By the time John, Peter, and Richard cut through the shower of globules, it was too late. He'd whisked Rasa away.

Rasa let him tow her across the room. First to the bar where he handed her another flute of champagne and took one for himself. Then, holding her hand as if it were made out of thin paper mache, he led her to a secluded corner.

She was glad to be away from the other men. She gave him a genuine smile as she leaned back against the wall.

"In my dreams, we've met many times, Rasa." There was a slight slur in his words, but he had an earnest expression. He took a gulp of champagne, keeping his eyes on her. "Ahhh...Rasa," he whispered, lifting her hand to kiss it.

Rasa wondered how he knew her name. Probably Xander's doing. And if it was, she figured this man was the richest one here tonight.

"You know my name. So what's yours?" She ran her hand through his blond hair.

"Tom. Tom Franz." He put his empty flute on a nearby table. Then he cupped her face in his hands and said, "You're the most beautiful woman I've ever laid eyes on. But I think you know that."

With a sarcastic tone she said, "Yes, Mr. Franz, tell me something I haven't heard."

He let go of her face. He wrapped his arms around her waist, pulling her close. He was about six feet tall. She had to tilt her chin up to keep eye contact. His warm breath veiled her face. She got a whiff of a delicate bouquet of flowers. No thanks to Xander, she'd been with a number of ultra rich men and knew that this was the way a man's breath always smelled after he'd consumed more than his fair share of good champagne.

"Beauty like yours, it has to be guarded. Protected. Like a Gauguin painting," he whispered. His hands moved up and down her back and settled on her derriere. He gently rubbed it as if he were polishing two prized bowling balls. Then he said, "No other man is ever going to touch you again." He leaned down and brushed her lips with his.

VICTORIOUS ESSENCE

At Cliffs, the setting amber sun rolled a saffron sheen across the horizon. Swollen clouds drifted above. In the shadowy distance, a yacht's sail formed a black triangle. Like a floating three-cornered, nori-wrapped onigiri.

Jaya sat and waited for Rasa at the vegetation border. The coarse sand massaged his bare feet. He kept his eyes on the speck that was Rasa catching waves in the far-off swell. The early evening was quiet, but Jaya was charged. Anticipation of being near Rasa kept him in a state of high alert.

When he saw Rasa at the water's edge fifteen yards away, his heart went from a trot to a gallop, like a wild horse on an open plain. He watched her hoist her surfboard under one arm, adjust her grip, and then wade out of the rolling tide.

The eight days without her had been like a tortured year. An agonizing one hundred ninety-two hours sans Rasa's thoughtful words, soft lips, and tender hands.

But there was something else, something that Jaya hadn't told Rasa about yet.

A couple of days ago Jaya had stopped by Rasa's apartment unannounced. He was hoping she'd be free for dinner. He'd backed into one of the visitor's parking stalls at the same time as someone in a Benz pulled into the adjacent stall. They stepped out of their cars. Jaya made eye contact with a tall, built, red-haired and bearded guy. They both headed to the lobby.

The guy was a few steps ahead of Jaya. A second later, he stopped. He spun around and faced Jaya. His stance was threatening—narrowed eyes, a clinched jaw, arms crossed tight on his chest, and a slight lean back. "Jaya!"

How does this guy know my name?

"Yeah?"

"Rasa's busy tonight." His nostrils flared.

The dude was almost as tall and thick as Alika. And how was this old guy saying that Rasa was busy. Didn't this guy know he was Rasa's boyfriend? In an irritated voice Jaya asked, "And you are?"

The guy's face relaxed. "I'm her uncle," he said. Then he gave Jaya a smug smile.

Uncle Xander? How come there's no resemblance between him and Rasa? A hānai uncle?

Jaya opened his mouth and lied, "Oh. Nice to meet you. I-I'm on my way up to see her."

Her uncle's smile vanished. "That's not a good idea. We're gonna get going. We'll be really busy tonight. Maybe some other time."

Her uncle turned and headed toward the elevator.

Jaya couldn't move except to tug on his ear. What just

happened? Should he go say hi to Rasa anyway? Would her uncle get pissed off and do something? Should he leave?

He ended up leaving. He decided it wasn't worth causing a scene.

A gentle breeze circled Jaya. It brought his mind back to Cliffs. Rasa got closer. He tried to forget about her uncle.

Jaya flipped his black baseball cap backwards then pulled a few gelled spikes of his short hair through the hole above the plastic closure. He looked down, quickly inspecting what he was wearing. Hopefully Rasa would be impressed by the grunge-meets-baller look he'd taken great effort to present as effortless. He dusted the crumbs of sand off his olive-colored cargo shorts. He checked his black T-shirt: "Nirvana" printed in yellow over a happy face with X's for eyes. Jaya gulped a lungful of humidity and tried to settle down.

Rasa quickened her steps even though her feet were sinking in the sand. "Hey," she called out when she was within earshot.

"Hey yourself."

"Love your Downing board. Turns good."

"You mean your Downing," Jaya corrected. "I saw you out there before it got darkish. Lookin' good. Rippin those lefts." Jaya cringed at his surfer lingo. He didn't know what possessed him to say it. It sounded so fake coming from him—the guy who couldn't surf to save his life.

Rasa didn't seem to think anything of it. She smiled as she sat next to him. "Thankfully the wind went somewhere else. The waves were beautiful."

Jaya's face flushed because the first thing that popped into his mind was, "You are too." But there was no way he'd say something that cheesy and unoriginal to the girl he was trying to show off his most romantic side to. Besides, he couldn't imagine that she hadn't heard it a million times before.

So he didn't say anything. He inhaled a slow breath and stared at the ocean. Out of the corner of his eye, he saw Rasa dig her toes into the sand and slick back her wet hair. She wrapped her long locks into a tight bun on top of her head. Then she propped herself on her elbows and let out a sigh. "Thanks for bringing the board."

"Glad you asked," Jaya said. "I haven't been down here in so long."

"Yeah, well, since you keep blowing me off about the free surf lessons, I thought maybe if I got you to the beach, you'd wanna try. So, how about it?" Rasa asked, holding her crossed fingers next to her face. Then she elbowed him and asked, "Tomorrow?"

He laughed. "Nope. I'm better as a spectator. Professional, in fact."

Rasa smiled. They watched the sun slip below the skyline. After the last bit of golden color faded, Rasa sat up straight and inched closer to Jaya. So close that it was as if they were joined at the hip. She let her foot tilt out. It touched Jaya's. At the same time, she leaned her head on his shoulder.

Jaya racked his brain about what to do next. The most appropriate thing seemed to be to snake his arm around her. So he did. And that's when he got the most amazing combination of feelings ever. How weird, he thought, to experience total relaxation and arousal at the same time.

He stroked Rasa's arm, his fingers gliding over the layer of salty moisture that lingered on her skin. His desire went from a gust to a hurricane within seconds. He was afraid that if he kept touching her he might ignite. He wondered if she felt the same way. He forced his fingers to stop their covetous roaming by draping his arm over her shoulder. He clenched his toes in the sand with all his might. As if he were trying to crush the sand instead of his libido. It was all he could do to keep himself from jumping on her.

Jaya thought about Rasa all the time. He wondered if she knew that. He daydreamed about her. He caught himself staring into space with her on his mind. He pictured them talking. Laughing. A couple of times he heard himself say her name out loud.

Then there were the times when he was alone. The thoughts turned into erotic head trips. His body always reacted. The last week or so it had been many times a day. He'd have to make sure the door of his room was locked. Because he'd be thinking about her and his breath would get heavy. Almost labored. Everything throbbed and boiled. And his hands. Oh, his hands. They freaked out at how soft his own skin felt. Especially between his thighs...

Rasa sighed again forcing Jaya out of his X-rated mind. He fake-coughed. He pulled his arm off her. He sat up and used his finger to spell her name in the sand. "By the way, what's your name mean? It sounds so...I don't know...musical."

"In Sanskrit it means essence or taste."

"So mysterious."

Rasa smiled. She wrote his name in the sand. "How about you? What's your name mean?"

"Victory," he said. It sounded strange when he said it out loud.

It was the antithesis of how he thought of himself. He picked up a speckled white shell fragment. He ran his finger over its jagged edge. He chuckled. "Bet my parents regret that name choice. They probably should've named me the Sanskrit word for disappointment. I'm the opposite of the good, feminine, obedient Gujarati daughter they wanted. One who dreams of being a wife someday."

Rasa took his hand. She squeezed it. Then she glided her fingers over his tattoo. "Jaya," she said. She traced the Sanskrit lettering of his tat. "My victorious tritiya-prakriti."

Rasa had actually known what his tat meant when he translated it for her. She told him that her mother had been all into ancient Indian stuff, especially Sanskrit words. Her mother even used to call her svairini. Rasa said she thought that it was pretty uncool of her mother to cop Sanskrit words for herself and her children when they didn't have an ounce of Indian in them. "Talk about appropriation..." she'd said staring ahead of her.

Jaya raised his head to search Rasa's face.

Rasa took off his baseball cap. She ran her hand through his hair. "My victorious tritiya-prakriti," she whispered.

"Well..." Lightheadedness gave him a sensation of floating away.

They leaned in at the same time and kissed. She pulled back for a second. "I love you, Jaya."

"I love you too, Rasa." His body acted before he could exert any control over it. He tugged Rasa's hands. And Rasa followed his lead. Soon she was on his lap and their foreheads were touching. He tilted his chin up and grazed her lips with his. The dominoes fell and what happened next was uncontrollable. Like an avalanche on a Himalayan mountain.

Their mouths connected in a sugarcoated kiss. Their tongues spoke to each other with moist, delicious rapture. Jaya heard Nirvana's *Breed* in his head as his hands caressed the smooth skin of Rasa's back and glided down over her satiny bikini bottoms. His hands kept moving, like they couldn't make up their mind which treat they wanted. Finally, they moved up and tugged at the string tie of her bikini top. He could tell that she was as into this as he was.

But then it was as if someone aimed a fire extinguisher at him and pressed the lever. His flames went out when he realized that he didn't know what to do. The first time they'd hooked up, Rasa had stopped it from going further. Before he had a chance to overthink anything. But this time his mind flooded with self-doubt. What if he did the wrong thing? What if he disappointed her? Had she done this before with a guy who unfortunately had a girl's anatomy? What if she was turned off by his lack of experience?

So in between kisses, he managed to say, "Wait, wait."

Rasa stopped and asked, "What's wrong?"

"Nothing," he said, his breathing rapid. "I can't believe I get to touch you. I want to keep going. You're so awesome. But..."

"But what?" Rasa asked, her voice breathy.

"I've never done this. I really love you, but kinda think we should take this slower." Then he mumbled, "Not that I want to go slower. But I think we should."

Rasa's expression was quizzical. She lifted herself off him. She fixed her bikini top then laid down on her back, tucking her hands behind her head. Jaya figured she was disappointed. Or worse yet, maybe disgusted with his prudishness.

"I'm sorry," he said. Then under his breath he muttered, "Shit."

Rasa held his hand and said, "It's ok. Actually, it's refreshing." She turned on her side to face him, resting her head on her hand. She smiled. "No guy has ever used the words 'love' and 'slower' in the same sentence with me before," she whispered.

Jaya gave her a weak smile. He took her hand and reclined. Lying on their backs, their hands interlocked, they gazed at the blue-black diamond-studded sky. They listened to the soothing undulations of the tide. The breeze skated through the palm fronds, adding a hypnotic rustling that seemed to sprinkle happiness and optimism all over them.

Jaya's mind flooded with possibilities of the future. A future with Rasa. He waded through the options of living happily ever after.

He got stuck on one version of the future. A version in which he had control over his circumstances.

"Rasa, let's run away," he blurted. He was dead serious. He looked at her. In the dark he thought he saw her lips curve up.

"You don't know how much I'd love that," she said. "But I can't."

Jaya was puzzled. "Why not?"

"I just can't," she said in a brittle voice.

He caressed her cheek. It was wet.

ANYTHING FOR YOU

Chinatown woke up from its evening nap. It yawned, stretching its paved arms. The evening breeze carried with it the smell of fresh piss. The destitute crouched against storefronts. A strung-out man sat on a step and stared at the littered sidewalk in front of him. Across the street, a couple stumbled out of a bar. The woman pushed the guy off her and sprinted to the intersection. The daytime shoppers and workers had long gone home. Close to midnight, it was the Honolulu pleasure seekers' stomping ground now.

Rasa grabbed Jaya's hand as they walked a brisk pace on Hotel Street. One block later they spotted the line for Purple Lotus. A curving queue of mostly guys spilled down the street and wrapped around Nuuanu Avenue. According to Rasa, Purple Lotus was the new twenty-one-and-over place to be. She'd been wanting to check it out.

Jaya wasn't as keen on it. More so now that he saw the line. He groaned. "Oh boy. That's gonna take hours," he mumbled.

Rasa elbowed him. "Hey, don't worry. You're with me, remember?" She smiled a reassuring smile.

"Ha," Jaya said, nodding. "That's right. Queen Rasa doesn't wait in line with the common folk," he joked.

Rasa laughed. She led Jaya to the front of the line where she struttred up to the tall bouncer, pulling Jaya close behind. "Can my boyfriend and I get in?" she asked, twirling a lock of her hair. Then she dug around in her purse and whipped out a fake ID. Xander had gotten one made for her a couple of months ago.

"Can we?" she asked again with a babyish voice and a sweet smile.

Rasa knew exactly what she was doing, each detail perfectly orchestrated. The way she left her lips slightly parted as the bouncer reached for her ID. The way her finger brushed his as he took it out of her hand for inspection. The way she kept her eyes locked in on his. They way she licked her lips when he gave it back to her.

Jaya stood behind, watching the interaction in awe. The bouncer looked at Jaya next. Jaya got in on the act by shoving his hands in his pockets and throwing the bouncer a strong chin up.

The bouncer brought his eyes back to Rasa. She flashed him a sexy smile. He got this almost-dreamy expression. He didn't bother asking for Jaya's ID. Which of course Jaya didn't have.

"Uh, yeah, sure. Go ahead," the bouncer stammered, motioning with his head towards the door.

Her charm always worked. *Black widow skills for life.* She gave the bouncer a quick peck on the cheek and whispered *thanks* right into his ear.

Rasa led Jaya through the door into a narrow hallway. The red lighting and thumping house music excited her. She reached for Jaya's hand. They hustled through the maze of hallways.

They got to the main bar and dance floor. It was jumping. Rasa felt a surge of adrenaline. They wove their way through the already sweaty crowd and managed to find a small table in the corner with one barstool. Like a true gentleman, Jaya let Rasa have it.

"I can't believe you got us in like that," Jaya yelled over the booming music.

"You ain't seen nothin' yet, Jaya baby."

"I'm sure."

A waitress came by. Rasa ordered a Cosmo. Jaya got a beer. After the waitress left, Rasa asked, "Next song, let's dance?"

"Ah...I don't dance. No rhythm in these two left feet."

"I'll be the judge of that. Anyway after a couple of beers, I'll get you to change your mind." She winked.

The waitress brought their drinks. Jaya paid and tipped.

"Thanks. Cheers."

They watched the crowd for a few minutes. Then Jaya moved next to Rasa. He leaned in and said, "Hey, I've been wanting to check something out with you."

"What's that?"

He took a deep breath. When he opened his mouth, the words came out fast. Like the air from a slashed tire. "Last Saturday I stopped by your apartment to surprise you. I wanted to take you out. You know, sweep you off your feet and all that," he said with a shy smile. "I didn't get a chance to dial up because your uncle stopped me. He said not to bother. That you two were busy." Jaya stared at his beer bottle. He spun it around in his hands. "It was your Uncle Xander, right? Anyway, I know he's your uncle, but I got this weird feeling."

Rasa's eyes widened. She gulped down the rest of her Cosmo. Setting down the glass, she nodded as if she'd just remembered something important. "Oh yeah," she said. "That was the weekend I had to help him do some stuff for his business." She smiled. She put her hand on his. "So sweet that you tried to surprise me."

"Yeah," Jaya said. He took a swig. Then he scratched his head. "It's just..."

Rasa cut him off. "Don't worry, Jaya!" She reached up and ran her hand over the back of his head. "He's just my uncle. You, on the other hand..." she let her voice trail off as she drew his head to her. She brought her lips to his for a long, deep kiss. His eyes were still closed when she finally pulled her tongue and lips away.

"Better?" she asked.

"Uh-huh." He opened his eyes slowly. "It's good to be me right now."

Rasa grinned. She reached into her purse and took out a pack of Camel Lights. She was about to search for her zippo when she heard someone say Jaya's name.

"Well, well, well. If it isn't Jaya the carpet muncher."

Rasa forgot about smoking and turned her head. Two guys and a girl were hovering with anticipation in their eyes. Like shoppers at the front door of Walmart on Black Friday.

"What the fuck are these assholes doing here?" Jaya muttered.

"Who are they?" Rasa whispered.

"The biggest jerks at my school. Ron's the tall one with the beady eyes and butt chin, Steve's the short, squat guy, and Faye's twiggy girl."

Rasa giggled.

Ron took a step toward Jaya. Motioning to Rasa with his chin, he scowled. "How did someone like you score Jasmine? You aren't exactly Aladdin," he said.

Then Steve joined in. "More like Aladdin's nasty sister, Uglydin." He slid up on the other side of Rasa and put his arm around her. "Yeah, this fine Arabian princess should be with me," he said. His lisp seemed more prominent.

Rasa frowned. She looked at Jaya. She'd have no qualms about putting this guy in his place, but she was more focused on Jaya.

The next thing Rasa knew, Jaya stepped forward. He pulled Steve's arm off of her. Then he took Rasa's hand. "Let's go," he said tugging her towards the crowded dance floor.

Rasa looked over her shoulder as they escaped. She saw them laughing and pointing at Jaya and her. Faye made a licking motion with her tongue between her two fingers that were in a V. Rasa held Faye's gaze then gave her the finger. Faye stopped laughing. Rasa mouthed, "Fuck you," then fake-smiled.

Safe in the middle of a pack of dancing strangers, Jaya seemed to shake off the encounter. He embraced Rasa. "Guess I'm gonna dance. Guess you figured out that I'll do anything for you," he whispered.

SOMETHING WICKED
THIS WAY COMES

"I saw you and Xander," Jaya said, his voice flat like a robot's. He couldn't bring himself to look at Rasa. Instead he stared at a long procession of ants on the sidewalk. The full moon glowed quiet and sad in the night sky. The evening hadn't started out bad. In fact Jaya had earned over two hundred dollars for HHS from his Waikiki gig.

Through the two sets he played, people dropped more money than usual. Encouraged, he'd made some spontaneous changes to his set lists. He'd added a couple of non-Nirvana songs and ended the show with Radiohead's *Creep*.

When the last note drifted off his strings, his eyes feasted on the money in his open guitar case. He knelt down in front of the case to gather the bills into a pile, smoothing them as he went. He counted them, then stuffed the stack into his wallet. Pleased with the amount he'd donate the next day, he lifted his bulging wallet up to the moon, offering a silent thank you to the universe. He shoved his wallet into his pocket and clipped the chain to his belt loop.

He was sweating by the time he finished packing up his gear. He decided to take a quick break before heading home. He pushed his heavy cart to the side. Grabbing his water bottle, he leaned against the wall and let his head rest. He watched the thick crowd of tourists stream up and down Kalakaua.

Suddenly his eyes crashed into Rasa. He ran into the throng and stood at attention. He scanned the flow of people. His eyes found her again. She was walking next to Xander who had his arm around her shoulder. They approached where Jaya was standing. They were busy talking and didn't notice him.

Jaya held his breath as he watched Xander's hand drift from Rasa's shoulder, down her back, and to her butt! It stayed there!

Maybe he was seeing things. Jaya rubbed his eyes and looked again.

Xander's hand was still glued to Rasa's okole. A couple of seconds later Xander kissed her. On the lips!

Jaya craned his neck to keep his eyes on them. When Xander pulled his lips off Rasa, she gave him her best smile.

It was the same sexy, flirty smile Rasa had given Jaya. The urge to hurl overcame Jaya, but he hadn't eaten since late afternoon. There was nothing in his stomach. Instead his neurons vomited questions into his head.

Does an uncle grab his niece's ass? Does an uncle kiss his niece's lips? Does a niece wear an ultra short dress and stilettos when she hangs out with her uncle? Does a niece give a sexy smile to her uncle?

Jaya went on his tiptoes for another look, but they'd already been swallowed up by the mob. Jaya clasped his hands over his head. Then he turned around and huddled against the wall. He tucked his chin and beat the pinky side of his fist on the rough

241

concrete. He whisked around and stood with his legs hip width apart. He groaned as he crossed his arms.

He thought about chasing after them. Pulling Rasa behind him. Beating the crap out of Xander.

But he couldn't get his legs to move in their direction.

Eventually he trudged back to his car with his cart. It felt somehow heavier. He kept pondering the horrible possibilities.

The drive home was surreal. He didn't realize he was only going five miles per hour. Not until someone behind him honked. He snapped out of his befuddlement. He changed his mind about going home. He cranked the steering wheel and his tires screeched as he did an illegal U-turn on Kalakaua near Kapiolani Park.

He gassed it all the way to Rasa's apartment. When he jerked his car into the parking area, the first thing he saw was Xander's Benz in a visitor stall.

Jaya's head spun. He thought he was about to pass out. The deep breaths he took didn't calm him down. Not knowing what else to do, he turned the car around and raced home.

In his room he paced, wide-awake. He wanted to punch something. He ended up pounding the wall of his bedroom, leaving behind a couple of dents and a hole in the drywall. His knuckles were swollen and bloodied, but he hardly felt it.

He forced himself to lie down. But as soon as his head hit the pillow he sprung up. He ran out of the house and jumped into his Beamer. He drove to Rasa's place again.

It was 3 a.m. when he got there. Xander's Benz was gone. Jaya parked and called Rasa. She answered. "I'll be right down," she said.

"I saw you and Xander," Jaya repeated. He stepped on the trail of ants and dragged his foot to crush as many of them as he could. "You were walking on Kalakaua. His hand was on your ass. He kissed you."

Jaya inched his head up. He looked into Rasa's eyes. He noticed a band-aid on her neck. He would ask her about it later. "And why were you all dressed up like that? Why did you smile at him like that?"

"Oh, Jaya," Rasa whispered. She reached for his hand, but he pulled it away before she could touch it.

"Why, Rasa? I don't get it. Is he really your uncle?" A tear slid down his cheek. "He doesn't look anything like you."

Rasa wiped Jaya's tear away. "I know, but he really is."

"Where were you going?"

"To meet Sam and Ann for dinner."

In the silence that followed, Jaya hung his head. His eyes sunk downward from the weight of what they'd seen. His lips trembled. The sharp pain in his gut turned dull as if someone had plunged a rusty, blunt shovel in and dug out his innards.

His instincts told him something wasn't right, but he had no proof. Only Rasa's word. And Jaya had a feeling her word was a lie floating in between truths.

Is this how his mother felt when she confronted his father and he spewed lie after lie?

"Jaya?"

Her voice sounded far away.

"Jaya?" she asked again. She took his hand and kissed it.

He felt her soft lips on the back of his hand. Then she said something else about the cuts on his knuckles.

But Jaya didn't hear all of it because his head echoed with the radio version of *Creep.*

PUPPET ON A STRING

Rasa huddled into a corner of her bedroom. Nirvana's *Lounge Act* became the soundtrack for her convoluted memories. She slammed her eyelids shut and rocked herself as she tried to clear her head. She succeeded for a moment. She stopped rocking and enjoyed the dark stillness of her mind's eye. She let her eyelids drift open.

But then her imagination went haywire. A spotlight polluted her serenity with its brightness. She wrung her hands and squeezed her eyelids together again but couldn't stop what she saw—herself as a puppet on string. Suddenly Kalindi, all the men she'd slept with, Sam, Ann, Xander, and Mr. Tom Franz closed in on her. Puppet masters trying to pull her strings.

Rasa bit her knuckle.

No.

She dropped her hand, then shook her head.

No.

She got up and paced.

They're not controlling me. I control me. I choose the sex. I am a black widow.

She dragged her hands through her hair.

No. I'm not in control. I'm not a black widow. No more euphemisms. Let me call it what it is. I'm a sex slave. And now I belong to Mr. Franz because Xander says so.

It turned out that Mr. Franz had agreed to pay Xander a hefty chunk of change each month to be the sole recipient of Rasa's "services." Xander had informed Rasa of her new fate when he walked her home a couple of nights ago—right before Jaya had confronted her under the incandescent whistleblowing moon.

"No, Xander. I-I..." Rasa'd stammered. She knew what she wanted to say—that she had a boyfriend. Jaya. But she couldn't let that slip. She realized that Xander could, and would, hurt everyone she truly loved if she didn't comply. Maybe even Jaya, though as far as Xander was concerned, she and Jaya were just friends.

"No? Did you just say no?" Xander'd demanded. He pushed her up against the wall outside the lobby. He took out his knife and held the tip to her throat. "No?"

Rasa felt his furious breath on her face. "I-I can't. I-I don't want—"

"I don't care what you want," he said. He pressed the blade's tip into her neck.

"But—"

"But nothing," he said. He firmed up his hold on her. "You will fuck Mr. Franz whenever he wants." Then he cut her neck.

Rasa had screamed. A half-inch diagonal line of bright red blood appeared on the side of her neck. She felt cool wetness trickle down. He was still pressing her arms. She couldn't stop the blood.

Xander crammed the knife back into its holder. Then he wiped the blood from her cut in one swift motion with his index finger. A thinner line of blood replaced it. He shifted his eyes to his glossy red fingertip. He brought his finger to her mouth and spread the blood on her lips, the way she spread her lipstick—starting at the center of her top lip and working down each side then shifting to the bottom lip.

"Taste it," he barked, glaring at her.

Rasa licked her lips. The rusty flavor made her eyes fill with tears.

Xander ran his finger over the cut again. He drew a bloody line from her collarbone to the hollow between her breasts. "I can do worse to Ach, Nitya, Shanti...and Jaya."

Rasa buried her face in her hands and sobbed.

I'm trapped. If only I could call the cops on him.

Cops.

Rasa stopped crying. She dried her eyes with the heels of her palms. She grabbed her cell and scrolled her contacts to find Nohea.

You like me call da cops?

Maybe Nohea could help...

She was about to dial but then her cell rang. It was Mr. Franz.

Ugh.

"Hello?" She rubbed her nose to hide her sniffling.

"Hi Rasa, it's Tom." His voice seemed a little shaky.

"Yes. How are you?"

"Fine. And you?"

"I'm good, thank you."

"Listen, Rasa, I'll get right to it. I need to see you right now. What are you doing?"

In the past, this would've been Rasa's cue to turn up the charm. Pour it on. Lather him up with what she knew he wanted to hear.

"Rasa, did you hear me? I need to see you."

She twisted her face. Her black widow senses were nowhere to be found. But it didn't matter. Mr. Franz was going to get what he wanted with or without her black widow sweet talk. Her lip curled and the tip of her tongue stuck out for a second.

"Sure, Mr. Franz. I—" It came out flat and low. Like she was repeating back an order for the hundredth customer of the day at Bubbies.

He didn't notice. "Tom. Please. Call me Tom. What're you doing?"

"Waiting for you to call me," she said like an automated message.

Tom chuckled. With more confidence, he said, "Let's run away together. Go somewhere far away."

Go somewhere far away.

Rasa heard herself say, "That sounds nice." That's what she'd wanted to do with Ach and the girls—drive up to Waialua with Jaya and pick them up. Head to the airport. Maybe the five of them could fly away. Disappear. Out of the country somewhere. But she didn't have enough money saved up. It's not like she was getting much of the cash she was earning for Xander.

Xander.

Reality check—she wasn't going anywhere with anyone she loved. Not her siblings. Not Jaya.

She thought about Nohea's offer again. She shook her head. If she reached out to Nohea, there was no telling what Xander would do. She'd been silly to get her hopes up.

Rasa tapped her knuckles on her forehead and tried to banish all notions of escape. Of freedom.

Still, Jaya's voice echoed.

Rasa, let's run away.

The things Rasa really wanted she couldn't have.

TEN HOURS OF HAPPINESS

"Seriously, Jaya? It took you this long to let me meet her?" Alika questioned with a petulant toss of his head.

"Woah, take it easy, brah." Jaya held up an open palm. "Listen, even I have a hard time getting on her schedule."

Alika chuckled. His face relaxed. "Just kidding, I know," he said.

"Where is she?" Jaya mumbled, straining his neck to look out of his car's rear window.

A minute later Rasa knocked on Alika's window.

Alika hopped out of the car. "You must be Rasa. So nice to meet you," he said, leaning down.

"Same here," she said. She stood on her tiptoes and they exchanged a cheek kiss.

Alika held the passenger door open for her. "You ride shotgun."

Rasa half-smiled. "Why, thank you, sir." She slid in.

Alika jumped into the backseat.

Jaya started the ignition. "Let's get this show on the road."

"So where are we going, boys?" Rasa asked, looking first at Jaya, then at Alika.

"How about a drive to the North Shore. Check out some waves. Grab some shrimp. And hang out with Ach, Nitya, and Shanti?" Jaya suggested.

Rasa put her hand on her heart. "You're the sweetest thing ever, Jaya," she said. She blew him a kiss. "Thank you."

Alika smiled. "I have a feeling this is going to be a great day."

And it was.

On the drive home, Jaya and Alika decided to continue the hang at Jaya's house. They tried to convince Rasa, but she said she had other plans. When they pulled up in front of her apartment, Jaya made one more attempt.

"Come on, come chill," Jaya pleaded, tugging Rasa's hand, hoping for a miracle. "Pretty please..."

"I wish. But I can't," Rasa said.

Jaya recognized the reticent look in her eyes. The anxious way she twirled a lock of hair around her index finger. And the emptiness that invaded his being when Rasa was silent like this. It could mean only one thing.

F'in Xander.

"Let me guess. Uncle Xander?"

Alika stared at him, shocked by Jaya's biting tone. "Hold up, Jaya. What's your problem, dude?"

Jaya looked away. "Sorry," he muttered. He couldn't bring up his whole Xander paranoia in front of Alika. *Why do I put up with this shit?*

Alika tried to lighten the mood. He thrust himself forward between the driver and passenger seats. "Glad I finally got to meet you, Rasa!" he exclaimed. "Let's hang out again soon...next week?"

Rasa gave Alika a grateful smile. She went along with it. "Already on my calendar!" Then she leaned over and gave Jaya a peck on the cheek. "Talk to you later, ok?"

There was no way Jaya could pull off being all irked with the two of them acting so freakin' happy. He forced himself to drop his sternness. He joined in on the joy parade. "You're killing me, Rasa," he said, faking a miserable voice. Then he pierced a fake dagger into his heart, shut his eyes, and let his head fall back.

"Uh-huh." Rasa jumped out of the BMW. She closed the door, waved, and headed to the apartment lobby.

Jaya waited until Rasa stepped into the elevator before he started the engine. As he drove he asked as aloof as possible, "So what do you think?" He glimpsed at Alika.

Alika shook his head. "A girl that fine likes you? I mean the girl is like Beyoncé fine."

"Shut up, Alika! She loves my heart. Like she said, I'm the sweetest thing ever."

Alika laughed. "Yeah, I guess if Beyoncé loves Jay-Z, Rasa can love you."

"Wow," Jaya replied, grinning now. "What's wrong with Jay-Z?"

Alika kept going. "Next thing you know, you'll be shooting your own video for '03 Bonnie & Clyde. '11 Rasa & Jaya.'"

"Ok, ok. Enough already!"

"Sure thing, Hova," Alika said in all seriousness. He paused, then started to laugh, but sucked it back in and said, "We going to your place, Jigga?" He turned on the radio. He fiddled with the tuner until he found a suitable station that happened to be playing Jay-Z's *Izzo (H.O.V.A).* "Hey, it's your song, J-Hova," Alika blurted.

Now Jaya was cracking up. And even though Rasa wasn't in the car with them anymore, it struck him that he'd spent the day with his two best friends. There hadn't been a cloud in the rich blue sky all day. The forlornness that usually chained him for at least part of the day had set him free for almost ten hours.

But it came rushing back, manacles in hand, as soon as they pulled into his driveway.

"Dang, I've never seen one of those in real life," Alika said, staring at Sanjay's new black and orange Bugatti Veyron.

"Yeah. Well. It's his latest baby."

They made their way upstairs. His parents weren't in sight. *Good.*

They approached a dark wood bureau in the hallway. Sanjay's Glock rested on top like a piece of decorative art. A modern sculpture of death and destruction.

Why'd his father leave it out? Jaya hoped Alika hadn't noticed it. He was about to suggest they turn around and hang out on the deck.

Too late.

"Double dang. I've never seen one of those in real life either," Alika whispered.

"I know. Money doesn't just buy fancy things. It buys entitlement," Jaya said. He pressed his hands onto the bureau and straightened his arms. "Yup. This is my father's gun. He says it's for all those lazy bums who try to steal from him. They all deserve to be shot." Jaya shook his head and frowned.

"That's whack."

Then Jaya's eyebrows lowered. He squinted. He pulled back his lips to stop himself from spouting what else was on his mind. That Sanjay thought all Hawaiians were freeloaders. Even Alika's family.

Jaya wrapped his fingers around the edge of the bureau and squeezed.

Alika put his hand on Jaya's shoulder. "It's ok. Let's go hang out in your room."

"Yeah." Jaya took a step and stopped. He turned back to the gun and eyed it. "Let me just put this thing away." He looped his finger behind the trigger and lifted it. His mind flashed to the time his mother had held it to her head. He stretched his arm to the side so the gun was as far away from him as possible. Then he crouched down and opened the bureau's cabinet door. The shelves inside were full of linens. He tucked the gun under the silky white sheets on the bottom shelf. He shut the doors and stood up. "Ok, let's go."

They headed to Jaya's room. Alika diverted the conversation back to Rasa. "So does Rasa have an older cousin?" His face was hopeful. "A single older guy cousin?"

Good old Alika. Jaya threw his head back and guffawed. "Oh, man. If she did, I'd have hooked you up by now."

Alika hung his head in mock disappointment. "Guess I'll have to get used to being third wheel."

Jaya snickered. He pushed open the door to his room. "Don't worry, Alika, it won't be that bad."

"Sheeeeeit!" Alika hurled his muscled body across Jaya's king-size bed. He flipped over so he was on his back.

Jaya plugged in his Ipod and scrolled down to The Black Keys, selecting *Tighten Up*. He whistled along to the intro. When the drums kicked in, he started nodding.

Alika turned over onto his six-pack. He rested his chin on his crossed arms. "Rasa's great, man. I'm happy for you."

"Thanks, bro."

Alika opened his mouth to say something else but a loud crashing sound followed by shouting made him shut it.

"My parents." Jaya turned up the volume.

But Alika still heard everything. Loud voices in a language he didn't understand. Shattering glass. Thumping of heavy objects against the wall and the floor. Banging cabinet doors. More pounding. Then the roar of an engine and the screeching of tires. Alika was all ears, tuned into the conflict of Jaya's parents. This was a battlefield he'd never been on with his own family.

Meanwhile Jaya had tuned out. *Tighten Up* ended and Alice in Chain's *Would*? blasted. Jaya's mind sung the verses and screamed the chorus. The temporary scaffold of happiness he'd spent the last ten hours building with Alika and Rasa was destroyed in a couple of minutes by his parents' war.

ACTRESS

If Rasa had met Xander a year ago, the plush Waikiki penthouse
that he'd set up for her "work" with Mr. Franz would've been her
palatial web. The modern decor of the living room led one way—to
the bedroom, the center of the web—where she, the black widow,
patiently awaited Mr. Franz, her male prey—a victim fully aware that
she was about to use her potent love venom to extract as much cash
from him as possible.

But Rasa wasn't a black widow anymore. Ever since she'd met
Jaya, she'd been shedding her arachnid exoskeleton. Little by little.

Last week at Kapiolani Park, she'd stepped away from
spiderhood forever. She and Jaya had been loitering in the shaded
refuge of the thick, knotty aerial roots of the grand banyans. With
her back pressed up against the crowded roots and Jaya's lips
worshipping her with tender love kisses—not selfish, aggressive
kisses—she let go of her past.

There was also something else. The only people she'd ever loved
were Ach, Nitya, and Shanti. Rasa had always loved them. It was a
pure sister love. But the love she proclaimed to Jaya continued to

grow. It matured into a different love—a pure lover-love. Her first time. She liked to think of herself as a lover-love virgin until she met Jaya.

The only problem was that without her tough black widow façade, she was emotionally naked. She didn't have another kind of protective shell waiting underneath. She felt everything except powerful. Her moods ebbed and flowed, like the tides on the south shore. It was as if she had to relearn everything.

Including how to handle doing Xander's dirty work with Mr. Franz. There was no part of her that could be convinced that she actually enjoyed it anymore. Now she felt only complete and utter disgust. Even the coke was useless. All it did was make her crave Jaya more.

Rasa sighed. Mr. Franz would be here any second.

The doorbell rang.

Right on time.

With a couple of deep breaths, Rasa forced herself to become an actress. She slapped on an unreadable expression as she glided to the door, like a royal courtesan on her way to greet the king. Her hand clutched the doorknob. She quieted the last of her mind's frenzy. Then she opened the door.

"Ah, my gorgeous Rasa," Mr. Franz whispered as soon as he laid eyes on her. He took her hand and kissed it softly.

Rasa was unnerved. She was having to force all her moves. And now her words. She masked her fear by playing along with Mr. Franz's greeting. She lowered her head, lifting only her eyes to meet his. "I've missed you, Mr. Franz," she replied, soft and sweet. She stepped to the side and motioned for him to enter.

His roguish expression reminded her of what was about to happen. She considered bolting out the open door. Straight to Jaya. And taking him up on his offer to run away. But her feet remain planted, grounded in the reality of Xander's threats.

Mr. Franz's voice drew her back to the task at hand. She watched him survey the apartment. His smile grew with each step. He nodded his head, mumbling, "Yes, yes, this will do nicely." Then he whisked around. "Rasa darling, I have something for you." He held out a long turquiose gift box.

She hesitated, but took the box from him, forcing her finger to graze his as she did. "You shouldn't have," she said with a fake smile, though her eyes widened when she read the top. Tiffany & Co.

"Oh yes, I should have. And this is only the beginning," he said. "Open it."

She removed the top. She gasped. Inside lay a thick platinum chain with a gleaming oval yellow diamond the size of a nickel. It was surrounded by two rows of smaller white diamonds. It reminded her of the sun on a cloudless day.

"Do you like it?"

She pried her eyes away from the necklace and looked at Mr. Franz. "It's beautiful." Then she shook her head. "But it's too much. You shouldn't have..." She replaced the top and handed the box back to him.

"Nonsense." He opened the box and placed it on the coffee table. Lifting the necklace, he said, "Here, let me."

Rasa nodded. She gathered her hair into a loose, high ponytail as he positioned the necklace. He fiddled with the clasp. Finally he hooked it in place. "There," he said. "Now turn around."

She faced him. She felt his lustful eyes on her neck. In the past, she would've done something racy next. Like lick her lips. Then slowly catwalk over to him. Press her body up against his. Something that would send seismic waves of desire coursing through him. But today those things sickened her. So she stood there, sheepish.

Mr. Franz didn't notice. "Perfect." He sat down on the white leather loveseat. He patted the space next to him. "Sit with me." He stared at her cleavage.

She sat down at the opposite end of the sofa. She looked out the windows at the crowded gray landscape of Waikiki buildings. They seemed so small and far away.

"Come closer."

She slid towards him. He put his arm around her shoulder, drawing her into the angle between his arm and chest. Then it was like she was chewing on coffee beans. Because a bitter taste filled her mouth as she watched his hand run over her bare leg. His roaming fingers happened upon a thin, two-inch scab.

"What's this? What happened?"

She wanted to tell him that Xander had cut her a couple of days ago when she tried to get out of tonight's job. But if she said anything like that, it would start a chain reaction that would end up in her siblings and Jaya getting cut as well. So Rasa played it off.

"It's nothing." She lifted his hand off her leg and intertwined her fingers with his.

He massaged her arm. "My poor Rasa got hurt," he whispered into her ear. "Let me make you feel better."

She squashed the impulse to rip his old man paw off her. She tried to pretend she was in Jaya's arms instead. She closed her eyes. She pictured his smile and spiky hair. Her tense body relaxed in Jaya's imagined embrace.

I'm tangled up with Jaya. We're a mesh of young arms and legs...

"What're you thinking about?"

"Huh?"

"What's on your mind?"

She channelled her desire for Jaya to her current role, knowing the curtain hadn't come down on this show yet. "You, of course," she said with a half smile.

His hand clutched the top of her thigh, then coasted down and grabbed the underside. "So tell me about yourself," he whispered.

That's something she didn't do with these Johns. She wasn't about to start now. "There's not much to tell." She turned towards him and draped one of her legs over his. She leaned in to kiss his cheek. "I want to know about you," she whispered into his ear.

His breath quickened. "What do you want to know?"

"Tell me about your job, your family." She forced herself to lay her hand on his chest.

"I'm in real estate development. I'm single."

She could feel his breathe on her cheek. It smelled like tequila.

Her hand veered down. Down. Mr. Franz opened his mouth to say something else, but then he dropped his head and kissed her bare shoulder. "No more talking," he said. He stood up. He extended his left hand to her. That's when Rasa spotted a band tan line on his ring finger.

A liar like all the rest.

She took his hand. She let him lead her into the bedroom.

iN MY BLOOD

Bamboo tiki torches lit up the deck. Glowing string lights crisscrossed on the railings. Inside, delicate arrangements of white ginger and pikake filled the air with perfume, but it all smelled like indulgence, entitlement and pretension to Jaya. It seemed the more Jayshree overdid things, the more phoniness Jaya could count on as the evening progressed. And tonight Jayshree had gone all out.

She expected him to do the same. Hours before the party, she'd cornered him. Circling her shoulder and stretching her neck she said, "Wear that new salwar kameez with the gold paisleys. I laid it on your bed."

"Is it ok if—"

"Chuup. I don't want to hear it. Just wear it. It cost two thousand dollars. Don't waste it. And put on this kohl and lipstick." She handed two of her makeup tubes to him.

Jaya wrinkled his nose as he held the sticky tubes.

"But I want to wear—"

She cut him off again. "I want, I want...it's always what you want." She scoffed. Then she lifted her chin and turned away, muttering, "I don't ask for much."

Jaya hung his head. He sighed. Part of him felt sorry for his mother, for how hard she tried to fit in. But the other part was resentful of her unwillingness to try to understand her own son.

Secretly Jaya wished he had a suit that fit his female body in a way that would show off his true masculinity. A bespoke suit. A suit his mother would be proud of him in.

Jayshree dropped the pressure as soon as she got busy entertaining. And of course Jaya didn't change out of his T-shirt and shorts.

He scanned the living room and devised a plan to snag something to eat without being noticed. He stuck close to the walls to get to the food station. His guard was up. For good reason. The flashy dresses and the shimmery mood lighting hurt his eyes. The mix of colognes and perfumes made him feel sick.

A waiter walked by carrying a tray of champagne flutes. Like a pickpocket in a busy New York City subway station, Jaya hoisted one without him noticing. He guzzled it down.

Jayshree had stepped up tonight's extravagant affair by hiring a jazz band. They were pretty good.

His father was standing at four o'clock with two men, another couple of bigwig developers. Jaya honed in on their conversation.

"Progress can't be stopped by a bunch of bones," Sanjay said. The two men laughed and chugged their beer.

"Yeah, they need to get over it. This is the U. S. of A. Money talks, right?" one of the men chimed in.

Jaya knew "they" meant Hawaiian people.

The three men raised their glasses in a toast.

Same old shit. Don't these losers ever talk about anything else?

The man with blond hair raised an eyebrow. "Speaking of money..."

"Yes?" Sanjay asked.

The man ducked his head a little to whisper something about "expensive young hookers" at "exclusive parties" on the North Shore.

Jaya grimaced. The man lowered his voice some more. Now Jaya couldn't hear the guy. He shifted his attention to eight o'clock, to his mother and four other women.

"How do you stay so slim, Jayshree?" one of the women asked. She held a champagne flute near her lips. Her arms were well-toned and glimmered with sequined body oil.

"Oh, it isn't easy. I'm on a constant diet. I count every calorie I consume," Jayshree said. "It takes a lot of discipline." Naturally, she left out the part about gorging and puking.

"I don't know how you do it, Jayshree," another woman said. "I've tried everything—diet shakes, fasting, laxatives, cleanses, throwing up—but I keep gaining weight. I'm thinking of going gluten-free. Maybe I'm allergic. Or maybe I should just give up carbs completely."

"You really have to incorporate an intense workout regimen," the woman with the buff arms bragged. "I do four hours a day."

Jaya'd had enough. He went straight to the chafing dishes to pile his plate with blue crab beignets and brie and fig jam mini tartlets. Then he crept up to his room.

He hopped onto his bed and devoured the delicious pupus. He set his plate on the floor and burped. He pulled his phone from the pocket of his shorts and dialed Rasa.

No answer. For the third time this evening.

So he texted her. He was actually resorting to texting. That's how desperate he was.

He stared at the screen. Minutes passed. No response.

His mind tortured him.

Xander's hand on her ass. Xander's lips on hers. Rasa is Dad, and I'm Mom.

And like his mother, Jaya wasn't buying the excuses anymore.

But...he also wasn't leaving her. Just like his mother never left his father.

He realized his body was covered in a cold sweat. He peeled his shirt.

He'd thought about following Rasa. But he couldn't resort to stalking. He'd lose the only shred of self-respect he had. Worse, he'd be invading her privacy. He didn't want to do stuff to her without being honest.

Where are you, Rasa?

He focused on his tattoo, but his thoughts kept plummeting.

He turned to Nirvana. He scrolled through his Ipod and selected *I Hate Myself and Want to Die*. Cranking it, he tried to find solace in the guitar, drums, and bass. He rubbed his wrist, hoping he could convince himself that his head was playing a cruel joke on him.

But it didn't work.

His eyes were wet now. He wiped the tears away. He thought about the irony of it all.

It was crazy that he could feel so depressed when he lived this life of riches. He was just as self-centered as all the partygoers downstairs.

Kurt's voice boomed. Jaya's thoughts became a repeating loop of the song's title—*I Hate Myself and Want to Die*.

ONE TRUTH

Rasa was a shrewd detective. She caught the disillusionment in Jaya's words. She pressed her cell harder against her ear.

"This one time I walked in on my dad kissing some woman," Jaya continued in a wobbly voice. "I never told my mom. Anyway, I'm pretty sure she knows he's been unfaithful to her for years."

Rasa lined up all the clues—the sad letdown coating his sentences, the questions about Xander, the revelations about his family—and figured things out. Jaya was still convinced that she was cheating on him with Xander.

"Jaya, I'm not cheating on you," Rasa pleaded. Well, technically she was cheating. But it wasn't her choice. She hated every second of it. And the lies were killing her, like a small spike in her heart.

Jaya asked the same questions again. "I can't get it out of my head. Why did Xander grab your ass? Why did he kiss you? Why would your uncle do that?"

Only now the words came out with a weariness that reminded Rasa of Natalie Imbruglia's song *Torn*. The spike became a large, serrated sword.

Tears streaked Rasa's cheeks. Her lips were in a pouty frown. Her nose, pinched up. Kalindi would not have recognized this Rasa.

She tried again. "Jaya, it wasn't like that. Xander's very affectionate, but not a perv. Maybe from where you were standing it looked worse than it was?"

You've got to believe me. I can't tell you the truth because if I do, he'll hurt Ach, Nitya, and Shanti! And you! Maybe kill you all!

"Please, Jaya, don't worry. I swear there's nothing going on between me and my uncle. That would be so gross!"

Jaya didn't say anything.

"Jaya, I love you!" It came out louder than she'd intended because it was the one truth she'd told during this conversation. "I love you," she repeated, softer this time. All she could think was how she'd never forgive herself if Jaya didn't have a change of heart. "You're the best thing that's ever happened to me."

A couple of stretched-out seconds later, Jaya whispered, "I love you too, Rasa. It's ok." He paused and groaned. "I guess I'm not used to family that's so—I don't know—close." Then in a dreary voice he said, "I'll get over it, I guess."

Relief melted over Rasa like butter on a stack of hot pancakes. "I know what'll make you feel better," she blurted.

"Oh yeah, what's that?"

"Come over and I'll show you."

SOUR MANGOS

"As if the most financially well-endowed school in the state needs more money," Jaya grumbled to himself. He hated volunteering at Manoa Prep's carnival, the school's annual two-day fundraiser. But more than irritated, Jaya was bummed.

All week he'd been anticipating his date with Rasa. It was the first Saturday night she'd gotten out of whatever "family thing" she'd been busy with for three weeks in a row. And even though they'd met up Tuesday afternoon, tonight's date seemed more significant. But then an hour ago, Rasa had cancelled. Her tired excuse, unchanged. Jaya's sadness and paranoia, reflex.

He and Jayshree drove home for a short break from their carnival duties. He let out a long-suffering sigh of yearning and suspicion. Jayshree didn't seem to hear because she began an excited recap of the record-breaking sale of mango chutney. Jaya nodded and tried to smile as his mother rattled on and on about the high sales.

"If we have the same numbers by this time tomorrow, it'll be a new bar," she announced in delight. The chutney-making process took a year of coordinated effort by a slew of parent volunteers. Jayshree prided herself on being one of the committee chairs. Most years, Jaya loved Jayshree's carnival enthusiasm. She seemed truly happy being a leader. He was glad when she was interested in something other than drinking, bingeing, and puking.

"Julie's sick. The flu, I think. Anyway she can't cover tonight's shift. Sanjay will have to fill in. It's time he helped out." Then she muttered, "The other dads do."

When they arrived home, Jaya collapsed on the living room sofa. He closed his eyes. Maybe a nap would help.

Jayshree flitted to the kitchen. Sanjay was standing at the counter, nursing a whiskey on the rocks. Jayshree walked to the other side and started fixing a sandwich for herself. "Sanjay," she said, "we need your help in the booth tonight."

Sanjay downed the rest of his drink. He poured himself another generous serving. He drew the glass to his lips. "I can't," he said.

Jayshree kept her eyes on the ciabatta. "Why not?"

"Business meeting."

"I didn't see it on your calendar."

"Something just came up."

Jayshree dropped the bread and pushed the plate away. She went into her binge routine, gathering all the snack foods she could find. She shoved chocolate chip cookies into her mouth. "Ok. What's it this time? Strip club? Bar?" Crumbs flew out of her mouth.

"It's not that, Jayshree. It's business." He polished off his drink. Then he lifted the entire bottle of whiskey to his lips and chugged.

Jayshree uncorked a bottle of red and took a swig. "Sure. Right. Business." She yelled, "Business with another woman is more like it!"

Jaya shot up from the sofa. But then he relaxed. After all these years, his parents' fights brought him a strange comfort. It was what he knew. What he expected. He could predict how it would end. He was used to the kind of self-loathing he felt as a result of their conflicts.

All of this he'd grown up with.

These things didn't jar him to the core the way Rasa's lies did.

Jaya looked at Sanjay. His father's eyes grew large and red. He finished the rest of the whiskey in the bottle and flung it at the sink. It shattered.

In a scary flat voice, he said, "Yes, Jayshree. Another woman. Actually, other *women*." He pushed his tongue around in his mouth. Now came the part where Sanjay exploded with violent words. But there was only silence. Instead of delivering his usual tirade, he stood there, quiet, but his hand trembled on the edge of the counter. He took a few steps back, turned and marched out the front door.

Jaya heard the Bugatti engine roar. He listened to it rev, then screech off.

Jayshree wolfed down some chips and gulped more wine. Jaya tracked her steps to the bathroom. The sound of her gagging and vomiting brought another moment of relief to Jaya.

His mother was acting the same. But Sanjay was acting different.

Jaya rocked back and forth with one arm crossed and one arm propping his chin. Yeah, Sanjay was piss drunk. Yeah, he threw the bottle. But his voice. It didn't break through the walls the way the whiskey bottle broke in the sink. It didn't batter Jayshree with its usual repetitive unkindness. Sanjay had skipped that part of the typical fight before storming off.

Jaya acted on instinct. He rushed out the front door and climbed into his BMW. He pulled out of the driveway and raced off in hot pursuit of his father.

THE FINER THINGS

Rasa despised everything about this evening with Mr. Franz. Sure, the setting was perfect. The breezy Waikiki night. The relaxed vibe at The Royal Hawaiian Resort. The outdoor, oceanfront table at the upscale restaurant Azure. The delectable seafood meal. Mr. Franz's polite conversation.

But Rasa could barely taste the fancy food, let alone take another second of his boring flattery. She kept her eyes on him but pictured herself plugging her ears with her index fingers and shouting "Lalalala...I can't hear you!"

Mr. Franz didn't seem to notice that his expensive seduction wasn't putting Rasa in the mood for the sex that would come. He had no idea that even the coke she'd done earlier or the costly alcohol she'd guzzled within the hour weren't helping. She continued to waffle between jonesing for Jaya and drowning in the shame of her newfound realization that she was nothing more than a prostitute.

Still she kept up the charade with Mr. Franz. She leaned forward and batted her eyes at him. She laughed at his jokes. She touched his hand and teased him.

When it was finally time to go, Rasa swallowed the huge sigh of relief trying to escape her mouth and blew him a kiss instead.

Mr. Franz smiled and held up his finger for the waiter.

"Check, please."

"Right away, sir."

Mr. Franz looked at Rasa. "So. How was your chocolate tart?"

"Lovely." She tilted her head back and sucked down the last couple sips of her sparkling wine.

"Not as lovely as you." He bit his bent finger and shook his other hand. "What I'm gonna do to you..."

The waiter came back with the bill.

Mr. Franz dropped his eyes to his wallet and Rasa immediately scrunched her face.

"Here," Mr. Franz said to the waiter, handing him a credit card without even glancing at the amount. The waiter disappeared again and Mr. Franz looked back at Rasa.

Rasa quickly straightened her face.

"Where were we?" Mr. Franz asked, taking Rasa's hand and stroking it with his thumb.

He was wearing his wedding ring. He hadn't even bothered to take it off! With her free hand, Rasa grabbed onto her armrest and squeezed.

She plastered on a fake smile. The waiter came back in record time. While Mr. Franz calculated the tip, Rasa closed her eyes and thought about Jaya. *What was he doing right now*?

"Ready?" Mr. Franz asked.

Rasa opened her eyes and nodded. He helped her up and then offered his arm. She wove hers through it. They walked out of the restaurant, Mr. Franz with his head lifted and chest out while Rasa looked down. A light rain sprinkled on them as they waited outside for his Jaguar. Mr. Franz took Rasa in his arms and ran his fingers through her hair. Then he leaned in for a kiss. It was a deep, long kiss. So deep and long that Rasa didn't get a chance to see who pulled up to the valet.

EVERYTHiNG'S A LiE

Jaya slammed on his brakes in front of the Royal Hawaiian. He watched Sanjay hand one of the valets his keys. The front of the elegant resort was crowded with guests waiting for their cars or taxis. Sanjay hurried inside.

Jaya unbuckled his seat belt, ready to get out and follow his father. But when he glanced up he saw—Rasa and his dad's developer friend making out!

He watched them kiss for what seemed like hours. Finally the old guy peeled his lips off Rasa. He smiled at her. And she smiled back!

Jaya forgot about his father. He continued to spy on Rasa and his father's friend. They climbed into a black Jaguar and pulled out of the Royal Hawaiian driveway. Jaya drove after them, yanking his seat belt back on as he turned a corner.

He tailed them through Waikiki. They turned into the small parking lot of an apartment building Jaya had never been to. He waited five seconds, then pulled in after them.

The old guy opened Rasa's door and gave her his hand. She took it and let him help her out. He shut the door behind her. Rasa started to walk towards the lobby, but he grabbed her hand. He pulled her to him and pushed her back against his Jag. His hands roamed up and down her back as he kissed her. She wrapped her arms around him. She tilted her head back a little.

Jaya clenched his jaw. He pounded his steering wheel with his palms. One deep breath later he kicked his door open and jumped out. A few raindrops skimmed his arm. He looked up. The cloudy sky was starting to percolate.

"Rasa!" he shouted, as he rushed towards them.

She turned to look at him. "Jaya?"

"What the fuck, Rasa?" He opened his mouth, but nothing came out. He lost his nerve. He dropped his head, then backed away from them. He did a fast pivot and fled. Tears rushed down his cheeks like the Kahala Stream after heavy rains.

Rasa tried to push Mr. Franz away, but he kept a tight hold on her. "Jaya!" she shouted. "Wait!"

But Jaya was already in his car. He peeled out of the lot. Five minutes later he was in the left lane on H1 East. He gassed it to seventy miles per hour. He didn't know where he was going. Each breath he took sounded like Darth Vader's mechanical inhale and exhale. His thoughts gyrated like a toy top.

My girlfriend.

My dad's friend.

Together?

My girlfriend.

My dad's friend.

Together?

Jaya pulled his cell phone out of his pocket. He speed-dialed Rasa. No answer.

Everything's a lie.

Even me.

I'm nothing.

The wind howled outside his window. The car oscillated in the strong, irritable gusts. He swerved, almost hitting the car in the next lane.

The clouds burst. Sheets of rain drenched the road. The windshield wipers were on high, but he could barely see the green exit signs. Without looking, he veered into the right lane as he passed the 6th Avenue exit. The lane turned into the Koko Head off ramp.

Jaya ran the red light and turned right. Green Day was singing *21 Guns* on his stereo.

21 Guns.

He reached over and opened the glove compartment. His father's Glock was still there.

Of course it was, Jaya thought.

I put it there.

He'd been planning on getting rid of it that night.

He smiled.

The weather raged outside, but an eerie calm descended in his mind. The clouds in his head parted. It was clear to him that even though his despair came and went, it always came back. And things could, and would, and did, get worse.

He headed back to Waikiki.

NAKED TRUTH

"Let me go!" Rasa struggled to escape Mr. Franz' strong arms.

He tightened his hold. "No! Not until I get mine." He yanked her into the lobby. "I'm paying for this and I'm going to get it," he growled. He pushed her to the elevator, twisting her wrist until they got to the apartment.

The light rain turned into a torrent. While the storm thrashed Waikiki, she swore she heard the howling wind outside screaming the names of her brother and sisters.

Midway through, he flipped her over. She hugged the pillow, imagining the pounding of the rain against the windows to be Jaya pounding at the door.

Oh, Jaya. His dark eyes. The sound of his first Nirvana serenade. The way he smelled, his delicious cologne. The touch of his fingers on the small of her back. The sweet taste of his mouth.

Mr. Franz finished. He zipped his pants and left without looking at her or saying a word.

"Thank God," Rasa mouthed to herself. She grabbed her phone and dialed Jaya.

"Where are you?"

Silence.

"Jaya?"

"Downstairs."

"I'm coming down."

The rain had stopped.

Jaya was leaning against his Beamer, his back to her. She walked around and stood in front of him. He was cupping his forehead in his right hand like he was in pain.

Rasa saw what he was holding in his left.

"Jaya...?"

He cut her off. He tossed the gun between his hands, muttering fast and hard. "I was going to get rid of this Glock, it's my dad's, he bought it to shoot people who try to rob us. Ha! No one's gonna break into our freakin' maximum security mansion so I figured he didn't really need it plus who the fuck is he to decide who gets shot for what? Sometimes my mom goes crazy because he's cheating on her and she threatens to shoot herself with it, I have no idea if she'd really do it or not, maybe she would, maybe she wouldn't, but he keeps cheating, so why take any more chances? I found it lying around so I thought, dump it." He looked up. "Dump it!" he screamed.

Rasa jumped.

He locked eyes with her, pushing close into her face. "It's not like I haven't thought about killing myself too, did you know that? I guess you knew that, what with me not being the daughter my parents want and them being so fucked up, my father cheating, my mother bingeing—which is another reason I figured I'd get rid of this death machine."

"Good idea," she whispered.

Jaya took a sudden step back and stood up, tall and erect. He pushed the Glock's muzzle into the side of his head. "I'm so very glad I still have it."

Rasa's eyes pooled with tears. "Stop! What are you doing? You're scaring me! Let's talk about this."

"Talk about what? That you're fucking around? Oh yes, you're fucking around with every single guy you meet. How could you do this, how could you do this to me, how could you lead me on like that? Didn't you know how I felt about you?"

"It's not what you think!"

"Oh, really? It's not what I think?"

"Jaya..."

"No, no, it's exactly what I think. I saw what you were doing. Twice now! First, your so-called uncle and now this! Did you know your Jaguar boyfriend is my dad's work buddy? Did you know that? You've probably fucked every single one of my dad's friends. Maybe you've even fucked him, huh? Did you? Did you?" He pushed her.

Rasa was bawling. "Jaya, stop. Please stop. Let me explain."

"Explain? Oh, this is gonna be juicy, better than my mom's Bollywood films, lemme grab some popcorn..." Jaya clutched the Glock to his chest.

"Put the gun down first. Please. I'll tell you everything, but please put the gun down."

"Don't tell me what to do! Don't you dare tell me what to do! Don't you ever ever tell me what to do again."

Rasa took a step toward him.

"Stop! Come any closer and I swear I'll..."

Rasa held her hands up and open. Then she wiped her nose with her forearm and exhaled. "Xander's not my uncle."

"I knew it! I knew it all along!"

"You were right."

"You lied to me!"

"He's my pimp."

Jaya's face crumpled.

"He arranges hook-ups with guys and I have to go. I sleep with them, he makes me." Fresh tears coated Rasa's cheeks.

Jaya snickered in disgust. "He makes you...? That's good, that's really good."

"If I don't do what he says then—"

"What? If you don't sleep with whoever he says, what?!"

"He'll hurt Ach and the girls," she said.

"Oh yeah, right." Jaya scratched his chest with the Glock. "That's so hard to believe. Why didn't you just call the police?"

"I can't. Xander will punish me by hurting them."

Jaya glared at Rasa. "Damn it! I can't get it out of my head," he said bringing the Glock's muzzle back to his temple. "You touching all those guys! Them touching you! Their hands all over you. You together with them like you've been with me. Oh, it makes me crazy! It's all just a lie!"

"Jaya, please, you've gotta believe me."

"No! No, Rasa! I don't believe you!" he shouted. "I don't believe anyone. I'm done." He shut his eyes and pulled the trigger.

NO NiRVANA

Nothing happened. No pain. No blood. No nirvana.

Jaya opened his eyes slowly. He shifted his eyes to his left hand. It was still pushing the Glock into his temple.

"What the fuck?!" he muttered, lowering his hand to examine the gun. "Why the fuck didn't it go off?"

"Oh my god," Rasa breathed. New tears flowed, but she brushed them away and then blinked hard to make the crying stop. She crept up to him and wrapped her hands around the Glock. "Let me have it."

Jaya looked up at her and squinted. "Huh?" He frowned. "No!" He whipped his back to her. He hunched over and fiddled with the Glock again.

Rasa slunk around to the front of him. She stroked his busy hands.

Jaya flipped the Glock over and over trying to figure out what the problem was. "The firing pin?" he asked himself. "What is it? What the hell, why didn't this work, I need to kill myself, and the goddamn thing doesn't work! I can't even kill myself. I can't stand this anymore. I can't live like this. The one thing I thought I had is just a lie."

"Jaya, Jaya. Look at me. Please."

He kept his eyes fixed on the Glock.

"Jaya, I didn't want to do it, any of it."

Jaya stopped messing with the Glock. He stared at Rasa. "Whatever," he said, waving the Glock around. "You're a liar and a cheat just like everyone else. My life is filled with fucking liars and cheats. Everybody lies, everybody cheats, everybody hides. My father, my mother, now you."

"I lied to you. I did. But I had to, I have to protect my brother and sisters."

"Seriously? Really? You really think you couldn't do anything about it? I mean you must've slept with hundreds of guys. You should've told me right from the start."

"You don't get it, Jaya," Rasa whispered.

"Sure I do!" he yelled, spitting his words at her. "You were partying and sleeping with half of Oahu because your pimp made you. But not once did you try to get out of it. What the fuck?" Jaya stopped. His upper lip curled. "You must have liked it. You really really must have liked it!"

"Liked it? I-I—"

"That's it, isn't it? You liked it! You liked getting fucked by all those guys! Bet you think they're real men, huh?

"What are you talking about?"

"You should've told me what was going on! Right from the minute you met me!"

Rasa shook her head. "No. Xander would've cut me, choked me...you don't know how scary he is."

"Why didn't you tell me he hurt you?"

"I couldn't. I didn't know how—" Rasa stopped. She took a deep breath. "There's so much you don't know about me," she whispered.

"Like what? That you're a liar and a whore!"

She turned away from him for a long minute, her shoulders heaving. She took a deep breath and turned back, glaring at him and shaking her head back and forth.

"You have to stop this, Jaya," she said. "You just have to stop." Now she was in his face.

"What?"

"You have to listen to me," she hissed. "You don't know me at all." He stepped back, staring at the ground.

She poked his shoulder with her finger. "You look at me when I talk to you!" She pointed to her tattoo. "See this black widow? You see it? This is my mom. She was a prostitute. Yeah, she was a prostitute. You got that right. She was hardly there for us growing up. We had no money, we didn't eat half the time. And then one day—poof!—she was gone." She clapped her hands together hard.

Jaya blinked, then squeezed his eyes shut.

"Look at me, damn it!" She pushed him again. "I don't know where she is. Maybe she's dead now. Who knows? I never met my father. I don't even know his name or who he was. I didn't get to go to school much because I was taking care of the kids. I was basically Mom. I did the best I could. I was twelve the first time I had sex. It was pretty much rape. But the guy was one of my mom's regulars and he paid me for it. Yeah, you got that! He paid me! And with that money, we ate, me and the kids! I started turning tricks just to survive."

"Rasa…"

"No! You be quiet! You're not getting it! All I could think about was taking care of my siblings. I didn't have anyone to turn to. I couldn't tell anyone what was going on or we'd get split up and put in foster homes. And then we did—get split up and put in foster homes, just like that! I was separated from my brother and sisters, but I still had to take care of them—only now it's making sure that they're safe." She shook her head. "I hate who I am. But it's what I know to do. You got that?"

"Oh, Rasa…" He rested the Glock at his side.

"It was already happening long before I met you. Xander already owned me."

Jaya sank down onto his haunches. He sobbed.

Rasa kneeled down next to him. "I wasn't trying to hurt you. I was just so happy with you, I didn't want it to stop. I didn't dare tell you anything because I thought we would be over. Please don't leave me," she whispered. Then slow and steady she maneuvered her fingers around the Glock.

Jaya didn't let go or resist.

"I thought maybe Xander would hurt you too. He knew we were close."

"We are—" Jaya stopped. His bottom lip quivered. He closed his eyes. "But tell me the truth, Rasa—is this going to keep happening? Are you going to keep fucking everyone you meet?"

"No. I'm done," she said.

"You're done? You've been doing this since you're twelve. What's to make you stop?"

"Love, I guess. You'll have to trust me. You'll have to help me."

Jaya breathed deep. "I keep picturing you having sex with some random dude, and then, in the next minute, I see you by yourself floating deep in the perfect ocean." He opened his eyes. "That's the real you, isn't it? Remember when you told me about how you used to free-dive all the time in Hau'ula?"

Rasa nodded. Jaya's face strained in a half smile.

"I don't know anyone who can dive that deep for that long." He pressed his lips together. Then he looked away and mumbled, "I've never known anyone who's gone through what you've been through." He let go of the Glock.

Rasa gripped it and carefully put it behind her.

"The first time I saw you on the Ma'akua Ridge Trail, I thought you were a goddess." Jaya hung his head. "I guess I assumed goddesses had easy lives." He rubbed his eyes with the heels of his palms. He stared at the ground. "No one took care of you. No one helped you. And people hurt you. Over and over." He looked back at Rasa. "How did you get by?" He took Rasa's hand.

She squeezed his hand. "I can't lose you."

"No, you can't lose me. I can't lose you."

HUNTED

Rasa shivered.

Jaya wrapped his arms around her. "Are you cold?" he asked, rubbing her back.

She shook her head. "No," she whispered. "I just remembered. I didn't get the money from tonight's job. Xander's gonna be looking for me. He's gonna want his money." Her eyes widened. "Xander's gonna kill me."

Jaya took her hands in his. "No, he's not. We'll figure this out."

"You don't know what you're talking about! You don't know Xander," Rasa cried, her eyebrows raised. She pulled her hands out of Jaya's and stroked her X-shaped scar. "I can only imagine what he'll do if he doesn't get his money."

Jaya touched her scar. "Did Xander do that?"

"Oh shit."

"What?"

"Xander's on his way. I know he is..."

"On his way?"

"He doesn't like to wait for his money. He always comes here to collect after a trick."

"Let's go then." Jaya grabbed her hand.

Soon they were speeding down Kalakaua towards Diamond Head.

"What if he's following us?"

Jaya checked his rearview mirror. No cars were behind them. "He's not. We're ok." He raced down Diamond Head and onto Kahala Avenue. "What should we do?" he mumbled to himself. He drummed his fingers on the steering wheel. "We gotta clear our heads."

"Where are we going?"

"I was going to take you to my house."

"Your house? That doesn't make any sense. What would your mother and father do with me?"

"Yeah, you're right. What would they do with you, with you and me together? But we can't go there anyway."

"Why not?"

"Xander will put two and two together. He'll know you're with me. I'm sure he can figure out where I live. It's all online and stuff." He made a sharp left turn on Kealaolu Avenue and then a right onto Kalanianaole Highway going east.

"Shit! Shit! Shit!" she cried, wringing her hands. Then Rasa cupped her mouth. "Oh my god! Ach, Nitya, and Shanti! If Xander can't find me, he's gonna go for them! She pulled out her phone. "I'm going to call them."

No one answered.

"Shit! What if something bad has happened to them already?"

"Xander can't be up there yet. Waialua is an hour away. They're probably all asleep. We still have a little time."

"You're right," she said. But then she inhaled sharply. "But you don't know Xander like I do. Turn the car around. Please. I gotta go back to Waikiki. I gotta find Xander. I gotta explain to him about his money. I gotta promise to make it up to him. That's the only way to make sure my family is ok."

"No, Rasa. That's not a good idea. You're not thinking clearly. You have to go to the cops. You have to get help."

"No, no! I can't go to the cops, no, we can't do that." Rasa shifted around in her seat and looked out all of the windows. "We gotta do something. He's gonna be hunting for me."

"I know a place we can be safe for just a little while." He changed lanes then said, "Xander will never think to look there."

NO MORE SECRETS

Jaya drove to China Walls in Portlock. He parked his car just outside the cul-de-sac leading to Koko Kai Mini Beach Park. He turned off the ignition.

Rasa dropped her head and sobbed.

Jaya stroked her back. He lifted her hand and kissed it. "He'll never find us here. We can take a little time and figure what we should do," he said. "Ok? Come on now."

They got out of the car. The wealthy neighborhood was quiet and dark. But the full moon glowed high in the night sky. It illuminated their way down the cul-de-sac and through the tiny park. They reached the cliffs.

The water below was calm and flat. Then, without warning, a set of three waves crashed against the rocks below.

"Just like that, everything can change..." Rasa whispered.

Jaya lowered himself to a place where the grass ended and the wide cliff began. He stretched his legs.

Rasa sat next to him. She leaned her head on his shoulder and put her hand on her heart. "My heart's finally back to normal. It was going so fast..."

Jaya put his arm around Rasa.

"Xander won't find us here, but we can't hide forever. I gotta do something ASAP," she said.

"Yeah."

"Ok." She closed her eyes.

A delicate breeze crept through the two clusters of palm trees behind them. The fronds swished, crinkled, and murmured.

"I love the way the palms do that," Rasa said, "Like they're whispering secrets to each other."

Jaya smiled. "I was just thinking the same thing."

Rasa turned her head to look at Jaya. "My sad sad secret almost killed you. My secret hidden life."

"Rasa, listen, I must have lost my head, I can't believe I wanted to do that, thank God, thank God that stupid gun didn't work..." He shuddered. "I could be dead..." Jaya shot up to a stand. "Oh shit. The Glock. It's still in the car. I have to get rid of it!"

"Oh, Jaya, don't—just forget the gun, please. You can get rid of it later. Sit down, please don't go back there." She pulled on his hand.

The palm fronds rustled again.

"I guess the Glock was my secret. It wasn't just today that I thought about getting rid of it. I've been thinking about getting rid of it for years." He sighed. "But I never did. I guess I wanted it in case I needed to...just in case. I never told anyone about the gun or about my parents."

"I wish you'd told me. You have to keep talking to me all the time. We have to keep talking to each other. You can't ever do that again."

Jaya nodded. "I wish I'd told you. We do, we have to keep talking." He looked at Rasa. "I wish you'd told me about what Xander made you do. I still don't understand why didn't you go to the cops? They could've protected your family."

Rasa shook her head. "No, they couldn't. No way. Xander would've found out. For sure he'd have done something bad to my family first."

"Maybe he was just bluffing. You should've tried something."

"I couldn't—"

"You definitely should've called the cops."

"I couldn't. He would've—"

"I know, he would've hurt your siblings."

"He would've..."

"Geez, why didn't you tell your foster parents? I can't believe they didn't notice something was wrong."

"They're the ones who sold me to Xander."

"What! Sold you? Things like that don't happen here. In Hawaii of all places? That's more like that temple prostitution shit in India."

"I'm not making it up. Xander, Sam, and Ann worked this together. Xander paid them so he could have me."

"What about your school counselor? Wouldn't they have to call CPS?"

"CPS placed me with Sam and Ann! I didn't think I could do anything about it. I felt so trapped."

Jaya put his hand on hers. "You're not anymore."

A strong gust of wind made the palm fronds crackle.

Rasa stared at the ocean. "You're the only person in the world, other than the people responsible, who knows what I've done. What

I've been doing." She stopped. Then she whispered, "I'm not proud. It's a sad sick way to grow up, don't you think?"

Jaya nodded. They sat quiet.

Then Rasa turned and stared hard at Jaya. "I thought I couldn't say anything because I had to protect my family. But you could've died because I didn't tell you. I think I need to try a new strategy. Like not keeping things secret anymore. Like not hiding."

"Are you saying what I think you're saying?"

"Yeah, I should go to the police and tell them everything."

Jaya took a deep breath. "Yeah." He grabbed her hand. "Let's go."

"Oh Jaya...no! I'm afraid." She was trembling. "I need a minute. Just give me a minute."

"I know what'll make you feel better," Jaya said real quick, pulling out his cell phone.

Rasa shook her head back and forth.

"Come on," he said, "this will make you happy." He put his hand on her back while he scrolled his photos until he found the selfie of him and Rasa at the fruit stand in Hau'ula. "Remember this? When we first met?"

"Ohhh..." she sighed. We're such a cute couple." She cried and laughed at the same time. She looked at the photo again. "You're such a stud..."

Jaya half-smiled. "If my parents saw this, I think they'd have to start trying to understand the way things really are for me."

"Yeah."

"Jaya," Rasa whispered. "There's something else I have to tell you."

Jaya eyes widened and his eyebrows rose.

"You know that day we were making out in your guitar room?"

"Yeees..."

"Well, the reason I stopped is because your mom walked in. But she left before you noticed and I didn't tell you because I didn't want to mess the day up. It was so great."

Jaya stared into space. "Huh. So that's why she got all aggro with the matchmaking photos..."

"Are you mad?"

"No. But I'm glad you told me." He leaned over and kissed her lips.

"From now on, no more secrets. I will tell you everything. If you ask me something, I'll tell you the truth. And I want you to ask me whatever's on your mind." She leaned over and kissed his lips.

"Ditto," Jaya said. Then he put his phone on its camera setting. He held it in the air facing them. "Let's take another selfie of us. To memorialize our new beginning. We can look at it when we're eighty and remember the day we vowed to have no more secrets. It's a big deal, don't you think?"

"Yes, it is," Rasa said.

They brought their heads together. Jaya took the photo. They looked at it.

"Perfect," Rasa whispered.

"Like you," Jaya said.

Rasa giggled.

"Hey, I couldn't resist."

"Jaya..."

"Yeah?

"I'm ready to go to the police."

"I'm ready too."

Rasa put her hand on Jaya's thigh. "Is this for real?"

Jaya turned to Rasa and held her face in his hands. "Yes, it is," he whispered. He let go of her face and wove his fingers into hers. Then he leaned in.

Rasa met him halfway.

ACKNOWLEDGMENTS

Many thanks to Cinco Puntos Press and the Byrds—Bobby, Lee, & John— for believing in my stories. Lee, I am forever indebted to you for your guidance in editing. You are always right!

My deep appreciation to Ezequiel Peña for his cover art that brought me to tears.

My gratitude to Rob Bittner for reviewing an early draft and offering his expert comments regarding Jaya and trans representation in YA literature.

My thanks to Annis Lee Adams, Jill Bell and Robin Kurz for reading a draft and asking savvy questions that helped me with Rasa's character.

I am obliged to J.L. Powers for reading the "final" draft and offering feedback that took the actual final version to another level.

And to James, Maya, and Joaquin Manaligod, thank you for sharing my enthusiasm and love for Jaya and Rasa.

AN EXCERPT

DUE OUT IN 2018

STONE

On rainy Seoul afternoons my bumo drink makgeolli and smoke Dunhill Internationals on the balcony of our penthouse—Eomoni nestled in the corner of the black-cushioned acacia wood loveseat and Abeoji in the matching armchair next to her. The view of the city is incredible even when it's pouring. Especially when it's pouring. Because all the tall buildings are gray and wet but way down on the street the open umbrellas look like the colorful round beads in my kaleidoscope. Sometimes I aim a pretend kaleidoscope at the street and turn the end of the tube slow and steady. The pattern shifts as the people underneath their umbrellas walk.

The moisture hangs heavy on this wet afternoon. So does the sound of my bumo's opera. They always listen to opera. Though their record collection is impressive they typically select one by The Three Tenors. Today is no exception.

I'm sitting cross-legged just inside the balcony. The Onkyo is behind me. My head is tilted back a little, my eyes closed, and my lips slightly parted as I try to listen to the rich sounds of *Nessun Dorma* with my entire eight-year-old body. I open my eyes and the first thing I see are the heavens crying to the powerful voices of the two Spaniards: Plácido Domingo goes first followed closely by José Carreras. Then the Italian enters with his solo and my eyes spit out tears. How can a voice be so fearless, yet so lonely?

Eomoni walks in. She bends down and kisses the top of my head. "Oh, if Pavarotti knew his voice is the only thing that can move my little Stone," she says, wiping a tear from my cheek.

Stone is my nickname. Abeoji gave it to me. My real name is Yi Kyung-seok but he said, "Seok can mean stone. The look on your face never changes. It's immutable, like a stone."

Eomoni pats my head and smiles. She's a beautiful lady. But when she smiles I think maybe she's a real angel. To the rest of South Korea, she's Gil Bo-young. The man on the evening news once called her "the country's most famous film actress this decade."

"Are you hungry, my little Stone?" she asks.

I nod.

Eomoni stares at me for a second. She shakes her head. "Your eyes. Icy cold black like your abeoji." She winks. "They make you dangerously handsome. Just like him." She walks towards the kitchen.

I don't know about me being "dangerously handsome," but people say Abeoji is very good-looking. My kajok talk about his wide face and square jaw, his thick eyebrows (I think they look like fuzzy black caterpillars), his full lips, and his sleek gakdoogi hairstyle—shaved on the sides and longer and slicked back on top.

Halfway to the kitchen, Eomoni stops. She turns her head back. "Haemul pajeon. And spicy pork, with extra gochujang?"

My mouth begins to water. My hand drifts to my stomach. I nod. She knows haemul pajeon is my favorite. She also knows that I like everything a little extra spicy—she's proud of me for it.

She smiles and disappears into the kitchen.

Eomoni is famous within our kajok for her haemul pajeon. I don't think anyone in Seoul makes it as crispy on the outside and as tender on the inside. Not anyone. And she always uses fresh oysters, shrimp, clams, mussels, and squid.

Abeoji stubs his Dunhill in the ashtray and gets up. He takes off his black suit jacket. He goes to the railing. He stands there with his left hand on his waist and his right hand on the top rail. He likes to enjoy the view. I can see the tats on the back of his hands. On one, the head of a fierce red dragon breathing fire on a black heart. On the other, a ferocious black tiger surrounded by flames, its eyes glowing orange. The bodies of both creatures extend up his arms.

Some mornings I hang out in his bedroom when he's showering. When he comes out with his towel wrapped around his waist, I get to see the rest of his tats. He's a human canvas, his entire upper body tatted up in multicolor designs. He's also got three black stars, five centimeters in length each, inked across his chest. Last time I took my own shirt off and looked in his mirror. I frowned at my paleness, so plain and boring, but with so much potential. My skin was like a sheet of Abeoji's blank parchment stationery, waiting to be inked. Maybe, I thought, when I grow up I could be a walking masterpiece too.

Abeoji exhales then turns around. He tucks his chin and lowers the middle of his eyebrows. His face is a strange combination of menacing and cool. He reminds of me the Admiral Yi Sun-sin statue at Gwanghwamun Plaza. Eomoni takes me to the statue often. The 12.23 Fountain in front of it shoots up water to commemorate the Admiral's achievements.

I finally know what those achievements are. Early this morning, I started a two-hundred page book on Admiral Yi. I snuck into Abeoji's den. I sat on the leather chair at his desk. I do that once in awhile. It's fun to pretend to be "taking care of business" the way he does. Like most "only" kids, I'm good at entertaining myself. Anyway I was talking to my pretend client when the book caught my eye. I slid it across the desk. Under the thin layer of dust on its cover, which I wiped off with my palm, was a scene of an intense naval battle on rough waters. It intrigued me.

When Abeoji strolled into his den around lunchtime, I was on the last page. He tousled my hair and waited until I finished. Then he asked me about it. I spouted off my favorite parts—the exact details of the four campaigns of 1592. I wanted to tell him some more, but he said he had a lot of work to do.

Abeoji picks up his jacket. He finds his Dunhill cigarette tin. He always keeps it in his suit's inner pocket. He opens it. He runs his fingers over the cigarettes, then plucks one out. He lights it, takes a drag, and exhales a ring of smoke. I love watching his smoke tricks. Multiple rings. Waterfalls. Thick clouds.

He walks inside and gives me a half smile. The only two people he smiles for are Eomoni and me. "Stone," he says. "Come with me. I have something for you."

I follow him to his den.

"I was going to wait until your ninth birthday to give you this," he says. He opens the tall persimmon wood chest. He takes out a flat black leather box. He lays the box in my hands. "Open it."

I lift the top and my heart skips a beat. There's a shiny stainless steel bisu inside. The kind assassins use. I know because I've read Abeoji's book on Korean knives.

"This bisu matches mine," he says. "It was made by a craftsman in Busan who specializes in ancient Korean weapons. Go on. Pick it up."

I lift it. I inspect the blade from all angles. It seems to radiate death. I check out the handle. This time my heart flutters. My name is carved in Hangul on one side and there are three stars carved on the other.

I really want to hug him. I really want him to hug me back. But instead I bow. "Kamsahamnida," I say. I examine my new bisu a bit more. I think about the three black stars tattooed on his chest. I ask, "Abeoji, why are there three stars?"

"Ahhhh," he says, stroking my head. "I will tell you. But it's our kajok's secret, ok?"

I nod.

"One star for each Yi hyungje. Me, your Keun Abeoji, and your Jageun Abeoji. Together we are Three Star Pa."

Pa. Together we are Three Star Pa.

My kajok? Pa?

I've seen all the Korean gangster films. My bumo let me watch with them. One pa battling another pa for this reason or that. The fight scenes are violent. And not just with punches and kicks and gunshots. Some are bloody cinematic displays of bats crushing skulls, knives slashing and stabbing, chainsaws cutting, and axes hacking.

I can sit through all the films from beginning to end without flinching. I know it's only fake blood and guts.

Eomoni has starred in several of these films. Always as the mob boss' girlfriend or wife.

I hold my breath for a second.

Is Abeoji a mob boss? Is Eomoni a mob boss' wife in real life?

Abeoji nudges my chin. "Someday you'll be one of the stars."

I don't know what to think. My mind is racing.

That's when we hear Eomoni's voice. "Let's eat," she calls out from the kitchen.

"Coming," Abeoji calls back.

I slice the air with my bisu, then thrust it into the heart of an imaginary foe.

Abeoji laughs. "Tomorrow we'll go the park at sunrise. I'll teach you to cut and throw." He lifts my chin. "With practice, you can control any fight. You can hurt someone. Or kill them. It's you, not the knife, that decides."

I watch his lips move, taking it all in. Then I look at my bisu, wondering if real blood looks as watery red as it does in the movies.

He holds up the leather box. He motions for me to put my bisu back. I hesitate.

"Tomorrow," he promises with a hard nod.

I carefully place my bisu back in the box. He closes it then returns it to the chest. He walks to the packed bookshelf. He glides his index finger over the spines on the middle shelf. He stops on an olive-colored spine. He pulls it out. "Here. Study this tonight. It's the best," he says holding it out. "Learn it well."

He knows I can do it.

I take the book and read the cover. The Netter Collection of Medical Illustrations: The Cardiovascular System. I flip it open and skim a few pages. There are detailed, colorful illustrations of the inside of the human body. I close the book. I cradle it against my chest. Then I look at Abeoji.

"You need to know the human body if you want to be a true bisu master." He points to the book. "Open it again."

I turn to a random page. There's a color drawing with the words "exposure of the heart" printed above it.

"The red blood vessels carry the clean blood to the body and the blue vessels carry the dirty blood back to the heart then to the lungs for cleaning."

I stare at the drawing. I'm already memorizing. Aorta. Superior vena cava.

"You'll understand it better when you read the descriptions."

I look back at him.

He pokes his chin out. "Remember, the red ones are your targets."

"It's getting cold," Eomoni calls out.

"Let's go eat," Abeoji says. He pries the book out of my arms. "You can start after we eat." He lays it on his desk.

He walks to the door of the den. I can't stop thinking about the bisu and the book. I want to start reading right now. I reach for the book.

Abeoji turns around. "Stone," he says, "Not now. We've kept Eomoni waiting long enough. Come on. Besides, a Three Star Pa bisu master needs to eat. He needs his strength."

I nod once. I follow him to the dining room.

As usual, Eomoni has a grand spread of banchan, rice, and soup on the low table. Abeoji and I sit on the floor across from each other.

I'm still thinking about my new bisu. "Abeoji," I say, "May I please show Eomoni the bisu?" My heart begins to speed up as I wait for his answer but I keep my face steady. I focus on the yakgochujang and even try to look bored.

"Yes, Stone. Go get it," he says.

My eyes widen, but I catch myself. I was hoping he'd say yes but I can't believe he really did. I want to leap up and run to his den but I make myself get up slow and walk. When I return with the black box, Eomoni's walking to the table with a large, sizzling cast iron skillet.

'O Sole Mio comes on. The aroma of the scallion, ginger, and garlic floats off the hot haemul pajeon and teases me. My eyes don't move from the skillet. I decide to show her my bisu after we eat. I put the box on the floor next to me, opening it for a quick peek.

Eomoni kneels and puts the skillet in the middle of the table. She removes her mitts. She serves Abeoji first, then me, and then herself.

"I appreciate you preparing this meal," Abeoji says.

"Thank you for preparing the food," I say.

Eomoni and I wait until Abeoji starts eating before we dig in.

I'd just dipped my first bite into the sauce when I hear our neighbor's dog bark. That small dog is well behaved. I've never heard him bark. Sometimes I forget they have a dog. It barks again. Something's not right. I feel it in my bones.

Abeoji senses it too. He reaches under the table. He brings out a gun. He doesn't seem ruffled.

Neither am I. I listen.

Abeoji keeps his eyes on the door to the dining room and says, "Stone, hide in the chest. Now."

I bow my head. I lay my chopsticks down. Quiet as a mouse I get up but not before I grab the box with my bisu. I hide it in front of me as I open the ginkgo wood chest and climb in. I close the doors gently behind me.

I've always wondered why there are big chests in every room of our penthouse with nothing in them.

Is this why?

There are tiny decorative holes near the top of the door. I can see Abeoji and Eomoni.

Suddenly a loud crack and thud. Then quick footsteps. Six or so men in pinstriped suits with red silk shirts swarm into the room. They have guns. One man I see through the holes has the intense look of a warrior going into battle.

A loud pop. Abeoji shoots the man in the chest. He drops to the floor. The other men step over him, and I hear the scream of my eomoni followed by several rapid gunshots. I cover my eyes. I want to cover my ears, but I don't have enough hands. The cracking sound hurts.

Then silence. And a slightly sweet burning smell. I drop my hands and peek through the holes. A few of the men chuckle. One of them stubs his cigarette on the back of Abeoji's head. Another one says something about what a shame to kill such a "sexy woman" before he had a chance to…he thrusts his pelvis back and forth.

My cheeks burn.

The men file out. I slowly open one door, but it creaks a little. I stop. I don't move or breathe. I lift my eyes to the holes.

The men are still leaving. But then the last one stops. "Go on ahead," he calls out to the men. "I'll be right there." He turns his head back. He's got this scar on his right cheek that looks like the number seven.

His eyes are on the chest.

I stiffen and don't even let myself blink. He looks away. I breathe a quiet sigh of relief. He walks over to Abeoji. He reaches into Abeoji's pocket and bring out his wallet. His eyes bulge when he opens it. "You rich bastard," he mutters, "Carrying around this much just because you can." He plucks out all the bills and throws the empty wallet on Abeoji's lap. Then he spits on Abeoji's back.

Stop disrespecting my abeoji! I must've lifted the bisu out of the box at some point because it's in my hand. My grip tightens. My neck and jaw feel tense. I can't take it anymore. I push the door open. I scramble out, brandishing my bisu.

The man with the scar looks up. When our eyes meet, he smirks. Then he laughs. "What are you going to do, little man?" he asks. He doesn't wait for an answer. He turns around and leaves.

I'm left with my feet stuck, my teeth bared, and my bisu as nothing more than a useless accessory in my stiff hand.

The Three Tenors record is skipping. It always does that near the end of 'O Sole Mio. From the open balcony door, I can hear the pounding rain. A flash of lightning. A moment later the boom-boom-boom of thunder.

That's when I realize what I'm looking at. The table is a mess of banchan and blood. My bumo's heads are buried among the scattered wedges of haemul pajeon. They aren't moving. I tiptoe around the table to them. They still haven't moved. I touch Eomoni's shoulder. "Eomoni?" I whisper. Nothing. I try the same with Abeoji. Again, nothing.

I scan the table. My bumo's thick, darkish red blood coats the banchan like extra gochujang. It isn't at all watery like in the movies.

I get dizzy and queasy.

I'll never eat Eomoni's haemul pajeon again. I'll never eat her spicy pork again. She'll never ask me if I want it extra spicy...Who will make my food extra spicy?

I look at my bisu. *Who will teach me how to throw and cut? Who will...*

My stomach contracts. Automatically I clutch it. I heave. I manage to turn around before I throw up. The congealed contents of my stomach lays in a slimy puddle at my feet.

I trudge to the kitchen sink to clean up. I cup water to my mouth, rinse and spit. I reach for the dish towel and see that it's yellow, Eomoni's favorite color. A deep sigh leaves my lungs and I fall to my knees. I howl, and howl, and howl.